"Remarkable. The very best in today's baseball fiction just got a little better."

  —Don Williams, retired sports columnist, *Newark Star Ledger*

"A moving story about an exceptional boy with uncommon athletic ability. This novel harkens back to the days when baseball was King."

      —Chris Platt, award-winning YA author of *Storm Chaser* and *Star Gazer*

"Frank Nappi knocks another one out of the ballpark! If there were a Hall of Fame for Baseball Books, this heart-warming Mickey Tussler series would be in it."

   — Betty Dravis, author, *The Toonies Invade Silicon Valley*

SOPHOMORE CAMPAIGN

ALSO BY FRANK NAPPI

The Legend of Mickey Tussler

Echoes from the Infantry

SOPHOMORE CAMPAIGN

A MICKEY TUSSLER NOVEL

FRANK NAPPI

Sky Pony Press
NEW YORK

Sky Pony Press books may be purchased in bulk at special discounts for sales promotion, corporate gifts, fund-raising, or educational purposes. Special editions can also be created to specifications. For details, contact the Special Sales Department, Sky Pony Press, 307 West 36th Street, 11th Floor, New York, NY 10018 or info@skyhorsepublishing.com.

Sky Pony® is a registered trademark of Skyhorse Publishing, Inc.®, a Delaware corporation.

Visit our website at www.skyponypress.com.

10 9 8 7 6 5 4 3 2 1

Library of Congress Cataloging-in-Publication Data is available on file.

ISBN: 978-1-61608-663-3

Printed in the United States of America

AUTHOR'S NOTE

In an effort to replicate personalities and scenes from a most regrettable period in American history, and in order to tell a realistic story that avoids sanitizing the events herein to the point that they are perceived as both contrived and unrealistic, *Sophomore Campaign* employs certain language, themes, and events that may be offensive to some readers. The use of certain vernacular and epithets, while entirely unacceptable today, provide a gritty yet realistic glimpse into a period in time that we can happily say has passed.

Note to baseball historians: certain artistic liberties have been taken with regard to timelines and the chronology of other baseball occurrences in order to facilitate the telling of this story.

For Julia, Nick, and Anthony

*And for my father, Francis Nappi, whose
undaunted spirit and love of the game
continue to inspire me*

Baseball gives every American boy a chance to excel, not just to be as good as someone else but to be better than someone else. This is the nature of man and the name of the game.

—TED WILLIAMS

SOPHOMORE CAMPAIGN

MILWAUKEE—1949

It was one of those classic autumn days, replete with crisp jets of air and a wide, bright sky. The trees were golden brown, glistening ever so softly with remnants of an early morning frost, and the crops were heavy, saddled with a restless weight that matched the heaviness under which Arthur "Murph" Murphy's mind labored. It had only been a few of weeks since the loss—a bitter defeat at the hands of his nemesis, Chip McNally, and his Rangers. Murph was still reeling from the callous machinations that Fate had rendered his way. He had lost games before. He was used to that. It was all part of the toiling in the minor leagues. He had lost plenty. A promising career to a freak injury; a promotion to the big show as punishment for his managerial efforts with the hapless Brewers; and now quite possibly that job as well. But it was the way he had lost that last game that bothered him most—a loss that occurred without his young star pitcher Mickey, who had spent the afternoon of that championship game languishing in a damp prison cell for an insidious crime that had forced its way into his life. That was something that really stuck in his craw.

There were many things, however, for which he was thankful. Molly was certainly one. She had remained with him, and so had

Mickey, for the duration of that summer. It certainly was not the plan. She had only intended to teach her insufferable husband Clarence a lesson. But she never felt more alive than the moments when she was with Arthur. She never expected, when she went there to live for a while last summer, that every thing that passed through her eyes and into her imagination would ignite in her brain this conflagration of possibility for a life—a real life, one filled with laughter, discovery and fulfillment. She was singing again, and playing the clarinet. She found herself to be lighter somehow, walking through each day unencumbered by the silent fear of vituperation and brutality that had always trailed her back on the farm. True, there were moments when she felt this morbid guilt rise up in her throat. It was so bad some days that she considered just abandoning this new vision of hers and returning home. But after the horrible incident between Mickey and Lefty Rogers, something inside her snapped, came undone, and she was sure that she would leave Clarence for good, a bold step for such a meek woman.

Murph recalled the great trepidation that Molly had when the time had finally come for her to go back to the farm, one last time, to collect her belongings and say goodbye to Clarence, once and for all.

"I don't know if I can go back there, Arthur," she said with roiling tremors of panic and indecision. "You don't know how he gets when he's angry."

"I'll be right there with you," he assured her. "And if it makes you feel any better, we'll bring some of the fellas along too."

They both laughed now, weeks later, at the overwrought absurdity attenuating the scene on the farm that day.

It was late afternoon and the air was crisp, clear and blank. Clarence had been laying on a cot inside, with two or three empty beer bottles balanced precariously on his heaving chest. He got up and staggered to the window when he heard the car door slam outside. Through the square panels of dusty glass, the petulant farmer could see the orange sun sinking slowly behind the line of trees. His eyes also found Molly, who was with Murph, making her way slowly from the road up to the walk. He gazed at them for a while, his mouth half open, as though they were just part of another one of his fitful dreams. He froze, unable to conceptualize the one thing he had known, since the day she left, would eventually happen.

His head, a block of chiseled stone, remained still, pointed in the direction of the intruders. He stood still, soundless on his bare feet. Then, like a statue suddenly come to life, he rubbed his eyes, grabbed his shotgun off the floor, and blasted through the shroud of the foggy daydream full speed, whipping the front door open and emerging, wrathful and unsteady, on the front porch.

"That's jest far enough, little Miss Molly," he warned, cocking the rifle and taking aim. "Ya got some nerve, showing yer trampy face round here. You, and that no good washed up jockstrap boy-friend of yours there. Both of you. I'll shoot both of ya, just as sure as I'm standing here. Now turn yer sorry selves round and shove off! Go! You got no business here no more."

Molly shut her eyes and cowered next to Murph. He stroked her face and whispered something soft in her ear, all the while glaring at the unbalanced miscreant spewing his venom. Murph imagined his voice penetrating the viscous layers of the simpleton's dark, inaccessible psyche, arresting his bilious advances, even though he knew, somewhere deep within his own mind, that it would never happen. A man like Clarence could never listen.

Murph tried anyway. He took one step forward, leaving Molly shaking in his shadow. His eyes did not shift and his muscles tensed in preparation for what was to be an ugly exchange. Then he fired his opening salvo.

"Step aside, Tussler," Murph yelled back. "It doesn't have to be like this. She just wants to get what's hers. That's all. Then we'll be gone."

Clarence's face grew infinitely sad. His eye caught the whirl and dash of two ground hogs foraging in the lengthening afternoon shadows. He looked as though he would drop to his knees and surrender to the heartache ripping him apart, until he broke out in a violent sweat that revealed the true urgency of his present situation.

"I'll blow yer damned head off, baseball boy," he replied. "You just try me now. Come on. I'll take both of ya out with one shot."

Murph was unmoved by the perilous warning. He just stood there, feet set firmly between the divots in the gravel walkway, like an actor awaiting his cue.

"Well, come on ya lily-livered piece of crap," Clarence said. "You want some of me?" Murph stepped back to Molly and steadied her with a firm hand to the small of her back. Then he looked directly at Clarence, who was squinting through one eye with the shotgun pressed firmly against his cheek, placed two fingers in his mouth, and let fly a whistle that pierced the cool air like an alarm. In a fury of abhorrence, two pickup trucks appeared from nowhere, their tires coming to a violent skid in front of the property. Out of each stepped three men, each one wearing a baseball cap and brandishing a wooden bat. Included in the group was Raymond Miller, the fiery catcher and Brewer captain—the heart and soul of the team, the man the other guys all called Boxcar because of his solid build. Last season had taken a lot out of him. They all noticed it. He looked smaller somehow, and not even the brightest of afternoons could light the darkness looming behind his eyes. Still, he remained their undisputed leader.

With Boxcar were Woody Danvers, the barrel-chested hard hitting third baseman, Clem Finster, keeper of the opposite infield corner, right fielder Buck Faber, second baseman Arky Fries and Jimmy Llamas, the eccentric centerfielder who was always up for a challenge. They walked steadily, purposefully, and joined Murph and Molly at their side. The scene turned perfectly motionless. Murph folded his arms and smiled at the fuming farmer. The confidence in Clarence's visage was invisible now—only the bushy overhang of his tangled brow which seemed to slump downward toward his feet in silent submission was discernable.

"Mr. Tussler, I'd like you to meet some of my best hitters," Murph announced ominously. He glanced proudly at the lineup he had assembled. "Yup, each one of them hit well over .300 last season. They don't miss very often."

Clarence stood uneasily, trying to appear impenetrable. "A wood bat ain't no match fer a bullet, city boy," he shouted back. "You should know that."

Murph's brain split suddenly into two parts. The half nourished by the blood and adrenaline rushing through his body wanted to just overrun the smug bastard, take from him the remaining shreds of self respect he was struggling to preserve. The other half, however, had the effect of cold rain on a camp fire, dulling the raging flames with a more conservative, methodical approach. "True. Yes, that's true. But unless that shotgun of yours can fire more than one shot at a time, Tussler, I reckon you got yourself a little problem."

Murph and Molly were able to laugh now at the dissolution of Clarence's tyranny, as he just stood there like a little boy, surrounded by Boxcar and the others, scarred, frustrated and helpless, while Molly proceeded to empty the house of her belongings, closing the chapter on the most regrettable period of her life. Both of them— Molly and Murph—had come a long way in a very short time. Their lives, separate from one another, were riddled with unspoken longings and frustration; together, they had assumed a far more definitive shape, one that appeared safe and promising. She was happier. And he was okay, for the first time, outside the white lines. There was even some premature talk of nuptials, somewhere down the road. Yes, life was good for both of them. All that remained now was the question of Murph's job for next year—would Warren Dennison renew his contract as manager of the Boston Braves minor league affiliate Milwaukee Brewers, or was his tumultuous career to end so abruptly and unceremoniously? The meeting with Dennison was brief, and came sooner than he thought. Murph had agreed reluctantly, after the final loss to the Rangers on the last day of the previous season, to discuss his fate with the Brewer's capricious owner sometime before Thanksgiving. But here it was, just two days before Halloween, and he was on his way to Dennison's office for yet another one of these now infamous sit downs.

The sun was darting in and out of a line of white, downy clouds stretched across a wide canvas of deep blue, creating unannounced spikes in the temperature that afternoon. One minute Murph was chilled, the crisp autumn jolts of air nipping at his face, and the next he could feel the sweat rising to the surface of the skin on his neck and lower back. He could not decide if he was hot or cold. The vacillation was irritating. He was also having some trouble reconciling in his head the myriad rumors afloat regarding his future with the club. Some said he was finished, washed up for good. Others thought he was being reassigned, as a scout or head of player development. He couldn't be sure. He even heard some conjecture that he would be replacing old man Thompson, the grounds crew icon who had been working the diamond at Borchert Field since its inception. He said he didn't care— that what was to be was to be—but everyone knew he was lying. "Mr. Murphy," Dennison said upon Murph's arrival. Dennison sat recumbently in his chair, feet on his desk, a mere phantom shrouded in shadows, holding a freshly lit cigar in one hand and a sheet of white parchment paper in the other. "Come on in, sit down. I've been waiting for you."

The unregenerate old man just sat there, smiling oddly. He did not speak, but merely placed the sheet of paper down on the desk and with his wrinkled hand motioned toward a stack of invoices and ledgers sitting innocuously on the middle shelf of a three-tier mahogany book case. Murph's eyes narrowed. He could not make out what was going on inside the man's head.

"It's the paper on top," Dennison said. "That's your copy."

Murph dragged his feet across the floor, and pulled the top sheet off the pile. "I don't understand," he said with a clear note of liberation in his voice. "Everyone said—"

"I know what everyone's been saying, Murph," Dennison remarked, placing his cigar in his mouth and his feet firmly on the floor. "And don't think for a second that each and every scenario wasn't, at some point, a distinct possibility."

Murph's eyes scanned the paper incredulously.

"Well, this is great then," he said, shaking his head in disbelief. "Really. I don't know what to say, Warren. Thank you. I'm stunned. Really. I certainly appreciate you giving me another shot."

Dennison puffed vigorously on his cigar, then pulled the tiny brass chain dangling from his desk lamp. "Hold your horses there a minute, Murph," he said soberly. "You might want to read the fine print there—the part about Mickey—before you start falling all over yourself."

A blinding brightness fell on Murph's face, gilding the premature tears still resting on his cheek. He read the paper again, this time with a far more meticulous eye. "You mean I will only be asked back if I can get Mickey to come back too?" he asked dejectedly. "Is that what this means?"

He sat down across from Dennison and slouched over in his chair, as if being suspended by an invisible chord stretched somehow from a point in the ceiling to the center of his back. Mickey? Playing baseball again? After all that transpired last year? Hell, that was never going to happen. Murph could still recall vividly the glare of the sheriff's car lights and the exanimate body of Lefty, a crumpled heap of flesh laying quietly at the feet of Mickey, who was just rocking, his mouth opening and closing in catatonic recitation. It had all happened so fast. Murph's fortuitous discovery of the boy on a scouting trip; Mickey's precipitous rise to prominence on the baseball diamond; Lefty's betrayal and ill-fated plan to stop Mickey from pitching that last game in order to ensure the Rangers' victory.

Then there was Mickey's violent outburst after Lefty assaulted the boy's pig, followed by the arrival of Sheriff Rosco and the subsequent incarceration of Mickey for attempted murder. It was all just a kaleidoscope of misfortune, all of which the boy was ill-equipped to understand. Months later, even Murph had trouble sometimes accepting what had happened. If it had not been for the governor— who orchestrated a pardon for Mickey for all that he had done, not only for the town, but for his sickly grandson—the story would have ended right then and there.

"Are you kiddin' me, Warren?" Murph asked desperately. "You can't be serious. You remember what I told you. The kid is traumatized. Wrecked. He told me he was finished. All that stuff last year with Lefty and the sheriff? Even a kid in his right mind would be rattled. Besides, his mother would never go for it. There ain't no way he's coming back to play. No way. Hell, after what happened last year, I'm lucky they still want to live with me."

Dennison scratched his chin and stood up, detaching himself from the transitory hold of Murph's emotional plea, and with a scathing eloquence, proceeded to explain his position to Murph, who just looked at him with a sick stare.

"Listen, Murph. Let's be real here. You, and the entire team for that matter, are nothing without this kid. Nothing. Now you get your chestnuts out of that little lady's purse and be a man. I don't care how dim-witted he is. *He* puts fannies in the seats. *He's* the one all the papers write about. *He's* the one who somehow, some-way, does something superhuman just about every damned time he takes that mound. He's the 'Baby Bazooka,' the darling of this city."

Dennison raised his eyebrows expressively and smiled at Murph, rendering him more and more diminutive in his chair. He slumped gravely, his chin disappearing partially behind his shirt collar, until he all but vanished completely beneath the suffocating wave of Dennison's steely eyes and tobacco stained teeth.

"So you see, Mr. Murphy, the way I figure it, without him, the season's a bust anyhow. So I have nothing to lose by changing managers here."

Realizing the futility of his predicament, Murph just sat, almost completely crumpled now, floundering in a squall of visible relinquishment. What the hell was he going to do now? Dennison continued pontificating, something about giving the people what they want and opening new doors, but Murph said nothing, his mind drifting in and out of hearing. *All these years*, he thought. *So many innings. So many games, each now seemingly dreamlike and purposeless. What had he become?*

When Dennison paused his diatribe just long enough to relight his cigar, Murph got up, nodded in the old man's direction, and swallowed hard. Then he turned his head and left the room, with self pity and loathing leaking from his eyes.

It rained heavily that evening, big violent drops that puddled Diamond Drive in a matter of minutes. It made Murph's trip home all the more trying. His tires protested loudly against the wet surface, and at every bend in the road, the line of weeping willows that framed the picturesque landscape with restless hands seemed to lunge forward, driven by the intermittent gusts, closing in on him ominously through the gathering darkness.

The car came to rest quietly at the edge of the road. Out his window, clouded now by the remnants of his heavy breath, loomed his modest home. He sat for a while, listening to the rain beat against the rooftop. What on earth was he going to tell Molly?

His paralysis lasted only a short time. In the sheen of some passing headlights, he emerged from the vehicle, worn and defeated. His gait was unsteady though deliberate. As he drew closer to the door, he thought about all the times he had returned home, the house empty and dark as a grave—the only thing waiting for him an amber bottle of Irish whiskey and an empty chair. Now the tiny house was lit by the warmth of Molly. Her touch was everywhere, from the carefully sculpted flower beds in front to the white lace doilies and country curtains in every room. Even his baseball room fell victim to this most wonderful metamorphosis, with the collection of photographs, trophies and other game paraphernalia, once just a messy amalgam of keepsakes and mementos, now assembled in artful fashion. Through the damp autumn air he could see her through a window whose shade had not been lowered. God, she was beautiful. Standing there, with the rain now sideways at his face, the bitter irony gnawed at him, mocking the landscape of his past. He always had baseball, and all the energy and fulfillment that went along with playing the sport professionally. It was in his blood. But he never had a woman. There were plenty of dalliances with young girls who longed for the attention of a budding star. But there was never anything of substance— never anyone real to share it with. Now that Molly stepped into his world, and had shown him how glorious life outside the lines could be, baseball had betrayed him, playing the part of the fickle harlot, threatening to leave him for the next diamond idol waiting in the wings.

And, it was Mickey who was the reason.

The minute he hit the door, she called to him from the kitchen. There was a fire going in the den; the heat felt good against his damp skin. He could smell the chicken and dumplings, and the apple pies cooling on the window sill.

"How'd your meeting go, Arthur?" she asked. Mickey was in the kitchen as well, slicing carrots and placing them in neat rows on a porcelain serving plate.

"Okay, I guess," he shouted back. "I really won't know anything for a while."

With the sound of Arthur's voice, Mickey bounded out of the kitchen. He was young, and so uncertain and fearful. When Murph looked upon the boy's simple face and saw again his unmanageable mood, and recalled the disappointment of last season, it seemed to him that he was looking not at the boy but rather a demanding, threatening creature of which he was now the victim. He fought hard against the insidious emotion.

"Hey, Murph," the boy said, holding a plate of carrots sticks neatly aligned. "Mickey's gonna go out back and feed Duncan and Daphney. Wanna come?" For a minute, Murph resembled a statue. Mickey appeared concerned. "It's okay, Murph," the boy continued. "There's plenty for both of us."

"No, no, Mick," he said, ashamed suddenly of the embittered feelings festering deep within his gut. "Not right now, thanks."

It was half-past seven, much later than he had thought. He muttered something about his aching back as he sat down across from Molly. He wanted to tell her how nice it was to see her, and to thank her for keeping his dinner warm, but under the weight of Dennison's ultimatum, he felt fettered and tongue-tied.

"Getting those silly rabbits to replace Oscar was a great idea," Molly said. "It's all he talks about."

"Yeah," Murph replied. "He seems happy."

"Well, they sure aren't as colorful as that damn pig, but they're a hell of a lot easier." She paused long enough to take a sip of her tea. "What about you?" she asked, dabbing her lips with a napkin. "You look so down. Is everything okay?"

He sighed. His eyes remained fixed on a catcher's glove resting on the table just below the window. "Yeah, I'm okay. Just tired, that's all." Molly fixed his plate and placed it before him.

"Well, you'll feel better after you eat something," she said. "Can't understand why that man would keep you so long if he wasn't going to tell you anything."

Murph considered her comment attentively. "I'm sure everything will be fine," he said. "A new season has a way of healing old wounds." He paused reflectively and looked slightly the other way. Would it be totally shameless to dupe the kid into another season? To make a promise to Molly that the boy would be okay, even though he knew he could not guarantee such a thing? He hated to take the risk, and almost swallowed the impulse, but realized that he loathed the idea of hanging up his spikes forever even more. "I think that even Mickey would find that the same is true for him. You know, a little hair of the dog, so to speak."

Molly's eyes narrowed; it was evident that her guarded imagination had stumbled on this final aside. "Mickey's not playing this year."

"I know. But if he were to play, I just mean that—"

"Look, Arthur, we've been through this already," she said. "He said he does not want to play again."

He sighed. "I know, Molly, but there's nothing to worry about anymore," Murph explained. "All that crap is behind us. And Mickey has an entire town behind him. He really has a special gift. He hasn't even scratched the surface yet. There's so much more waiting for him out there. It would be the best medicine for him."

Murph was on one knee now, his arms outstretched in convincing fashion. He wrinkled his nose playfully, and his eyes shone with the optimism of a crafty politician. He was charming as hell. How could she possibly say no?

"Stop that foolishness," she said, tugging at his arm. "Stand up. This is not a joke."

"I'm not joking, Molly," he said, rising again to meet her gaze. "I'm serious. I really think that Mickey can—"

"Enough. You know how I feel about this, Arthur," she said, her arms folded tightly against her chest. "I know you do. I was very clear about this last year. But if you need me to remind you, that's fine. I will. For the last time—no baseball. None. Mickey has played his last game, do you hear, his last game—for you, or anyone else."

HARVEST FAIR

The sky that morning was a bright pink, bathing the awakening earth with a peculiar light that seemed to intensify everything in its wake. Murph sat on the porch, coffee cup in hand, rocking ever so slightly to the rhythmic call of the osprey stirring in the distance, his mind filled with more thoughts than his consciousness could hold.

The crowding made him feel so lonely. Numb. He sat for a good while without moving, paralyzed by a heaviness he had never felt before. Then, without warning, the ferocity with which this loneliness arrived rose up and struck at him. It wasn't the fact that his baseball career was over; he had expected, as all ballplayers do, that it would have to happen one day. It was the way it had all unfolded that galled him. How could Dennison give him such an ultimatum? Where was the justice in that? He was no more responsible for what Mickey did and didn't do than Dennison himself. Sitting there uncomfortably, he considered telling Molly. Telling her everything. Explaining to her that Mickey could save his job. And that all of them would be fine. It was so clear to him. So simple. But Molly didn't see it that way. He might be able to convince her, to alter her way of thinking so that she too might see the benefit in Mickey taking the field again. It seemed as though it was worth a try. The thought of upsetting her, however, and of possibly alienating her and losing her too was enough to suffocate the impulse.

"Hey, you're up early today," Molly said, peeking her head out the front door. "Wanna help me put the finishing touches on my pie? Only a few hours till show time."

"I thought you finished that last night," he said.

"Well, I did," she said, swinging open the door and stepping outside. "But I think I'm going to touch up the crust with my famous brandy and vanilla glaze." She raised her eyebrows playfully and smiled, but he looked right past her, still feeling this desolation which was clearly now his and his alone.

"Hey, is everything alright?" she asked. "You look upset, Arthur."

She was staring at his eyes, glassy and vacant, and at the tiny shaving nick on his neck, and the way his Adam's apple seemed to protest as he swallowed. He returned her stare, looking up at the intersecting planes of his life, now embodied painfully in her presence, with a vague sense of sadness and defeat.

"No, everything's fine," he answered, his heart beating in his throat. "I'm fine."

The Bowersville Harvest Fair was the pride of the modest bucolic hamlet, drawing every last denizen within its tiny borders—and many from neighboring towns as well—to the autumnal celebration, like moths to an open flame. Some said it was the smell of the homemade pies and other delicacies that was the allure; others cited the firehouse band and the array of carnival games and rides. All agreed, however, that they arrived each year like pilgrims because it was tradition, a weekend of rapture and revelry that they shared not only with each other but with the ghosts of thousands of other "Bowersvillonians" who had come before them. Truth be told, it was all those things, but mostly it was the ineffable longing in every human heart that stirs this time each year—the desperate need to grasp one last dalliance with Mother Nature before winter dropped its icy veil.

This year, the fair was imbued with additional meaning. Times were bad, and the tiny town needed something to smile about. Everyone in Bowersville was still reeling over the shocking reports of alleged Ku Klux Klan activity in the sleepy hamlet, the most recent incident involving a heinous attack on a young black couple from Kentucky that occurred while they were traveling through town en route to a distant relation in Minnesota. The ghastly crime happened on a Saturday night, not long after most of the houses in the area had dimmed their lights for the evening. It was one of the local farmers, Hank Kaestner, who found the girl that Sunday morning. She was lying in a field, in the open air, only partially clothed. Her face, dirt stained and swollen, was pressed up against a damp clump of earth that appeared to be dislodged during some sort of scuffle. Kaestner looked at her and grimaced, the mournful silence and gloom eclipsing the morning light.

Not too far from there, another grisly discovery was being made. It was the young girl's husband, mouth gagged, arms pinioned behind his back with chicken wire, his inert form dangling and twisting ever so slightly underneath a flaxen rope affixed to the lowest branch of the enormous Sycamore tree just outside the Protestant Church. The minister was the first to discover the evil design; he called Sheriff Rosco immediately. Rosco did his best to quell the hysteria attenuating the scene, assuring everyone that this event was in no way related to the other incidents that had occurred recently. They all wanted to believe his words, and some did, until news leaked out about the note Rosco found stuffed inside one of the man's pockets:

GREETINGS FROM THE KNIGHTS OF THE KU KLUX KLAN OF WISCONSIN

Gossip held the next few days, creeping into every house and igniting a maelstrom of rueful speculation. Nobody had an answer. Many of the old timers in town spoke about Klan activity some twenty-five years earlier, and how it damn near destroyed all of them. It was a time, as Kaestner put it, "to be ashamed." It took many years for the town to expunge the stain of racial unrest.

"It wasn't easy," the farmer recalled. "But we did it."

Now, years later, for some inexplicable reason, it was back.

Murph, together with Molly and Mickey, was one of the first to arrive at the fair. He was holding the prize-winning pie for Molly, careful not to tip it to one side or the other, all the while trying in earnest to mask the continuous pounding in the back of his head, a ceaseless knocking that poked urgently at him like something had gotten trapped inside and was fighting to escape. It was a cool night, the darkening sky providing a velvet backdrop for the thousands of festival lights that glowed like a ceremonial gathering of fireflies. Mickey walked deliberately, his eyes darting wildly between three juggling clowns, a hand-painted carousel featuring a menagerie of mythological creatures and chariots, and the throng of children lined up for rides on a Shetland pony everyone called Jake.

"What do you think, Mickey?" Molly asked. "It's really something, isn't it?"

"There are twenty-one kids waiting for pony rides," he answered. "Twelve girls, nine boys." Then his eyes shifted once again, to the carousel, where he noticed that there were exactly sixteen hand-carved animations: eight horses, four unicorns, two dragons and two eagle chariots. He watched momentarily, as each whirled round and round to the inimitable sounds of a Wurlitzer band organ, delighted by the symmetry and repetition of the scene.

"Do you want to ride anything, Mickey?" Molly asked, "or play any games?"

Mickey smiled. He was about to answer, the words forming precipitously on his lips, when he caught sight of a decorated stand next to the cotton candy machine. A tall man with a painted face and a ten-gallon hat was standing behind a table adorned with a neat row of multicolored balloons, crepe paper streamers, and a series of plastic bags, each one containing a tiny goldfish. Mickey swallowed his thoughts and was off like a shot.

"Would you look at him, Arthur," Molly said, shaking her head with wonder. "Amazing, isn't it? You would think he was still a ten-year-old boy."

Mickey walked deliberately to the table, as if negotiating the perimeter of some invisible island between he and his intended destination, and stopped before the painted man, who stood now like some cartoon figure beneath the ridiculous brim of his hat.

Nothing about the boy stirred except his eyes, which traced with great precision the outline of the festive table.

"Howdy there, partner," the man called. His face exploded into a full blown smile. "Try yer luck?" he continued, flicking the feathered end of a wood dart while chomping on a wad of chewing gum. "Break a balloon, win a fish."

Mickey said nothing. It was an odd, waiting silence. His mouth had formed a lopsided grin, yet there was a severity to his look, a limitless rumination in his eyes. "Well, what's it gonna be, young fella?" the man prodded. "Try yer luck?"

"Your table is crooked," Mickey said, pointing to one of the four table legs that was slightly shorter than the rest. "The fish on the left are lower than the fish on the right."

"How's that?" the man asked.

"The left side of your table is almost an inch lower than the right."

The man, irritated by the observation, rolled his eyes. He was chewing his gum slowly now, as if he were keeping time with the music in the background. "Well, I tell you what, partner," he said, scratching his head. "You're making a bit of a scene here. Weirding people out. Know what I mean? But if you run along now, and keep this whole table thing our secret, you can pick out one of these spectacular gold fish."

Murph and Molly had busied themselves as well, stopping to try their luck at the carnival wheel after submitting Molly's pie to the judges. They stood next to each other, watching glumly as the magic wheel of fortune clicked and turned past their hopeful predictions, time and again.

"Must not be our night," Molly laughed. She closed her eyes, delighting in the ambling breeze that swept across her face, and let her hand fall cheerily on Murph's shoulder. "Let's try again anyway," she said. "Our luck's bound to change."

She kissed him gently on the cheek, her lips soft and warm against his skin, whispered loving thoughts in his ear and convinced him to play again. Murph sighed loudly, dropped another quarter on the table with reluctant fingers, and spun the wheel. It just wasn't meant to be. After several more unsuccessful spins, followed by a series of Murph's loud, emphatic swearing and histrionics that seemed to release itself from somewhere deep within his soul, they walked away, three dollars in the hole.

"Calm down, Arthur," she said. "What's wrong with you? Why are you getting so upset? It's just a stupid game."

In a moment, things righted themselves. Mickey, now finished with his business at the goldfish table, ran into Pee Wee, Woody, and Jimmy Llamas, and all of them joined Murph and Molly just as they were about to try their hand at Tic Tac Toe.

"Hey, Mickey," Pee Wee said. "Watcha got there in the bag?"

"Fish," he replied.

"Where'd you get him? You ain't holding out on your best friend now, are you?"

"He was the fourth one. Fourth from the left end."

"Nice job, Huckleberry," Woody teased. "Did you win him or something?" Murph, aware of Molly's watchful eye, shot Danvers a look.

"No, Mickey did not win him," the boy answered. "I just got him. From the man over there."

They each took a turn tossing the plastic balls onto the Tic Tac Toe grid, with only Llamas managing to get the required three in a row. After watching the mercurial character dance around with a rubber dog in hand and listening to him extol his prowess as "simply the best there ever was," they moved on.

They walked slowly, eyes lit by flickering bulbs, feet moving collectively to the Polka tunes emanating from the Bowersville Fire Department band. Murph was enjoying himself as best he could. But his interest was waning. He moved listlessly, the frenetic surroundings connecting themselves somehow to his subconscious mind. He gasped, and lagged behind Molly's gait, as if he were suddenly realizing the harvest of bitterness and regret he was sowing by not pursuing the issue with Dennison and Mickey.

"What are you chuckleheads doing here anyway?" Murph asked. "Someone lock the door at The Bucket?"

"No, we thought we'd come here first for a while, have some laughs," Llamas replied.

"Where are the rest of the guys?" Murph continued. "I thought Boxcar was going to be here?"

"Yeah, he was supposed to be," Woody explained. "He was all set, but then he said he wasn't feeling too good. Don't reckon I know about the others."

Murph found himself growing more and more restless. He abandoned the jocular façade for good and by varying degrees peered warily into the eyes of his star third baseman. "Damn shame," he said. "I really needed to talk to him." He paused momentarily, placing his hand on Woody's shoulder indulgently. He was running out of time and the path of his inner demon was easy to follow now. "Maybe you have a second, Woody. I sure could use it."

The two men distanced themselves from the others and spoke in hushed tones beneath a sky that was now entirely black. Murph just wanted to be cleared of all the angst. From the way things looked now, he felt as though his life as a baseball man was over and he needed to begin the arduous process of moving forward, to clear his mind through some sort of formal acknowledgment or announcement. To say the unspeakable out loud just might clear his mind. And to have his mind cleared would be ecstasy—a definable, liberating purification. He longed for that now above all else, the way he had longed for Molly, with a simplicity of the heart that was deep and true. *Just let my head be clear*, he thought, *and I can move on*. Everyone else could either support the decision Dennison had made or scream foul and rally to his defense. He just wanted to be finished with it.

"Now listen to me," he began, his face flushed and broken. "What I'm about to tell you, Woody, stays right here for now."

His heart beat like a heavy church bell. A strange light thrown from the street lamps painted both their faces a peculiar green. Murph's lips, chalked now with the residue of fear and finality, kept any other words from escaping his mouth. Maybe this was a mistake. Maybe Molly was the one he should be talking to. Was he really ready to just acquiesce—to wave the white flag? And what about Woody? Even if he managed to get the words out, would Woody even care? He sighed heavily, then plunged his hands in his pockets and tried to appear unaffected by the galling indecision.

"I'm—I'm awfully sorry," he said, his eyes grey under the shadow of his furrowed brow. "But I'm afraid I will not be coming back next year, Woody."

Woody's jaw dropped. "Not coming back?" he repeated. "What the hell are you talking about?"

"Just what I said," Murph explained. "Seems that Dennison only sees my value to this team in terms of what—uh, who—I can bring along with me." He raised his eyebrows and looked past Woody's twisted visage and over his shoulder in the direction of Mickey, who stood impatiently behind a line of others all waiting to try their luck at the Milk Bottle Toss.

"Are you kiddin' me, Murph?" Woody complained. "Is that what he told you?"

Murph shrugged his shoulders and frowned.

"What a dirty son of a bitch. That stupid mother—"

"Hey, don't go getting yourself all crazy now, Woody," Murph warned. "That's not why I told you. It is what it is. Mickey's not playing. I tried. Nothing more I can do. I'm not happy about it, but that's it. It was a good run, but that's it." He tilted his head to the side, his lips retracting just enough to reveal a row of teeth that formed a bitter parody of a smile. "It's fine, Woody. Really. I just needed to tell someone, that's all."

Woody prattled on about a team meeting with Dennison and how all of them should force the cantankerous owner to do the right thing, but Murph only half listened. None of it mattered. From where he stood, it was simple. No Mickey, no Murph.

Under that same black sky, now big and bright with the sudden awakening of winking stars, Mickey stepped to the front of the blue and white canopied booth, picked up one of the hard rubber balls and rolled it in his hand. It felt good, like a jaunty drive through a familiar neighborhood. He smiled. His eyes darted wildly from side to side, his entire body tingling, jolted to life by currents of memory. He placed the hand with the ball firmly in the other, rolled his arms, wound and fired, scattering the display of bottles as if they had been struck by a missile. The tiny crowd of onlookers erupted in applause. Mickey smiled again, as if he knew how extraordinary the blow appeared to the crowd, then picked up another ball and proceeded to dismantle the next pyramid of bottles, sending the burgeoning throng that had formed around the boy into bristling vibrations of animation and awe.

"Do it again, son," one of the men in the crowd pleaded. "Please." The captivated stranger placed a quarter on the counter and rubbed his hands together furiously. Mickey looked at him with quizzical silence, then noticed the dirt under the man's fingernails. He shot up both eye brows and wrinkled his nose.

"You a farmer?" Mickey asked.

"How's that?" the man replied.

"Mickey grew up on a farm. Back in Indiana. Had me a big ole pig named Oscar. He were mine."

Immediately, there came from the man a look of impatient bewilderment. "I ain't no farmer son," he said. "I build houses. You know, with wood, nails. All that stuff. But pay me no mind now. I just want to see you knock them bottles over again. What do ya say?"

Mickey's eyes tightened and became fixed and intent in their gaze, a penetrating stare that narrowed in once again on the man's fingernails.

"Mickey will do it," he said smiling. "Then I will show you Oscar. I got a picture of him. In my pocket."

Mickey's elation rose precipitously as the sudden attention and adulation stirred in him feelings of joyful days now gone. He sighed nervously. He thought he heard the fain't echo of stamping feet and his name being screamed by the masses in rhythmic time. Standing now behind a mask of momentary aplomb, the boy seemed to flourish beneath the starlight. He licked his lips and looked forward, like a hunter eyeing his prey. Then he rolled his arms and began firing the rubber balls, one after another. He was perfect every time. Each ball that whizzed through the air, obliterating another pyramid of bottles, was like the song of Hera's sirens—made the passersby not only stop talking but slow down, pause, and ultimately join in the spectacle unfolding before them. With a swarm of onlookers now fully mesmerized, Mickey continued to do the impossible. Each one of his tosses found its mark, punctuating the crisp night air with the inimitable sound of clinking bottles, followed by a chorus of raucous cheers and wild applause. Waves of excitement eddied through the crowd, bathing each spectator in the warm exhilaration of improbable vision. They "ooohed" and "aaahed" riotously as Mickey, in the light of his skillful display, slowly ascended the ladder of commentary to heights of folk hero status. "Unbelievable," they just kept repeating. "Truly amazing. Who is this kid, anyway?" And then it happened. Out of the bristling throng of flickering eyes came a voice, small but certain. It came quickly, and with excitement and impatience, its owner's eyes fixed upon the scene in front of him.

"Hey, I know him, Daddy," the little boy declared. "I know him. I do. I do. That's Mickey. Mickey. You know, the Baby Bazooka, from the Brew Crew!"

In the dimly lit darkness, the boy's words filtered through the crowd, gaining momentum with each pair of lips that repeated the startling revelation until all at once the entire group was ensconced in a frenetic buzzing that vibrated underneath the diamond-dotted sky for several minutes before finally erupting into a rowdy incantation.

"Mickey! Mickey! Mickey!"

Murph and Woody, still engaged in their heartfelt exchange,

heard the commotion and, together with Molly, ran to the scene with dire concern. By this time, the bodies lined up to see the spectacle had formed an impenetrable wall against which the three were powerless.

"Do something, Arthur," Molly pleaded. "Do something. I don't want him there by himself."

Murph went one way, Woody the other. Each jockeyed from side to side, trying to negotiate the obstreperous mob. Once or twice Murph thought he had found a fissure in the mass, an entry point through which he could squeeze, only to be thwarted by another also seeking a closer look. Frustrated and out of patience, he tapped on one of the shoulders in front of him.

"What's going on?" he asked impatietly. The man held his hand to his ear and shrugged with noticeable irritation.

"I said, what's going on?" Murph repeated louder.

"Some kid's putting on a real show," the man replied loudly over the deafening mantra. He craned his neck to get a better view. "It's really something."

"Mickey! Mickey! Mickey!"

As the rhythmic chanting rose to a crescendo, Mickey's face assumed an expression of blissful retrospection which would have exploded into a full-scale smile instantly had it not been frozen momentarily by utter amazement. The young star of the fair sparkled with this new sense of energy and activity that had seized his complacent heart, reveling in the landslide of handshakes and affectionate pats on the back spilling from the crowd.

"Good to see you, Mick," one of the admirers said, gushing with heartfelt affection and enthusiasm. "Can't wait to see you and the rest of the Brew Crew out there again this spring." Mickey smiled and exhaled deeply, liberated by a feeling of fulfillment that surprised as much as buoyed him.

"Baseball in the spring," Mickey said. "Yeah, baseball."

Murph arrived at the front of the crowd just in time to witness the exchange. All the life in his body was now in his eyes—two glinting stars that lit up his face, incinerating the melancholy mask he had worn for so many days. Sure, nothing had changed really. Molly had yet to withdraw her definitive proclamation about her son's immediate future. But the hope that Murph now felt became indissoluble. He knew the look on Mickey's face. Recognized it right away. It was baseball fever. Once the germ got in your blood, there was no antidote—no way to arrest the rushing tide of electricity spawn by the feel of cowhide and lathed white ash or the smell of grass or the sound of legions of worshippers bellowing your name in tribal recitation. Yes, Murph knew the look, and the doubtless ruminations behind it. Baseball fever. It was a wonderful affliction. That night, under a winking moon many miles away, Mickey turned and fired his final ball to the delight of the crowd while Murph smiled, took a deep breath of crisp air, and nodded confidently in Woody's direction.

SPRING TRAINING—1949

The eager sun stretched and yawned before giving itself over completely to the beckoning earth, dropping yellow ribbons of warmth that fell from the sky like heavenly breaths, rousing everything in their wake. The grass at Borchert Field, tiny soft shoots that had slipped quietly out of the awakening ground, winked now with knowing approval and danced gaily in the temperate breeze. All around, the distant song of yawning birds and the sweet redolence of lilac and wisteria thrilled the air and settled gently across the pristine diamond, bathing the ballpark in warming splashes of familiar brilliance.

The players felt it too. It had been a long, cold, lonely winter. They arrived that morning with swollen bags and impatient hearts, like orphan sons, returned at last to their mother. This was home. The ballpark. The one place in the world that mattered. The one place in the world that did not morph in the tumult of the universe. It was safe, predictable. Each smiled as he stepped onto the field and filled his lungs with the seasonal sweetness, stirring in each of them the latent mysticism that flagged all of their hearts and ushering them back to life.

Yes, life was beginning, all over again; it was baseball season.

"He's only playing as long as *he* wants to, Arthur," Molly said, trailing behind both Murph and Mickey as they made their way to the locker room. "We have an agreement, understand? I still do not like this. Not one bit. And I swear to God, if he is unhappy, and you do not tell me about it, I'll—"

Murph could barely hear her over the galloping of his heart. "Yeah, Molly. Sure. Absolutely. I told you. Whatever he wants. For sure."

Life for Murph was starting all over again as well. And not just his existence as baseball manager, which had all but been extinguished with the belief that Mickey was going to hang up his spikes for good. It was Molly too. They had only talked briefly about making their union formal once she was free legally from Clarence. Of starting over again, fresh. They both agreed they'd have to wait. That they would just take it slow—one day at a time. But the night they consummated their relationship, everything changed.

He had taken her in his arms, under a moon that was slowly sinking into insignificance, and felt the warmth beneath her clothes. She was still a married woman, and had no real right even being there, with him, but she needed him as badly, as he did her. They both knew it.

The kiss was awkward at first, the two of them fumbling blindly with a passion both mastering and uncharted. "Let's go inside," she said, drawing a gasping breath. Murph could only stare at her, paralyzed by the startling emotion behind her words.

Afterward, they lay there together, their legs intertwined, heads resting up against each other. Although Murph's stomach growled, he felt full, as if all that he would ever need had already been provided. With his eyes closed, he listened to Molly's breathing and delighted in the warmth of her soft skin. Once or twice the harmony was disrupted by Molly fidgeting in the sheets.

"Is everything okay?" he asked her.

She drew in a deep breath of air and propped herself up on one elbow, sliding the pillow underneath for support. "You ever think about the future, Arthur?" she asked.

He locked his hands behind his head and cleared his throat. "Are you kidding? That's *all* I do. That's all any baseball man ever does. But it's a tough nut to crack because there are no guarantees in this business."

"Is that it?" she replied.

He turned on his side and looked in her eyes, soft and fading. "What do you mean?" he asked. "Is what it?"

She ran her hand along the sheets until it found his. Gently, she slid her fingers, one by one, in the spaces in between his, and squeezed tightly.

"Well, what about us? Do you ever think about us? You know, what we're doing? Where you think this whole thing is heading?"

Murph licked his lips as if about to speak but said nothing.

"Because I have to tell you, Arthur," she continued. " I do love you. But I cannot—will not—ever again be held prisoner by another man."

He looked at her quizzically. "Where is all of this coming from?" he said. "I mean, didn't we talk about all this? About getting married once all this mess with Clarence is finished?"

"Yeah, well—"

"Well, isn't that enough? I love you, Molly. That's all. I don't want to control you, like he did. That's crazy. That's not who I am at all. Why would you say that?"

She frowned, having failed miserably at what she was trying to say. She loved and admired and truly respected him, unconditionally. She felt as though, from the very first moment she met him, that she saw inside his soul and discovered that it was pure, filled with truth and decency.

"It's not that, Arthur. I know that's not what you are about. It's just—well, take this whole thing with Mickey. I told you I did not want him playing again. His world is a lot different from yours. He might be able to throw a baseball through a wall, but all the rest of it is beyond him."

Murph sighed ruefully. "I told you, Molly, and I meant it. He will play only for as long as he wants to. That's it. If he decides to quit, and Dennison fires me because of it, so be it. I will deal with it. I just don't want you to worry."

Molly rubbed his face gently with her index finger and smiled softly.

"Now try to relax. Tomorrow will be just fine. And Mickey and I will be home after we're finished at the park. Please. Do not worry. I am telling you he'll be fine."

"Not worry?" she said. That was something she wished for every day. Her frown deepened and she shook her head. "Not worry?" she repeated. "I think that ship has already sailed."

A short time later, the locker room was alive, the musty air punctuated once more by the sound of clinking metal doors and mindless banter. All around the room the players sat, hands busy with the contents of their bags, mouths engaged in the sharing of their off season exploits and ultimately their expectations for the upcoming season. Those who had arrived early, like Pee Wee McGinty and Arky Fries, were sitting across from each other, embroiled already in yet another contest of Canasta.

"You gotta be kiddin' me," Danvers said smiling as he slipped past the two. "You guys are at it already?"

"We got a lot of catching up to do," McGinty replied, making the cards dance in his hands with his patented riffle shuffle. "It was a long winter."

"Well you might want to take a little break, McGinty," Danvers continued. "Your boy, Mickey, just came in. And he was asking for you."

Mickey sat quietly at his locker, removing one article at a time from the gunny sack that Molly had taken from the farm before she left for good. First were his socks—six pairs in all, separated carefully by length and degree of wear. Next came his cleats, which he always placed at the bottom of his locker, each on its side, with the spikes lined up in perfect accord. Then came the baseballs. Fifteen brand new, pearly white Spaldings, which he set on the top shelf in five rows, each three deep. He had just begun to hang his jersey and fold his pants when he heard from around the corner the familiar sound of his best friend on the team calling his name.

"Mickey Tussler. Where are you boy? Cripe, I know you can't be hiding!" Mickey's spirits soared when he caught sight of Pee Wee, who sat down next to the boy and shook his hand. Pee Wee was Mickey's refuge on the team, the one guy who, from the very beginning, watched out for Mickey, particularly when he first arrived and the others razed the hulking pitcher unmercifully. He was Mickey's mentor, at Murph's behest, but had grown to really love the kid. He remembered just how much when he finally saw him.

"Well ain't you a sight for sore eyes," he said. "I heard you weren't coming back." Mickey stared back blankly, but was enormously pleased.

"Nah, Mickey is playing baseball, Pee Wee," he said. "I love baseball."

"Well, I'm glad to hear it, Mick. Really." Pee Wee folded his arms and smiled. A slight moment of awkwardness fell on them, as

Pee Wee struggled for something to say. It had been so long. And so much had happened. "So, what did ya do all winter, big fella?" he asked. "You all settled at Murph's place?"

"Mickey made snow balls, Pee Wee," he answered. "One hundred eight. Lined 'em all up in the yard. It was cold outside, and my feet got all wet. You should have seen."

Pee Wee chuckled quietly as the familiar patterns of discourse emerged once again. "That's great, Mick. Really. We had some snow in Chicago too. I did quite a bit of shoveling for my mom."

The two of them continued to volley tidbits about the past few months, stopping only once or twice to allow Mickey to finish his sorting and organizing. Pee Wee watched as his friend transformed his locker into an orderly masterpiece.

"Well, whatta ya say, Mick," he said. "You ready to go win us something special this year?"

Mickey stopped and rolled his arms wildly, the same way he did before every pitch he delivered. Pee Wee stood before him, silent. It really had not been that long, yet he found himself amazed by the startling reality that this enigmatic kid, who was riddled with all these peculiarities and idiosyncrasies, was the team's most valuable player. He watched him, trying to delve deep behind the eyes, and thought that perhaps the boy finally got it. What he meant to all of them. Christ, he was the Baby Bazooka, the talk of the town.

Surely he had to know by now.

"Well, Mick? How about it?"

"I'm sorry, Pee Wee," he said. "They all melted now. The snowballs. I can't show you."

One by one, the others trickled in. Each brought with him his own story. Clem Finster arrived sporting a full beard, and spent a good fifteen minutes explaining to all of them how his facial hair had changed his life immeasurably.

"I'm telling you guys, it's amazing. Everyone treats me differently. Guys are afraid of me. Nobody wants to mess. And the women? It's crazy man. The women are always looking. Christ, it's awesome. It's like I'm a new man."

Buck Faber, who had shown up twenty pounds heavier than when he had left in September, laughed and poked at Finster playfully. "Well, does a new batting average come with this new man?"

A wave of raucous laughter rose from the ranks.

"Good one, Bucky," Rube Winkler said, rushing to Finster's defense. "But at least Finster there is sharing *his* news. Looks to me like you've been holding out on us."

Faber scrunched up his nose and shrugged. "What the hell you talking about, Ruby?"

Winkler smiled and patted his belly gently. "Heck, is this the way your good friends have to find out? Why didn't you tell us you were expecting?"

One of the last ones to arrive was Jimmy Llamas, whose penchant for making an entrance had not diminished any in the off season. Each year, Llamas came back to camp with a new persona. Some identity he had adopted as his own. He was lost in a perpetual search for self, so most of them just laughed, knowing full well that it would never last. That by the second week of spring training, he'd be James Borelli again — "Jimmy Llamas," the same old puffy lipped, gap-toothed cartoon character whose very being provided more comic relief than Bob Hope. But his antics, as benign as they were, really irritated Woody Danvers, who was a bit of an egotist himself and perhaps the most irascible guy on the team. Danvers thought he had cured Llamas of these sophomoric antics the year the kooky centerfielder came to spring training with a pipe and smoking jacket, professing to have discovered "culture." Danvers, unbeknownst to Llamas, mixed a little cow manure in his tobacco blend. Later that day, Llamas lit up, puffed hard on the pipe while pontificating about "the finer things in life," only to fall to his knees, hands clutching his throat, when he realized what had happened.

"Howdy, partners," Llamas bellowed, entering the room wearing a ten-gallon hat, leather vest, and black lizard skin cowboy boots. "How do I look?"

Here and there were whispers and muffled laughter as the attention of the entire room turned immediately to Danvers, who had stood up, slammed his locker door, and narrowed his eyes in Llamas' direction.

"Like you just took a ride on the idiot wagon, and hit every bump along the way before finally falling off."

The entire room roared. Llamas blushed and fired back, mumbling something about Danvers's mother. Everyone laughed again. That drew the ire of the chiseled third baseman even further.

"Okay, numb nuts," Danvers warned. "It's a little early, but you asked for it."

Danvers rushed for Llamas, collared him and cocked his fist behind his ear while the others looked on. This was usually the time that Boxcar stepped in, right before anything really serious transpired. He was the law. But he was noticeably absent, which left the responsibility to Murph and his sententious assistant, old man Matheson.

"Enough already," Murph hollered. "It's way too soon for you two idiots to be doing this. I have enough of my own crap to worry about without babysitting you two jackals. Okay? Am I clear? Now get your crap together and make sure you're on that damned field in twenty minutes."

Murph stormed off, leaving a trail of overturned laundry bins and batting helmets in his wake. They all just stood around for a moment, stunned by Murph's explosive rant, uncertain what to make of the atypical outburst. It was only Matheson's inane commentary that shook them from their collective stupor and sent them all scrambling for the field, while he just continued to spew his vapid remarks.

"Well, what are you all standing around for, hunched over like a pack of dogs crapping razor blades. You heard your skipper. It's show time. We've got a clean slate. Yeah, that's right. Atta boy, Woody. You too, McGinty. What about you, Finster? Ha ha. That's what I'm talking about. Hustle out there. Go get 'em. Slice the melon. Fly in the face of it. This here's a hard row to hoe fellas, and believe me when I say…"

Baseball was back everywhere. High above, as though suspended by invisible strings, a band of crows flew idly, listlessly, desultory stains pressed against the pale blue sky. With eyes both dark and ulcerous, Chip McNally stood, arms folded, and spoke passionately with his Rangers about the upcoming season. It seemed impossible that anyone should be unhappy on a day such as this, when the world had burst open once again. Who could find fault with today, especially McNally, whose team was coming off a rousing victory over Murph's Brewers en route to the championship. "Last year is last year, boys," he began, pounding a fist into his open palm. "It means nothing right now." He shook his head violently, and a reckless rage settled around his heart.

"And, we shouldn't be too proud of ourselves. We barely hung on. Christ, to have those rat bastards nipping at our heels on the very last day. Inexcusable. Completely inexcusable. We will bury them this year! All of 'em. From that whining has-been Murphy to Mickey, that freakish wonder boy. Ya hear me. Bury them! I will settle for nothing less."

Lefty Rogers, whose face and neck bore the painful reminders of his run-in with Mickey just months before, listened quietly in the lengthening shadows of the others as McNally continued his harangue.

"And we open up with those turds in just about a month. So we need to be sharp. Ready. There's not a minute to be wasted here."

The manager's words filled Rogers with an unavailing wrath. Since that fateful day last season, when he lost all hope of nailing down a championship for the Rangers and most likely a call up to the big show, all the workings of Lefty's frustrated imagination had been concentrated on vengeance. It's all he thought about. Dreamt about. He had carried it with him all winter. He held it at the hospital, as doctors worked tirelessly to put his battered body back together. It haunted him at night, when he lay his head on the pillow after hours of rehabilitative exercises. It trailed him everywhere, this frustration, a roiling pulsation that ate at him mercilessly in the absence of a tangible outlet. Oh, how he had waited for this day. A chance for redemption. Vindication. His frustration, now unfettered, held up a torch to the fragile fabric of his inner demons, illuminating the pitcher's festering malevolence.

"I'm all for that, Mr. McNally," he said, stepping into the center of the group. "Count me in. Just hand me the ball and point me in the right direction. I'll be there."

Back at Borchert Field, under a sky splashed here and there with rectangular strands of white filament, some of the Brewer pitchers began loosening their arms, the annual ritual of resurrecting those muscles which had lain dormant for many weeks. Gabby Hooper grabbed a ball and paired up with Rube Winkler. Packey Reynolds did the same with Butch Sanders, and the foursome headed down the left field line, moaning and jawing about sore shoulders and stiff biceps.

"Hey, Mick," Sanders called back. "Wanna join us over here?"

Mickey, who had spent several minutes studying the pattern of the laces in the webbing of his glove, started to yawn, as if a simple game of catch was of no interest to him, then emptied a bucket of balls of his own at home plate and scampered down the opposite foul line, stopping when he reached the right field corner. With a quick smile and a jovial, audible "perfect," he placed the empty bucket on its side, then trotted back down the line and proceeded to line up the mess of baseballs—four perfect rows, each five balls deep.

The foursome continued to throw softly, struggling with the rust that had formed on each of their arms with the five-month lay off. It was evident that none of them was any better off than the other, but bravado soon got the best of all of them.

"Jesus Christ, Hooper," Winkler said. "That's all you got? Hell, I've seen better arms on my grand daddy's chair."

Sanders, who caught Winkler's eye and was suddenly aware of the public scrutiny, shot him a quick grin before throwing his next ball to Reynolds with a little more zip on it.

"Yeah, you should talk, Ruby," Hooper fired back. "You couldn't break a pane of glass with that puss ball you've been throwing."

They all laughed, and began peppering each other with a litany zingers until, through the mist of insults, a thunderous sound, like a gun being fired in a stone canyon, halted their attack and left them wide eyed and gape jawed.

"Holy shit," Winkler said. "I don't believe it."

There was a moment of pure, motionless disbelief, when all else seemed to stand still, as the four of them watched with astonishment and incredulity as Mickey bent over to pick up another baseball.

"Did he, uh, just do what I think he did?" Hooper asked, shaking his head rigorously as if to extricate the madness which had entered his head and altered his senses. "From over there?"

They had scarcely reconciled the enormity of the feat when Mickey rolled his arms, licked his lips, and let fly a second baseball. The little white sphere rocketed through the still air like a meteor, its trajectory crisp and true. With eyes wide with wonder, Hopper, Winkler, Sanders and Reynolds stared as the ball careened off the center of the bucket, splitting the silence with a deafening crash.

"That's 329 feet away, guys," Winkler gasped. "On a line."

The others shook their heads. As the display continued to unfold, they all became increasingly preoccupied. There was talk about calculating velocity and power and all kinds of wild speculation about just how far his arm could reach. Someone even whispered the name Superman.

"Hell, I thought it was crazy last year," Sanders said. "But this? I'll be damned if this don't beat all."

Mickey continued firing baseballs, one after the other, and each followed the same path, seemingly wedded to the same destination. The befuddled pitchers just stood and watched, pale-faced and open-mouthed, with a wild stare that slid away only after Mickey had hurled the final ball. They tried to bring what had just transpired into some definite relation to themselves and ended up frustrated and noticeably envious but mostly just dumbstruck by the boy's raw ability. Hooper was the only one who could manage to break the silence.

"Unbelievable," he mumbled. "Un-friggin'-believable."

Murph, who had just stepped onto the field to hit fungos to some of the outfielders who had followed him out, was rattled by a discovery of his own—one that crept up on him eerily before fanning out across the entire ballpark like a storm cloud. It was Boxcar.

The team captain walked slowly, deliberately, a dwindling figure moving languidly in Murph's direction, half extinguished by the rise in temperature, or worry, or perhaps something far more formidable.

"Holy Hannah, Boxcar," Murph gasped once the catcher was close enough to receive the words. "What the hell happened to you? Where the hell is the rest of you?"

He was almost ghostlike in his appearance, his once burly frame reduced now shockingly to a skeletal form that swam awkwardly in his uniform. His face was wan and faded. In his eyes, which were sunk deep now in the dark folds of his lids, was a look of grim determination struggling against an unforeseen peril.

"Sorry I'm late, Murph," he said, his eyes far away from what he was saying. "Let's play ball."

Murph, along with several others who had trotted over once Boxcar had arrived, looked at him with alarm. Something was very wrong.

"Wait a minute here, Box," Murph said. "Just slow down a minute. What the hell is going on with you? Look at yourself. You look awful."

"Ah, I just got a bug or something, that's all. Ain't been feeling too good the last few weeks."

"Did you go see a doctor?"

Boxcar scoffed and thumped his chest with his fist. "Doctor? What the hell for? What do they know? It'll pass, same way it came, and I'll be good as new. I'm fine. Really. So quit your gawking. All of you."

A veil of sobriety fell over them as they listened to Boxcar plead his case, their hopes rising and falling like skittish birds balancing on a tree limb. It was all too much. This was their captain. The last bastion of vitality and unadulterated strength. The rudder of their ship. How could this be the same guy? Their thoughts were killing them. A big part of each of them just wanted to run, to dismiss what had now become so painfully evident. A small part of each of them was already in flight.

"I mean it. Enough with it," he demanded, nostrils flared, his tongue passing recklessly over chapped lips. "Why do you keep looking at me like that? Let's get to work. I don't know what the hell is wrong with all of you. Standing around like a bunch of cackling old hens. *What's wrong, Boxcar? Why are you so skinny, Boxcar? Go to the doctor, Boxcar.* Blah, blah, blah. Holy Christ. Enough with it. Okay? I can't understand you guys. Behaving like a bunch of wash women. Jesus Christ. Did everyone forget why we're here? Don't we have a season to prepare for?"

APRIL

The early morning sunlight spilled across the countryside and dripped gently over Murph's tiny house like golden honey over the side of a glass jar. Murph and Molly sat across from each other, sipping coffee and picking at the banana bread she had made the night before.

"Well, you've been awfully quiet lately," Molly said, playing with the frayed ends of her napkin. "How's everything going?"

"Okay, I guess," he replied. "Most of the rust is off. Guys are hitting and throwing pretty well."

"So what's the long face about? It sounds pretty good to me."

Murph held her off momentarily with a quizzical look that was neither hard nor inviting. He really did not intend to discuss team matters at home. 'Don't crap where you eat' he heard Matheson telling him. He was pretty sure it applied. It was one of the few times the old coot made sense. He was quite certain the comment would just pass, and that he could successfully move the conversation in another direction. But when he felt, all at once, a certain current being turned on somewhere deep within, he could no longer be silent.

"It's Boxcar. Something just ain't right. You should see him.

Looks like a damned corpse. All skin and bones. And he's been dragging himself around the field like every step may be his last. It's a real problem. I can't seem to stop thinking about it."

Molly took his hand and held it to her cheek. Then she smiled.

"I'm sorry, honey. That's awful. But I think maybe I can help you take your mind of that." She darted out of the room, and returned shortly after, with a fairly sizeable box wrapped neatly in brown paper. Her eyes glowed with excitement.

"Seeing it's your birthday and all next week, I suppose you can have this now." She handed him the package. He tugged at the wrapping methodically, then slit the sides of the box with his pocket knife. The longer he spent, the more intrigued he became, until finally, after all the wrapping was gone and the box top removed, he began rifling through the packaging materials inside until he saw it. "Molly, you gotta be kidding me. How did you—"

"Do you like it? I know how you are always losing your notes after the game. And let's face it. Your handwriting isn't getting any better. Now you can just speak your ideas into the machine and it will all be recorded for you. Right there."

Murph shook his head. She had touched him in a place few had ever found. "This is really swell, Molly. Really. But you shouldn't have done this. God. Imagine me. Arthur Murphy. Country boy from the sticks of Wisconsin. The proud owner of a portable wire recorder. Amazing, but I still don't get it. These things are expensive. How on earth did you afford it?"

Her eyebrows danced playfully atop her forehead and she giggled. "Compliments of Clarence Tussler. I received the first part of my settlement a couple of weeks ago. And I wanted to say thank you. For all you've done."

He walked over to her and kissed her lips softly. "You're the best, Molly. Really." He sighed as the euphoria of the moment yielded once again to the grim reality of the situation with Boxcar. "Now, can you fix my catcher situation?"

She laughed at first, until more sober thoughts replaced the frivolity. "Well, does Boxcar have a doctor? What does *he* say?"

"That's the trouble. He don't want to hear nothing about any doctors. Insists he fine. His body may be different but that rock-hard head of his is as thick as ever."

Molly sat stiff and pensive in her chair. "What are you going to do?" she asked.

"Don't really know exactly. I mean, Matheson brought in Hobey Baker. He's okay, but he's all glove and no stick. I also got my eye on another guy—young man who works a couple towns over, at the lumber mill."

Molly scrunched up her nose and shook her head gently. "Arthur, I'm sure you know what you're doing and all. Really. And I am certainly no expert. But if this guy's so good, why isn't he playing for someone else?"

Murph raised his eyebrows and smirked oddly. "He is. Sort of." He got up from the table, cup in hand, and walked to the sink. All of his muscles suddenly felt weighted, by some ineffable force.

"Well?" she asked. "Why all the mystery? Who is this secret star?"

"He's colored, Molly," Murph said softly. "Plays for one of those negro teams."

Molly's face lost all its usual shape."*What?* Where did you find him? Have you seen him play?"

"No, just heard about him. But I did see him swing an axe. Like nothing I've ever seen before. Wrists like lightening. Raw power. Not the big, burly type of power, like Boxcar. This kid's got long, lean muscle. I tell ya. He's the real deal."

Molly blinked her eyes as she stood thinking."Look, Arthur, I don't want to sound like an old stick in the mud, but do you really think that is such a good idea? I mean, this whole black and white thing has finally calmed down. People are starting to feel normal again. You know this will just open up the ugliness all over again."

"I don't see it that way," he replied. "Not at all."

"Well, what about Dennison? Are you sure he is ready for this? And what about the others?"

"Look, Molly, I'm just following the trend. Times are changing. They are. You've read the newspapers. It's not like it used to be. If Jackie Robinson can play for Walter O'Malley, why can't Lester Sledge play for us?"

"Hey, you don't have to sell *me* on the idea, Arthur," she said. "But you should remember that this isn't Brooklyn. And the people here are not as—let's say, cosmopolitan—as you and me."

His spirit sagged. Molly, aware of the damaging residue of her words, joined him at the sink, placing her hand softly on his face.

"Look, I'm sorry, Arthur. I should not have said what I said. I believe you know best. I do. Obviously you're very good at seeing things nobody else can." She smiled, then spoke again. "Speaking of which—how's *my* boy doing?"

"Great. Mickey is great. Truly. He hasn't skipped a beat. In fact, he seems more relaxed than ever. And you should see him throw that baseball. It still amazes me."

She folded her arms tightly against her chest and sighed, toiling with reminiscences both frightening and painful.

"Well that's good to hear. It is. But it's not the baseball that concerns me."

"I know what you're driving at," he assured her. "Trust me. Everything is fine. Everyone takes extra care to watch out for him. Come on now. Last year is last year. That will never happen again. He's right where he belongs." As if the mention of his name were like a bell summoning his presence, Mickey bounded in the kitchen holding a thin stack of yellow paper stapled together and a red pencil.

"Hey, Mick," Molly said. "Watcha doing, sweetheart?"

He set his teeth and for a moment his eyes went wide with concern. "Counting carrots. For Duncan and Daphney."

Molly and Murph both smiled. They sat back down for a moment. Mickey joined them, and began flipping through his log.

"Mickey noticed that some days Duncan and Daphney eat lots of carrots and some days not so many. I have to make sure it's always the same. Every day." He proceeded to flip through the pages, each containing a neatly drawn black line at the top on which the days of the week rested. Each day was divided by a vertical line, also black, that stretched down the page, forming a column in which a number was displayed in red pencil. "Mondays, Duncan eats three carrots and Daphney eats four. Mondays is always seven. On Tuesdays, I give them one extra. Tuesday is eight. Five for Duncan and three for Daphney. Wednesdays, Thursdays, and Fridays are the most. Wednesday is nine, Thursday is ten and on Friday, they share twelve. Twelve carrots. Six each."

Murph fidgeted in his seat, and thought about excusing himself, but knew better than to interrupt the boy when he was in the middle of something.

"On Saturday, they don't eat as many, on account of the lettuce they get that day. I have a book for that too. Saturday they get eight, just like Tuesday, but they each eat four, instead of five and three. And today, Sunday, I usually give them seven, but there were two left over from yesterday, so I didn't know if I should just give them five and leave the two in there or take them out put seven new ones in and change the number on Saturday from eight to six."

"Well, what did you decide, Mickey?" Molly asked.

"I gave them new ones," he said definitely. "You can't eat Saturday's carrots on Sunday."

Murph and Molly shook their heads. Neither of them, for a minute or two, could look the other square in the eye. There were so many moments like this one—moments that revealed the boy for who he was, and for what he was not.

"Uh, you know we have practice, right, big guy?" Murph asked, diverting the discomfort.

"Yes sir, Mr. Murphy," he answered. "Practice is at 9:00. It's only 7:56. We are leaving a half hour before, or maybe twenty-five minutes before, which is what we did the last time. That means I have at least 34 more minutes to get ready."

Once they arrived at the ballpark, Murph turned Mickey and the other players over to Matheson, while he made the onerous trip up to Dennison's office. It was sunny, and beginning to warm, but there was a high, cold wind blowing. He walked clumsily and struggled and strained with the specter of what he knew would be yet another frustrating exchange, pausing only for a moment for a mangy cat, haggard and tailless, who was busy examining the contents of its stomach which now lay in a steaming pile on the cement walkway.

As his feet pounded the familiar course, Murph scrunched up his face in protest to the biting air and the foul smell that had found his nose. He felt so terribly put upon. And useless. Like he had no definitive place in the grand scheme of things. Why was it that every time there was a little controversy, or something was a little amiss, he had to jump through these interrogative hoops, like a little kid, trying to defend his worth to this scornful curmudgeon. He was so sick of it. Sick, with a great angst—a sharp, galling angst that burned deep in his heart—as he entered the owner's lair.

It was cold and dark inside. Dennison was seated, as usual, behind his hand-carved mahogany desk, eyes narrow and wooden behind his glasses, his mouth busy expelling rings of smoke that hovered in the chilly air like white velvet ribbons.

"Come in, Murph," he said through the frosty haze. "Interest you in a hand-wrapped Cuban?"

"No, no thanks, Warren. Not now. I really need to get out to the field as soon as we're finished here."

Dennison nodded and rested his cigar on the glass ash tray to his right. Then, animated by what appeared to be a genuine interest in Murph's well being, he folded his hands and smiled behind the blurred line of smoke billowing from the idling stogie.

"How are you, Murph," he said. "Things good for you?"

"Sure, Warren. Things are okay. You know. The usual."

"The fellas all set to make another run at it?"

"Yeah, I think we're ready to go."

He picked up a baseball that was sitting next to the ash tray and tossed it playfully in the air. He wanted to feel relaxed, loose, but at the same time completely contained. Like everything was in order. "We've got the usual questions marks we have every year, but that's par for the course."

Dennison rose hesitatingly from his seat, pushing aside the pile of papers which lay between them. His eyes lingered on Murph's unusual countenance. The mercurial owner perceived, through Murph's transparent charade, that his manager was trying to get out of there before he was asked something which would undoubtedly throw a light on some of the uncertainty that was circulating.

"What's all this I hear about Raymond Miller—Boxcar?" Dennison asked. "Is that also part of the same course?"

Murph stood awkwardly and watched the smug Dennison, all the while repeating to himself that these words did not matter, and that he would be okay—stood there, with arms folded and lips tight, all in an effort to calm his growing irritation. "What are you talking about, Warren? Boxcar's not feeling so well. I know that. Everyone knows that. I'm not hiding anything."

"Well, now, I did not suggest you were. However, you have not discussed this with me. Or what you plan to do. You can't exactly win a championship without a catcher, now can you?"

"Won't have to," Murph said curtly. "Boxcar will get a shot, as long as he feels good enough. He's my starting catcher. And if that doesn't pan out, I got my eye on some young stud who would fit in here, just fine."

"Matheson's boy? That Baker kid?"

"No. He's not the answer. Never will be."

"Well, who is this mystery player?" Murph paused, as if measuring some weighty contents on an imaginary triple balance beam.

"Sledge. Name's Lester Sledge. Works down at the lumber yard, few towns over. Strong as an ox and has all the tools to sit behind the dish." With Murph's announcement came a thickening of his blood. There emerged a distinct tension in the chilly air. The old man seemed to be holding his breath, waiting for Murph's words to register. His eyes rolled at first, then shifted wildly from side to side. Then a look of revulsion and blinding incredulity hardened on his face.

"You mean the colored kid? You want to replace Boxcar—team captain and Milwaukee icon—with some work-worn blackie?" Dennison thundered. "Is that what you're thinking?"

"Listen, Warren. Nothing—"

"I swear to Christ, Murphy, you really have shit for brains sometimes. You know that? A colored kid. From some two-bit lumber mill. Hell, I'm surprised you just didn't take it all the way, and try to get Josh Gibson or Cool Papa Bell. Weren't *they* available? Heck, maybe Satchel Paige ain't doing nothing this year." He closed his eyes and ran both hands through his hair. "Christ almighty, Murph, I do not know where do you get these harebrain ideas from. Huh? Honest to God, what the hell are you thinking about?"

Murph looked away with impatience, myriad thoughts searing his forehead with lines.

"Jesus, Warren, we've been down this road before," he said, hands on his hips.

"Remember what you said about Mickey when I first told you about *him*?"

"The kid's colored, for Christ sakes. Don't you get it, Arthur?"

"He's a ballplayer, Warren. A damned ballplayer. It's that simple. So he's colored. Big deal. Everyone called Mickey a retard. Including you. And Pee Wee, who happens to be the best shortstop in the league, was just a midget. Words, Warren. Just words. Does it make them any less effective on the field?"

"You are talking out your ass, Arthur," Dennison said. "Apples and oranges. This ain't the same thing, at all. I don't need to lose any more fannies from our seats. And I certainly do not need any visits from the damned Klan. Have you read the damned papers lately? You are playing with fire here. These white folks work hard for their money. And they look forward to coming here to watch their team — a team of their own — play ball for them. I won't screw with that. I can't. I owe them better than that."

Murph wasn't listening anymore. He was so sick of Dennison's crap. Why did he think, even for a minute, that this arrogant, self-absorbed scumbag would be amenable to anything so unconventional? This man, who viewed himself, unjustifiable as it was, in such high regard. You think he would have learned his lesson with Mickey. But he just could not see beyond himself and his myopic ideas. He had this secret sense of power and control. God, it was sickening. He went about his business with this ineffable, inexpressible tyranny, something deep and twisted that suggested an unavailing need for control emanating from a truly insecure core.

"Well, I bet Walter O'Malley and a whole bunch of people wearing blue and white in Brooklyn are glad they didn't feel the same way. There's a colored boy over there who plays first base. I *think* his name is Jackie Robinson. You may have heard of him. Rookie of the year? Led the league in stolen bases? Helped get 'dem bums' to the Series?"

"Don't get cute with me, Murphy. Okay. I know all about that. Poppycock. This ain't the big city. Besides, that won't last. You'll see. Black and white? It just don't work. Especially here. Haven't you been reading the papers? Our people? They're just different here. And our players. What about them? Have you thought about them?"

Murph folded his arms and sighed.

"Listen, this is all sort of premature. Relax. But I'm telling you. I've seen him. And people I trust say he's the real deal. Negro league or not. He hits the crap out of the ball and has a canon behind the plate. I think once everyone sees that, nobody—not even you—will care *what* damn color he is."

Dennison continued to listen, unable to utter even a sound as his throat had thickened with abhorrence.

"Listen, forget about all this worrying for now," Murph continued. "Let's just see what happens with Boxcar. Maybe he'll snap out of it and all this bantering will have been for naught. But if he doesn't, and we still need to look for a catcher, you leave the fellas on the team and everything else to me. I'll put my job on the line, again, just to get this thing rolling. That's how sure I am."

Standing there, listening to Murph pitch his plan, Dennison thought about his manager and the last few years. All of the scheming and complaining. And all of the losing. The memory quickly became a burden. He had been thinking for a while that his interest would be better served with someone a little younger, someone who did not have so much baseball baggage and such an irritating penchant for challenging his authority with these chimerical ideas. All of these thoughts, and so many more, found their way to his thin lips, which suddenly morphed into a sadistic smile. "Job on the line, heh?" he said, raising his eyebrows. "I just may accept that challenge."

OPENING DAY

It was a dazzling, cloudless April afternoon, with a golden swim of light falling to the ground at Borchert Field in bolts of brilliant yellow that lit up the lush green grass as it danced happily in gentle wafts of wind. It was a classic spring day, and a beautiful day for baseball.

In front of a stadium filled to capacity with rabid fans who had awakened ravenous from their baseball hibernation, the Brewers and Rangers both busied themselves with their pre-game rituals. All across the field, players from both teams were fielding grounders, playing pepper, and shagging fly balls. While to the casual observer this appeared to be just another start to the season, most knew otherwise. Never before did one game possess so many subplots — issues that transcended the field into realms far more human and compelling. There was Arthur Murphy, pitted once again against his nemesis, Chip McNally, the man who crashed into him in the outfield years ago while chasing a ball that was clearly Murph's, destroying a career that was destined for Cooperstown. Murph never forgave him. And McNally still insisted it was his ball.

The bad blood had only escalated through the years, reaching an all-time high with last year's battle for first place that wound up going McNally's way after much controversy. Then there was the highly anticipated showdown between George "Lefty" Rogers, the ex- Brewer and fireballing ace of the Rangers, the man Mickey nearly killed after Lefty showed up at Murph's house and attacked the boy—and Mickey, the beloved, albeit slow-witted phenom who still did not understand everything that had transpired. After the incident, Lefty spent weeks in the hospital recovering from the injuries he sustained, followed by some time spent in the town jail for aggravated assault. Mickey was incarcerated as well, long enough to miss that last game against the Rangers, until a pardon from the governor released the boy once again. Now the two of them would face off, once and for all.

"Look at him over there," McNally said, pressed up against Lefty's ear.

They were watching Mickey loosening up on the foul line with Boxcar and Murph. "That retard messed you up last year. Bad. Now look at him. Everyone yelling his name, painting some picture like he's the next Warren Spahn. Pathetic. Are you gonna let that freak show get the best of you? Huh?"

Lefty's ductility was easily exposed. Somehow he had forgotten all about McNally and Quinton's role in what had happened. How the two of them used him, and set him up for the disaster that eventually befell him. Now all he saw was a monster on the other side of the field, one against whom all his anger could be directed. "I'll get 'em, Chip," he said, gritting his teeth. "I'll get all of 'em."

And then there was the less publicized, understated drama surrounding Boxcar. Were all the rumors true? The press had leaked the story just days before, and everyone was captured by the startling news. Would the heart and soul of this team, the captain both on and off the field, be able to play despite the illness that had seized him so unmercifully? Just the sight of him, noticeably thinner and much less demonstrative, was enough to fuel that fire.

Murph recognized all the commotion swirling on the periphery and was mindful to address it before the game. "Listen fellas, we waited all winter for this. A chance for redemption. But we need to focus here. Focus on the task at hand. Forget everything else. Clear your heads. Twenty-seven outs, boys. Twenty-seven outs and we're back on top. We can't get back last year, but we can sure as hell make everyone forget about it."

They were all huddled together, like a platoon preparing for an offensive, each man looking to the other for strength and support. All except Mickey, who was off in the corner of the dugout, rocking back and forth, eyes closed, lips forming the familiar words they had all come to recognize as his song of flight.

"What the hell is wrong with Mickey?" Murph asked. "Did something happen out there?"

"I think it was Lefty," Danvers said. "That jackass was jawing at him from the dugout, and making all kinds of gestures. I put a stop to it but I think it may have rattled him."

Murph saw the boy struggling, and was quick to intercede. "Hey, Mick, what's going on pal?" he said. "Everything okay?"

The boy did not move. Just stood there, catatonically, his fragile soul naked in his glassy eyes. He was remembering the last time he saw Lefty. And he could still hear the assailant's voice, cold and vituperative, and the pathetic cries of Oscar, his favorite pig, after Lefty plunged his boot into the porker's side, killing it instantly. Then there were the hours that followed, with Sheriff Rosco, and all the questions. So many questions. The recollection was overwhelming. Frightening. He just wanted it to all go away.

"'Slowly, silently, now the moon, walks the night in her silver shoon…'"

"Mickey, come on now. We're not doing that now. There's no need. You're home here. We've got a game to play here. Hear that crowd? Listen to them. They all came for you."

The boy's affectations were unchanged. He continued to stare vacantly, rocking back and forth, trying desperately to drive the hateful memories out of himself.

"This way and that, she peers and sees, silver fruit upon silver trees."

Murph put his hand on the boy's shoulder and squeezed gently. "Hey, Mick, you're okay. Save that poem for home. Come on now. Just you and Boxcar. Like always. Focus on that glove. Nothing else. Toss that apple right to the glove. Just like you used to do for Oscar. Right to the target. Can you do that for me?"

Maybe it was his manager's touch, and the way Murph's urgency flowed through his fingers and into Mickey's body like some electrical charge. Or maybe it was the mere mention of the name Oscar, said out loud, that made the difference. Maybe it was both.

Whatever it was, the boy began to free himself slowly from the demon that had seized him. He blinked several times, as if cleaning the lens to his mind's eye, and stopped his recitation of the poem.

"Oscar didn't like Lefty, Murph," he said. "No sir. Mickey don't like him much either." Murph grinned and shook his head.

"Don't sweat it, kid. Nobody here does."

The Brewers took the field moments later, led by their ace and fan favorite, Mickey Tussler. The crowd was bristling with an untamed enthusiasm, waving placards professing their unconditional love for the "Baby Bazooka" and chanting his name. In the wake of his superhuman exploits on the field, and all of the misfortune and injustice that had befallen him elsewhere, Mickey had become a cult hero of sorts.

Entire sections of stands at Borchert Field were commandeered by the most ardent of Mickey's followers. One area was claimed by the "Baby Bazooka Brigade," five rows behind the Brewer's dugout filled with dutiful, fanatical disciples donned in battle fatigues and army field helmets. Every time Mickey either took or left the field, the entire group would rise in unison and salute their hero until he had reached his destination.

Across the way, stationed behind the opposing team's dugout, was a group known affectionately as "Mickey's Minions," scores of men and women alike sporting cream-colored T-shirts espousing their slogan on the front and a big heart with the number 8 inside on the back. They had in *their* arsenal signs and noise makers and on occasion, bags filled with confetti, all designed to express their unconditional love for their favorite Brewer.

Mickey had captured the hearts and imaginations of the rest of the Brewers faithful as well; many of these less organized, less equipped worshippers were there that day too, roaring and clapping and rolling their arms in reverential pantomime, many dressed in Brewers shirts sporting Mickey's name and number on their backs.

Kiki Delaney led off the game for the Rangers. Delaney was their sparkplug, the catalyst behind a pretty potent offensive ma-chine. He led the league the last two years in stolen bases and runs scored and had been a real thorn in the Brewers' side. Both Murph and Boxcar reminded Mickey how crucial it was to keep Delaney off the bases.

"Don't play with him, big boy," Boxcar said after Mickey had completed his warm up tosses. "Just go after him."

Delaney stepped in, inched real close to the plate, and got into his crouch. He loved the ball low and away. There were very few who were as adept at fighting off anything that got into his kitchen until he got something over the outer half that he could drive the other way. Mickey stood tall on the mound, peering in at Boxcar's glove. The wily catcher was set up on the outside half of the plate, pounding his glove loud enough so that Delaney would know where he sat.

"Come on, Mick," he strained from behind his mask. "Hit that glove, kid."

Mickey nodded his head and, in typical fashion, placed his hand with the ball firmly in his glove and began the wild undulation of his arms, much to the delight of the eager crowd. Then he rocked back, brought his knee to his chest, and fired a dart just as Boxcar shifted over to the inner half of the plate. The ball whizzed through the frenetic air right for the glove, as if being pulled by some invisible string.

"Steerike one!" was the call.

The crowd roared. Delaney nodded his head curiously, as if to acknowledge that he had underestimated the velocity of the offering, and that he would not be fooled again. Mickey's second delivery, however, was equally elusive, a white streak of burning light that froze the hitter while shaving the outside corner for a called strike two.

"Come on, Kiki," McNally screamed from the bench. "That's all he's got. It ain't nothin'. Sit on the heater, for Christ sakes. You know it's coming again. There ain't nothin' else."

At those last words, something gloriously liberating and intoxicatingly delicious darted into Murph's mind. Now was the time. A special something was his and Boxcar's and Mickey's alone; a wonderful secret, something only theirs. He could still recall the days spent teaching the boy his latest skill.

"Grip the ball this way," Murph explained, showing Mickey the baseball, "and spin it like this—like you are snapping your fingers."

Mickey's head was the only thing spinning.

"But Mickey does not understand. If I spin the baseball, how can I throw it?"

Mickey's obtuseness challenged Murph's patience. It took some doing, and Murph almost gave up a few times, but eventually the young phenom got it. And it had remained a secret for months, suspended in designed dormancy. But now was the perfect time to summon the magical mystery and share it with everyone else.

"Mickey," Murph yelled from the dugout.

The boy turned his gaze toward the voice, as did Boxcar. Murph smiled, nodded his head, and, made a curious gesture with his hand.

"Come on now, Mick," he encouraged. "Just like we practiced."

Mickey's eyes studied Murph's face with discernable deliberation, as if the manager's instructions were slowly dissolving into an actual plan. He titled his head and scratched his cheek, remembering now what he and Murph had worked on previously. With this thought now fully hatched, Mickey toed the rubber and peered in at Boxcar, who was wiggling two fingers against the inner half of his right thigh.

Mickey nodded and fired what looked to be another missile, a shoulder-high delivery that was destined to land well above the strike zone. High fastball. Just a waste pitch. Delaney relaxed his bat, and the umpire ducked behind Boxcar, certain that he was about to take the wild pitch square in the face. Yet as the spinning sphere approached its destination, it dove sharply, suddenly, buckling Delaney's knees before plunging a good three feet across the center of the plate and into Boxcar's glove. The Ranger's leadoff man, stunned by the drastic change in trajectory, looked sheepishly behind him, waiting to be rung up. Boxcar turned his head as well, only to discover that the man in blue had only now just lifted his head back up into view.

"Ball one," he finally called.

Boos and jeers rained down from the stands. Murph, Matheson and the entire Brewers' bench launched invectives of their own.

"Where's your glasses and cane?" they screamed. "That's a curveball, ump.

Ever see a curveball? Pathetic. Jesus H. Christ! That ball was right there."

The umpire stood vexed as Boxcar returned the ball to Mickey, pretending not to hear any of what was being said. He had called Mickey's games before, but had never seen anything except pure heat. The error in judgment had him rattled.

"Sorry 'bout that, Boxcar," he finally whispered as he crouched behind the catcher in preparation for the next pitch. "I just missed it."

Boxcar, who was breathing heavily, answered without turning around.

"You better not blink again, chief. The boy will be dropping them yellow hammers all afternoon."

Now that the seed of doubt had been planted, Mickey and Boxcar owned Delaney. He didn't know what to expect. Mickey wasted no time cashing in on the indecision, freezing Delaney with a letter high fastball and sending him back to the bench shaking his head. The next two batters met with a similar fate, each going down on 0–2 curveballs that had the entire ballpark wide-eyed and speechless. Mickey had electrified the home town crowd as only he could. But it was time for the bats to join the party. The Brewers had played so many games last year that featured stellar pitching and anemic offense. Murph was mindful of the need to erase the trend.

"Okay now, fellas," he said, clapping his hands while pacing the front of the bench. "Let's get those sticks going."

Pee Wee waited in the on-deck circle, swinging two bats and eye balling Lefty as the southpaw completed his warm up tosses. There was certainly no love lost between the two, especially after Lefty used Pee Wee as a pawn last season in order to orchestrate the first deplorable incident with Mickey.

"How could you just leave him, Lefty? At a bar, all by himself? You know he can't handle himself that way. You said you'd take care of him."

The jealous hurler just smiled, his complexion waxy from a night of drunken debauchery. "Relax Pee Wee," he said callously. "He was with a girl. I did him a favor. You should be thanking me. Besides, you're the one who brought him."

The truth of the statement, although spun to suit Lefty's argument, stung mightily. It left the diminutive shortstop bitter and vengeful. He became very vocal about his feelings regarding Lefty before the surly pitcher moved on to the Rangers. And Lefty had heard every word of it.

The Brewers' leadoff man stepped into the box to a raucous chorus of "Let's Go Brew Crew!" Lefty stood still on the mound, his eyes dark and ulcerous, his mind echoing with accusatory voices, gobbling and jabbering in incomprehensible tones. The noise melded together with the shrill wail of police sirens and the cold clicking of handcuffs, until the cacophony rose up and filled the man with rage even he had underestimated.

This wrath traveled quickly to his left arm. Pee Wee had barely dug in at the plate before Lefty dusted him off with a two-seam fastball that whizzed by his head, sending the batter sprawling to the ground in a desperate attempt to dodge the ball of venom. The boo birds were off their roost again, this time showering the field with a deluge of apple cores and soda bottles. Lefty waved his arms to the crowd invitingly, his glove hand motioning for more trash while the other was pressed to his mouth blowing kisses.

"Do you believe this guy?" Danvers complained to Finster. "Incredible."

The two of them watched as Lefty continued to taunt the crowd and then Pee Wee, who had just stood up and cleaned himself off. "Hey, asshole," Danvers screamed from the dugout. "How 'bout dancing with me next?"

Some fragment of Lefty's attention was still lost in the crowd, but he heard the challenge and could not resist. He looked right at Danvers. He inhaled deeply and with nostrils flaring, began walking in his direction, ready to take on the Brewers' third baseman right there. He had all but reached the first base foul line when McNally's voice, harsh and savage, arrested his advance. "Rogers, you get your ass back on that mound and pitch goddammit! You don't get paid to screw around."

The grounds crew dispensed with the garbage in a timely fashion and the game resumed. Pee Wee swung and missed at the next pitch and took the next two outside to run the count to 3 and 1. Lefty was throwing hard; it seemed as though all the shenanigans had stoked his fire. Pee Wee knew he was not going to be able to get around on the fastball. He called time. With one foot inside the box and the other just outside the chalk, he held his bat with two hands, exhaled loudly, and brought the barrel gently to rest against his forehead, as if he were transferring his intention to the instrument. Then he glanced furtively down the third base line before climbing back in the box to resume his battle.

Lefty was still unhinged. His face burned in the hell-colored sunlight. He thought for a minute about throwing at Pee Wee again, just to teach him a lesson about making him wait. But the sound of McNally's voice, still shrill and admonitory, broke up the feeling into frenetic coils that festooned throughout his body. He sighed with frustration, passed his tongue over the outside of his lips, wound up and fired. It was a perfect delivery; knee-high four seamer that would have painted the black on the inner half of the plate had Pee Wee not run up, slid his hand up the barrel of the bat and dropped a perfect bunt up the third base line. Both Lefty and the third baseman scrambled for the ball, but by the time Lefty's fingers plucked it from the grass, Pee Wee had already crossed the bag safely.

"Way to go, Pee Wee!" Murph yelled. "Way to get it going."

Arky Fries was next. He saw just one pitch, a jam job that resulted in a foul out to the catcher. With the speedy Pee Wee still at first, Woody Danvers strode to the plate.

He too had a history with Lefty. Hated the guy. Some of it stemmed from the whole Mickey thing, but the truth was they never got along. Two egos that large were bound to bump into each other, and that's just what had happened, time and again. Now they were enemies for sure. And with Boxcar laboring under the weight of this undisclosed illness, Danvers remained the only legitimate power threat in the Brewers' lineup.

Danvers cut the tension with a few practice swings before stepping in to take his hacks. Lefty stewed, glaring at Danvers with intolerant eyes, gray and ominous. He felt the urgent need to carry out this furious, unflagging will for retribution as Danvers cocked and waved his bat by his ear, settling down only after Lefty had delivered his first pitch, a high hard one up and in that backed Danvers off the plate. The second and third pitches were exactly the same—more chin music. Danvers stepped out, tapped his spikes and grinned. It was obvious Lefty wanted no part of him right now. A fourth pitch, up and away, sent the Brewers' slugger to first with a base on balls.

The crowd began to stir now, intoxicated with the idyllic scenario that was unfolding before them. Mickey notwithstanding, Boxcar was the fan favorite. He had been with the team for years, and was the heart and soul of the club. The face of the franchise. He had spoiled them time and again with many a spectacular feat, so much so that the locals viewed him as a baseball deity. A man imbued with the ability to will his team to victory. They roared and chanted his name even louder now, for all of them had heard of the mysterious physical malady that had afflicted their hero and were thrilled to see him, as improbable as it seemed, in his familiar cleanup spot.

Boxcar! Boxcar! Boxcar!

He smiled, and tipped his hat to the adoring crowd, but there was something shadowy and vacant about the man. Ghostlike. He was thinking of years past as he stepped to the plate. And of friends and teammates from those years and how they knew him and his ways and how they had come to rely on and appreciate all that he could accomplish on the field. Of course, his mind also wandered to those moments of exhilaration, when his exploits, now legendary in their own right, led to victory for the Brewers and celebration for the entire city of Milwaukee.

Lefty grinned behind his glove. He too saw what they all saw. Boxcar was just a shell of his former self. The Rangers' ace wasted no time attacking, letting fly a rising fastball right down the center of the plate. Boxcar saw the ball okay, but his bat was late and sagged, and struggled to move through the hitting zone. The swing was awkward and spastic. He lost his footing and crumbled to the ground. A collective gasp swirled through the ballpark, as if the air from twenty thousand balloons had suddenly been released. It was painful to watch. They could not speak; all they could do was look on, silenced by the increasing drama, and pray silently that what they were seeing was not really happening.

Boxcar struggled to his feet, dusted off his jersey and readied himself for the next delivery. This time Lefty came inside, but the ball ran too far off the plate and was called a ball. The crowd began to shake itself from its stupor, trying to energize their exanimate hero with applause and cheers. Boxcar heard the tribute, like a sweet melody from days long since past, but could do little more than wave at the next pitch. Lefty sensed the desperation and went right for the kill, unleashing yet another tracer that whizzed through the still air, boring in on Boxcar's knuckles. The enervated catcher clenched his teeth and whipped the bat head through the zone with every ounce of strength he had. The crack of the bat was loud but deceiving. The ball struck the bat on the trademark, sawing it off in two. The handle remained in Boxcar's hands and the other half, jagged and splintered, rolled helplessly, along with the baseball, back to the Lefty who quickly scooped up the latter and fired it to second base to begin a nifty 1–6–3 twin killing. The inning expired before Boxcar even had the chance to run to first.

On the way in to the dugout, Murph stopped the winded idol. "Hey, Box, you okay to go another inning? You don't look so good."

Boxcar winced. His face flushed while he struggled with the emerging reality. He could choose, he thought, the easy way—the lesser of the two stances. He could be unfaithful to himself, and to the others, and just pack it in. Bag out, before it became too damned embarrassing and painful. For everyone. Or, he could play on, refuse to throw away his soul, the very essence of who he was, just because his body had chosen to betray him. "I'm fine, Murph. Ya hear? Fine. Don't you even think about it. I am finishing this game."

Mickey bounded out to the mound to begin the top of the second inning. He waited patiently as Boxcar donned the shin guards and chest protector. His eyes scanned the crowd. He saw so many colors—red, blue and off white mostly. The Brewers' colors were well represented that day. He marveled at the mixture, but decided that he'd much prefer to have all the colors separated from each other. Maybe have a section of stands for the people with red shirts, a section for blue, and one just for the off white. He struggled momentarily with what to do with those fans wearing shirts sporting an amalgamation of the Brewers' traditional colors. It was just his way. Everything had its place and order. Standing in the shower, the top half of the body got completely scrubbed first so that none of the dirt would run down onto clean legs. It was always pants first, then shirt. Right shoe and sock always went on before the left. Vegetables came before meat. And bread for last, except when it was liver. When it was liver, the liver went first, followed by the bread to soak up the juice and then vegetables to kill the taste. Dessert was no different. Pie and cake had to divided into squares of even proportions before eating. Brownies were okay as is, provided they were not cut too big, in which case alterations were a must. Cookies posed no problem at all, except in the case of oatmeal raisin or chocolate chip, where one of the raisin or chips extended beyond the surface area of the actual cookie. Then it could not be eaten. And it was green M & M's first. Then yellow, red, and orange. Brown was last. Always last.

Clarence tortured the boy his whole life, calling him names and mocking his unusual behaviors, all the while suggesting that Molly had somehow ruined him and needed to be held responsible. "What the hell's with this boy?" he always thundered. "Friggin' retard. That's what he is. I never saw such a boy as this. What in tarnation did you do, woman, to screw him up so?" It was only now, free from Clarence's tentacles, that they both finally felt as though they could be themselves. Standing there, waiting for Boxcar, Mickey began counting colored shirts when the tardy catcher jolted him away from his thoughts.

"Hey, Mickey, let's go here. I'm ready for you. Start warming up."

Seven tosses later, the cleanup hitter for the Rangers stepped in to try his luck against Mickey. He did exactly as McNally told him. Look for the fastball and adjust to the curve. But try as he might, he was just as ineffectual as the first three hitters. In fact, Mickey retired the side in order in each of the next six innings. Twenty-one up, and twenty-one down. Just like that. The kid was just un-hittable. Boxcar's glove was popping all afternoon like it was the fourth of July and Mickey was freezing hitters with a 12–6 hook that was rolling off the table. Everyone who was at Borchert Field that day said it was the best pitched game they had ever seen. The only blemish on the day was that Lefty had also posted all zeros on the board, so after seven full innings of play, the game remained knotted in a scoreless tie.

The Rangers managed to break up Mickey's bid for a perfect game with two outs in the eighth on a check swing dying quail that fell in between Arky Fries and Amos Ruffings. The crowd cursed the ill-fated knock but soon rose to their feet to salute the exemplary effort of their favorite pitcher. It was quite a run. Twenty-three straight hitters.

Mickey smiled, and tipped his cap to the adoring masses only after Danvers and Pee Wee had run in from their positions to tell him that such a show of appreciation was in order. Then Mickey thanked them all again by disposing of the next hitter with three straight fastballs.

Under a patch of late afternoon sky that had suddenly blanched, illuminating the silhouettes of the players in the field as though they were clay idols glued to a game board, Danvers walked to the plate to leadoff the home half of the eighth. Lefty, working on quite a gem of his own, readied himself for the next frame, vowing not to let Mickey and the Brewers get the best of him. He was thinking about a game last year, when he got too cute in the late innings trying to make the perfect pitch. He had been cruising along, just like today, destined for a win and all sorts of adulation and attention, when a walk to the leadoff man opened the flood gates and ultimately lead to a rousing Brewer comeback victory. His eyes grew dim remembering.

Danvers was recalling the same thing. Lefty was not that hard to read. Even though Boxcar was slumping, and had looked awful at the plate all day long, Lefty would not want to put the go ahead run on base to start the inning. The idea of pitching around him to get to Boxcar was absurd. With this thought planted firmly in his mind, Danvers dug in and waited like a dispossessed child standing at a candy counter, about to sample a delicacy he had not tasted in quite some time. *First ball, fastball*, he told himself, licking his lips. Here it comes.

Lefty did not disappoint. He reared back and grooved a fat, belt high heater that appeared to Danvers to be spinning in suspended animation. He could not recall the last time he had seen a ball so clearly. He laughed silently to himself as the laces spun closer and closer. How he had longed for this moment—when he could jam his bat up the ass of this pompous, self-absorbed jerk who had betrayed all of them. *God I can't wait to see his face*, he mused. It was the last thought he had in his head before the bat struck the ball cleanly, a thunderous crash that launched the little white sphere into prodigious orbit. A collective jolt of rapturous expectation followed. All eyes in the ballpark traced the flight of the ball as it soared and scraped the sky with a majestic trajectory that sent the hoards of Brewer faithful into a breathless frenzy while leaving Lefty and the entire Ranger contingent crestfallen once it had landed safely some thirty-five feet beyond the leftfield wall.

Danvers savored his trip around the bases, reveling in the shower of praise raining down from the fevered crowd. His gait was buoyant, his strides short and deliberate, celebratory steps that fanned the crowd's fire while drawing the ire of the humiliated pitcher.

"Don't dig in too far next time, pretty boy," Lefty jawed as Danvers continued his victory jaunt. "Or there's gonna be one less asshole to worry about."

With one run to his credit, Mickey seemed oddly taller, more powerful and looming as he stood on the mound with just three outs to go. The Rangers had scarcely touched the burly fireballer all afternoon. They had generated nothing at all offensively.

All they had to show for a day's work was a check swing dunker that had barely eluded the gloved of Arky Fries. And now they had just three outs to work with—three shots to get the game tied and back into the hands of *their* ace.

"Let's wake up, boys!" McNally barked wildly. He was looking into the Brewer dugout and scowling at the look of confidence, affixed to Arthur Murphy's face. "I will not—uh, *we* will not lose to this kid and this second-rate bunch of bush leaguers. Come on now. Let's go!"

The Rangers sent their seven, eight, and nine hitters to the plate in the top half of the ninth, hoping to manufacture some sort of threat. The bottom third of their lineup, however, proved no match for Mickey that day. He fanned each batter on three straight fastballs, running his strikeout total for the day to an unfathomable fifteen, sending the awestruck crowd into a dizzying display of boisterous celebration, culminating with the rhythmic chanting of their hero's name as he walked of the field. Afterward, the clubhouse was buzzing with reporters, all clamoring for a chance to speak with the star of the show. Murph stood at the boy's locker like a sentinel, buffering the hysteria and screening questions, all in an effort to quell any misgivings Mickey may have been feeling.

"How did it feel to go out there today Mickey and be so dominant?" one reporter asked.

"Good," Mickey replied.

"Did you think at all about last year when you were out there?" another inquired. "You know, Lefty Rogers and all?"

"No. I don't reckon so. There were lots of colored shirts out there today."

"What about the perfect game? Did you think about that at all at any point?"

"Nope."

The frustrated reporter squeezed the inner corners of his eyes with his thumb and forefinger. "Well, can you tell me anything you were thinking out there?" he persisted. "Anything?"

Mickey shrugged. "Nothing I suppose. Just lots of shirts."

"Nothing? Nothing? Aw, come on now, kid. Don't play with me. You must have been thinking about something out there."

Mickey sat calmly, his eyes affixed to something on the other side of the room. "Nope," he repeated. "Nothing."

The reporter shook his head. "Well what about now? Can you at least tell me what's going through your mind now?" Mickey swooned inside, then looked at Murph who was smiling.

"Go on, Mick," Murph said winking. "It's okay. Tell the man what you told me after you came off the field."

Mickey grabbed the edge of his locker door with both hands and pushed it shut. "Carrots," he said. The reporter squinted and his face contorted.

"Carrots?" the man repeated. "Did you say 'carrots?'"

"That's what he said," Murph interjected. Then the manager held out both palms and motioned to Mickey that it was okay to continue explaining.

"Duncan and Daphney eat carrots," he began. "Mondays, Duncan eats three carrots and Daphney eats four. Monday is always seven. On Tuesdays, they eat eight. Wednesday is nine, Thursday is ten, and today, which is Friday, they eat twelve. Twelve carrots. Except last Friday, it was only ten. Mickey thinks they may be sick. So I will go home now and count how many they ate."

The reporter stared for a minute, as if in that instant he were suddenly removed from and suspended above the vibration of everything that had led up to this one surreal moment. Murph saw his expression and couldn't help but chuckle. Then he pushed himself into the middle of the crowd.

"Okay fellas, you heard the kid," he announced. "That's enough for today. We have some important business to take care of at home."

The day should have ended there, at that moment. This glorious, seamless day that was filled with victory and merriment. It should have concluded with Mickey's final strikeout and the celebration that followed. But Murph still had one more task he needed to tend to.

During the seventh inning stretch, Dennison had sent a note from his seat to the dugout summoning Murph to a post-game meeting in Dennison's office. Murph was benumbed much more than he could have imagined. He sat stiffly across from the despotic owner, his mind lost in a momentary squall of swift visions and painful recollections not entirely unconnected to his present situation.

"I bet you're feeling pretty good about the outcome of today's game, Murph," Dennison said, leaning back in his chair while dabbing the moisture on his forehead with a cocktail napkin. "Always nice to start the year with a W." Murph's eyes were watching Dennison quietly. He seemed to be beyond him.

"Yes, yes it is. It was a nice win for us today. No question."

"Indeed it was," Dennison said, scratching his chin. "However, I could not help but notice that you guys were not exactly tearing it up out there. Your boy threw a masterpiece. That's not going to happen every day. We need to hit the ball, Murph. Put up some crooked numbers now and again. And we can't go into battle every day with a captain who's washed up."

"He's not washed up, Warren. Christ, it's the first game. He's just struggling a bit."

"Struggling a bit? Is that what *you* saw? I saw 0–4 with three strikeouts. I saw a guy who barely had enough energy to get the ball back to Mickey after each pitch. I saw a guy—a cleanup hitter mind you—who carried himself today like some second-rate weakling who has one foot in the grave and the other on a banana peel." Murph appeared to be watching something around Dennison's feet, and remained aloof as though he had not heard him, or as if his body had just quit functioning as soon as Dennison had finished speaking.

"What are you saying, Warren, huh?" he finally said. "Are you telling me you don't want Boxcar anymore? That you're just going to forget everything he has done—everything he has meant to this club? What is it that you want?" Dennison's face was dark and grave and oddly bemused.

"I'm not the heartless ogre you'd have people believe I am," he answered. "We owe Boxcar some sort of allegiance. He's welcome to be a part of this team. Of course he is. It wouldn't be the same without him. All I'm saying, Murph, is that I cannot tolerate having a catcher batting in the cleanup spot who can barely swing the bat and run to first. We cannot win that way. And, if I may be perfectly clear here, I am in this thing to win." An odd look came to Murph's face, as if Dennison had reached into the core of his soul, the vault of his innermost thoughts, fears and concerns, and suddenly exposed them to the light.

"I know what you're saying, Warren. I do. And I have been thinking about it. Believe me. I can probably convince Boxcar to take a back seat while he works through whatever it is that's ailing him. And, if you recall, I have just the guy to give us the lift you're talking about."

Dennison's eyes narrowed and he frowned. "No way, Murph. We have gone over this already. I have thought about your cockamamie proposal. No way. I will not replace a Milwaukee icon with some porch monkey from the lumber yard. You can play Matheson's boy. Or I'll get someone else myself. That's what we'll do."

"You're wrong, Warren. Dead wrong. Lester Sledge is the real deal. He is exactly what we need. And he's hungry, Warren. He wants it bad."

"He's colored, Murph. Did you forget that?"

"It's not about the color, Warren. I'm telling you. This kid is a stud. You think Brooklyn has flipped over Jackie Robinson? Wait till Milwaukee gets a look at this guy. It'll be like nothing you've ever seen."

Dennison got up and stood in silent agitation, his hands folded into his armpits. "I told you once before, Murph. This ain't Brooklyn. You cannot replace Boxcar with some farm-fed negro. These people are not ready for it. Black and white don't mix. You don't know what you're saying here. It ain't the answer. It ain't natural. It just ain't. And when the whole house of cards collapses, who do you think will be left holding the damned bag? Huh? Me, that's who. What are you going to say to me then—when the turnstiles stop clicking, and I'm out a ton of money?"

"I don't know, Warren. It's hard to say." He paused a moment reflectively. "But I know what I'll say to you now. Let me try this. I'll take full responsibility. For the whole damn thing. I'll do all the leg work. I promise you, you won't be sorry. I'm telling you. Between Mickey and Lester, we'll be the envy of the entire league. The fans will have to love us. Everyone loves a winner. And if things do go bad, and you need your pound of flesh, I'll be happy to provide it."

"Are you saying what I think you're saying, Arthur Murphy? You're serious? That you will put your job on the line? Just for a chance with this kid?"

"Just give me half the season, Warren. Half. If, at the half-way point, it has not been what you would consider to be a success, I will pack my things and be gone before anyone has any time to miss me."

Dennison responded like a mechanical toy, one whose buttons had been pushed in all the right ways. He was curiously at ease now, as if a wheeling grace had settled in between them and had come to pass. "So you'll leave—just like that? And Mickey is still mine? Is that what you're saying?" Murph nodded and extended his hand in Dennison's direction. "Well now, you've got yourself a deal there, Mr. Murphy," Dennison said, grabbing Murph's hand with one of his own. "The hand shake seals it."

They talked some more, about this and that, and shook hands one more time. Dennison seemed oddly at ease. So was Murph. He smiled, then turned and walked away dutifully, his thoughts unfurling like a beautiful picture on a boundless scroll of paper.

APRIL 19, 1949

Lester Sledge lived above Elijah Finney's lumber mill, a small, shingled structure just two towns over from Borchert Field. Lester was responsible for chopping, sawing, stacking and hauling lumber around from here to there; in exchange, Finney gave the young man a place to hang his hat. It wasn't much to speak of, but the price was right.

When Lester wasn't working the mill, he was throwing out base runners and hitting balls out of sight for the Milwaukee Bears of the Negro National League. The team had come into the league to fill one of the vacancies created in the NNL after the Cleveland Tate Stars and Pittsburgh Keystones had been dropped. But with limited financing and an inexperienced ownership, the team quickly dissolved and fell out of the running in the league. Most of the players, however, refused to let their dream of playing baseball die. With little more than just the shirts on their backs and some baseball gloves and bats, they formed a "pickup" squad that traveled around to neighboring cities playing against anyone who would have them. They had been very successful throughout the years, despite competition from minor league teams featuring all white rosters, particularly of late with the addition of players like

Lester, who continued to open eyes each time he stepped on the field.

Dawn had arrived suddenly, with a medley of firebrick clouds pressed softly against a sky of sea foam green, when Murph and Mickey arrived at the mill. Splashes of the early light fell on a tiny black and white kitten who had come out from under one of the piles of wood and scampered through an unhinged gate, finally coming to rest right in front of them, his tiny paws close together. He arched his neck and purred loudly when Mickey kneeled down to scratch the convivial creature behind his ears.

"Don't let him bother ya none now, ya hear? He's just looking for some more petting." Lester tossed the log he was carrying onto a pile and started for them. He was a lean yet muscular young man, with a thick nose, small eyes, and a sociable smile that belied all the hardship he had endured.

"Can I help you fellas?" he asked, his surprise at their presence largely diminished now.

"Morning, Mr. Sledge," Murph said. "My name's Arthur Murphy. From the Milwaukee Brewers? And this here is—"

The young man released a hearty laugh. "Are you kidding me?" Sledge said eyeballing the cap on Mickey's head. "I ain't living under no rock, Mr. Murphy. I know who he is." The exchange held a trace of affection. But Murph stood there, like a suitor about to drop to one knee, the sickening qualms of doubt hammering his insides.

"We won't take up too much of your time here, Lester," Murph explained. "I just want to talk to you about an idea I have."

Lester leaned for a while against the broken metal gate. He was remembering the words his mama taught him when he was just a child. *God loves the black folks, Lester, but he helps the whites. Ya hear? You best be looking out for yourself now.*

FRANK NAPPI

"How is it you know my name anyhow?" Lester asked. "We met somewhere before?"

"Murph thinks you're a swell baseball player, Mr. Lester Sledge," Mickey said, his eyes still fixed on the tiny cat, who he now cradled in his massive arms. "Swell."

Lester looked all at once thoughtful, his eyes lit by some realization flickering behind them. He stood with arms folded, studying their faces. "Oh, I see now. And here I thought you just come 'round this mornin' to play with Milo."

Murph proceeded to unveil his plan, once or twice calling on Mickey, who was now wholly distracted by the whimsical antics of Milo, for assistance in selling the idea. Lester listened intently. He thought of himself and his place in the baseball world of 1949; skilled enough to be playing the nation's favorite game, but not quite white enough to be considered a serious player. Sure, he could play with the Bears. No one said boo about that. "Monkey ball" they called it. It was harmless, and kept them all out of trouble. He also saw, stacked behind him like a row of weathered books, the myriad tragedies and failures that had befallen him in his twenty-two years. He often thought that he would, in years to come, look back on his life, and see nothing more than a painful succession of opportunities that were never really opportunities at all. Doors that were all ajar, just enough to let the light of hope through but nothing else. He hadn't been at Rayfield Grammar School more than two weeks, not even long enough to know what a grammar school was, when his father was stricken with a deadly illness that claimed his life just two months later, leaving young Lester and his mama to fend for themselves.

She went to work cleaning in some of the wealthier homes around Rayfield and Lester pitched in as well, taking any odd job he could find just so they could put food on the table. It worked for a while, until his mother fell ill too, leaving Lester, at the tender age of thirteen, to a world unwilling to open its arms to someone like him. He tramped around from place to place but never really found a home. It was baseball—the hitting of chestnuts or bottle caps or anything else he could find to whack with the whittled wooden stick he had made—that kept him alive. No matter where he went, he always found two or three kids to play with. He was the best. Wowed everyone who had ever seen him with his raw ability. He found it was easy to win over a kid, white or black, when you could do the kinds of things he could. But it always ended the same way— with Lester having to move on in search of work that could fill his stomach.

"With all due respect, Mr. Murphy, there ain't no colored folks playing in the American Association. This here's still a white man's world. You got your league, we got ours. I may not be educated, but I'm smart enough to know that's the way people are happiest round here."

"Are *you*?" Murph asked. "I mean, happy about that?"

"Don't reckon I ever gave it much thought. And I don't know why I would now. It ain't like it's gonna change anytime soon."

They stood for a while silently, each overcome somewhat by the other's presence, melting only when they both caught sight of Mickey, who had tied a machine bolt to the end of a piece of twine and was dragging it behind him, with Milo nipping playfully at his heels.

"Amazing," Lester said smiling. "I bet he don't even know what he's done, on the field and all. And he has no idea on this earth what other great things that lie in front of him."

"Yup, he sure is something. He's getting better, Lester. Every day. Last year was quite an eye opener. But we all got to watch out for Mickey," Murph explained. "He's special. Pure, with a heart as big as that pile of lumber over there."

"Yeah, and that boy sure can throw a baseball. Like nothin' I've ever seen." Lester explained that he and some of his teammates had caught a game or two last year, after Mickey joined the club. They were all amazed at the boy's simplicity, and of course, his pitching prowess.

"We was at the game when he broke 'bout five bats," Lester said chuckling. "Damn, it was sumpin'. And all my friends give me quite a ribbing too, saying the boy sawed more wood in two hours than I could in an entire day." They both laughed. Murph was heartened that their exchange had reached such a pleasant level of conviviality.

"Well, that's why I'm here, Lester. Because I see you two sort of the same way. Nobody thought they were ready for someone like Mickey on the ball diamond. Hell, most weren't. And some still balk. But look at him now. He's the darling of this entire town. He's got it, Lester. I saw it right away. And I'm seeing it again. With you."

Lester's smile sagged. Murph looked hard into his eyes, for the first time that morning, saw deep inside the young man. His own gaze penetrated the gregarious veneer and revealed a profound wound, a bottomless hurt that made his heart quiver.

"Look, Mr. Murphy. I appreciate what you is trying to do. I do. But this boy ain't like me. I may not be no college boy, but I read the papers. Sure, he's different from the rest. That is true. But you is forgettin' something mighty important. He's the right color. He may be off to some folks, but he's still the right color."

Murph shook his head with great agitation. "Come on now. Look around you, kid. You got nothing to lose here. Nothing. I'm giving you a chance, a real chance, to show off that talent of yours to some pretty powerful people. And if my hunch is correct, you just may find your black hind quarters squatting behind a white man's dish, maybe one day gunning down another pretty darn good player from Brooklyn. I think they call him Jackie?"

"Oh, come on now, Mr. Murphy. Do you mean to say that—"

"What I'm saying here son, is that you got talent. Loads of it. And the time is right. It's happening. Things *are* changing. Now. Screw these backward-ass country fools who still think only white is right. Robinson is the first. The first. But he sure as hell ain't the last. You got a real shot here, son, if you're smart enough to take it."

Their engagement rendered Lester stupid for the moment. He had never before entertained such an idea. "I want to thank ya and all, Mr. Murphy. Really. But it ain't no use. One man can't fight against no army. I know they out there. Can't see 'em none. But they there. Heck, I don't got much, but what I got, I'd like to keep. Don't need no trouble like what that guy from Kentucky saw. I think I best leave it alone."

The preposterousness of the plan suddenly revealed itself to Murph, who sadly, reluctantly, turned away. He lowered his head and kicked at some splintered shards of timber. The sense of energy and opportunity that had possessed him ever since his last conversation with Dennison drained from his face as if someone had just pulled a plug. "Come on, Mick," he called. "We need to be leaving now."

The two of them walked past the gate, with Mickey turning around after every other step to see if Milo was following. Murph's legs seemed much heavier than before, and grew heavier still each time Mickey asked him why Lester was not coming with them.

"I don't know, Mick," he said, his face awash with inarticulate despair. "I told you already, three times, I don't know."

As they approached the road, the seemingly endless consequences of his failure unraveled in front of him, as did the phantom image of Dennison's smirking face. He knew he needed to get home. He opened the car door for Mickey, but stopped suddenly before getting in himself.

"Do ya really think I'm good enough?" Lester called after him.

Murph smiled and stuck his right thumb in the air.

"I mean, not that I'm saying yes or nothin'," Lester continued as he came closer, "but if this has any chance of workin', I has got to be sure I'm good enough. Damn good."

Murph smiled again. From several feet away, he saw that the boy was now completely exposed. There was no hidden meaning or innuendo in what he said. The words themselves were enough to tell the story brewing behind the young man's eyes.

"Well, what are we waiting for?" he said, holding up a pearly white baseball he pulled from his jacket pocket. "Let's see for ourselves."

Murph fiddled around in the trunk of his car, then walked past the gate again and found a good spot. Then he proceeded to march off sixty feet, six inches. Just the thought of Mickey and Lester being teamed as a battery filled him with an excitement that the actual tossing back and forth raised to some ecstatic triumph. He watched from the side, and could not help but smile yet again with glorious satisfaction and anticipation as Mickey popped Lester's glove with every delivery while Lester was more than happy to return the favor with each toss back. The rhythmic thumping was music to Murph's ears.

"You guys were made for each other," Murph gushed, his heart now fully dilated. "It's beautiful. What a tandem!"

Lester smiled at the possibility of such a thought.

"Now what do ya say you hit a few for me too?" Murph asked. " I think Mickey's loose." In a mellow light, with only Mickey, Murph and a bevy of nature's creatures for an audience, Lester proceeded to light up the morning sky with long, arching blasts that streaked the pale blue ceiling, each climbing higher and higher as if ascending an invisible ladder before landing unceremoniously in the woods some 400 feet beyond the mill.

"That's four fastballs and four dingers, Lester," Murph said from his crouch behind the fledgling slugger. "Of course, Mickey ain't throwing his hardest, on account he'd probably kill me if he did. But not bad kid. Not bad at all." The energized manager pounded his glove feverishly.

"Okay, Mick, just a couple more now," he called out to the mound. "You're game, Lester, right?"

"For sure," he said. "Beats the heck out of cutting and stacking them logs." With another baseball now safely in his hands, Mickey plotted his next pitch. Murph had told him before they began to take it easy—"not too hard; just move the ball around a little" were his exact words. Mickey had done just that, and was ruminating over what he should offer next when Murph put down two fingers in between his knees.

"But, Mr. Murphy, I thought you said to—"

"It's okay, Mick," Murph reassured. "No big deal. Just do as your told."

Now, with the sunshine sprinkling through the slanted limbs of ancient oaks, Mickey turned the baseball in his glove, his fingers reading the laces as if they were stitched for the purpose of delivering some unknown story scribed in brail. *Yellow hammer,* he thought, his mind turning and feeling among his recent memory of baseball jargon he had been taught to describe things he scarcely understood. *Murph wants a curveball. I can do that. Sure. But we had a plan. 'Not too hard. Just move the ball around a little.' He didn't mention nothing about a yellow hammer. And why don't he just say curveball? Why yellow hammer? Or Uncle Charlie or yacker? And why two fingers? Why is a fastball one finger and a curveball two? Hammers aren't yellow anyway. Bananas are yellow. So are chicks and corn. But I've never seen a yellow hammer. Pa had a red one. And a green screwdriver. But never a yellow ham-*

mer. *And even if they was yellow, what has a hammer got to do with pitching a baseball?*

Mickey floated into an abyss of cerebration, his mind turning and roving in desultory circles from thought to thought until the insular meandering was shattered by Murph's voice.

"Mickey, let's go son! You know what to do now, right, kid?" His game sense now roused, Mickey returned and nodded in Murph's direction. He gripped the ball, just as he had been taught, began his motion, and with the morning light falling heavily on his furrowed brow, he reached back, curled his wrist, and broke off a beautiful curveball that tumbled across the makeshift plate and into Murph's glove like it had been dropped from an invisible ledge. Lester had watched the ball the entire way, his eyes two brown saucers wedded to the whirling white sphere, certain his bat was destined to strike the ball on the fleshy part. He swung virulently, with a trembling sense of expectation that engendered nothing but a sudden rush of air and an awkward buckling of the stunned batter's knees.

"Now what in tarnation was that?' Lester complained to Mickey. Then he turned to Murph with a sheepish smile.

"That ain't fair." All three figures flashed in the sunlight.

"Just keeping you honest, slugger," Murph said winking. "Don't want you thinking it's that easy. But no worries. You ain't the first to come up with nothing but air. Nobody can touch that pitch."

"I sure am glad I won't have to," Lester said, shaking his head. "Am sure glad this here boy's on our side."

"We're all on your side, Lester," Murph said. "I'll get the paperwork to you tonight—no windfall attached to it, but it's more money that you are making now—and you can stay with us if you like as well. It's closer to Borchert Field and it will give you and Mickey a chance to get to know each other really well."

Two days later, before Murph introduced Lester to the team, he sat down in his tiny office with Boxcar. They sat for a while, inanimate as the row of trophies displayed behind Murph's desk, just looking at each other, a tacit uneasiness hovering between them. Boxcar was pale and there were shadows under his eyes.

"I don't know why you're looking at me that way," Boxcar said with modulations of pride. "I ain't some charity case."

"Come on, Box. You know me better than that. I have nothing but respect for you. Always have. But we need to—"

"Talk, right? Is that what you were gonna say?"

"Look, Box, I don't like this anymore than you do. Neither of us asked for this."

"You don't have to worry, Murph," he said, leaning back and folding his arms tightly to his chest. "I know what's happening here. Dennison's riding you about me. I'm not stupid. Been around long enough to know you're only as good as your last game."

"Listen, nobody's saying that you're done here, Boxcar. Nobody. It's just that maybe it would be better, for you too, if you just took it easy for a while. Just until you're feeling strong again. You're welcome to stay with the team. And when you're ready to come back, your spot will be waiting for you."

Boxcar laughed uncomfortably. He leaned forward and grabbed a picture frame off Murph's desk, fingering a photograph with trembling hands of him and Mickey. Then he began to talk about Murph's design.

"So you think Baker can handle the load? I mean, he's still sort of green."

Murph frowned. Something anomalous in the question arrested him.

"Baker ain't the one I had in mind," he replied.

Boxcar looked at him quizzically.

"I just signed a real stud. Plays for the Bears. You'd like him, Box. Tough kid who can knock the cover off the ball."

A momentary flush passed over Boxcar's face.

"The Bears?" he asked incredulously. "From the Negro National League?"

"Yup. He'll be with us for the next game."

A veil of awe stole over the wounded backstop as he gazed blankly into Murph's eyes. "You're replacing me . . . with a negro? Are you kiddin' me Murph? That's what you think of me? Jesus Christ! After all we've been through. And what about the fans? Huh? Have you thought about that? Do you really believe this is going to fly with them?"

"Look, Box, I don't expect you to understand. I know you're upset and all. This has nothing to do with you. But you have to trust me. This kid is the real deal. I've seen him. He's legit. He can really help us now. Forget his color and all that stuff. He's a perfect fit for this team."

"Perfect fit? Are you out of your mind? You think these guys are gonna want to share a field, and a locker room, with some no name colored boy from the sticks? Come on, Murph. You're better than that." All around Murph swirled an unpleasant air of admonition.

"He's a guy, Boxcar. Just a regular guy. I'm surprised at you. Of all people. Who cares what color he is? If he makes us better, and can help us win, who really cares? He's just a another damn ballplayer. Puts his spikes on just like we do. And I'll tell ya something else. You would like him. Mickey's met him already and loves him. Can't stop talking about him."

"Mickey is simple, Murph," Boxcar shot back. "A child who doesn't know nothin' about the world and the way things work." Murph's blood was roused. His nostrils flared and the skin around his cheeks tightened. Boxcar was at a loss to handle the rush of exposure he suddenly felt.

"You know what I mean, Murph," he said painfully. His mouth was twisted, as though he were struggling with something inside of it, and his face remained slightly averted, as if to ward off the palpable feeling of change that was all around them. The conditions and unspoken truth that had governed their lives previously were now gone forever.

"With or without your stamp of approval," Murph went on, "I am walking in to that locker room and introducing him to the guys. He's playing with us, Box. Now I'd rather do it with you, but you can go if you like. It's your choice. And nobody will judge you. But this is *my* decision. And like it or not, I've made it."

Moments later, in a semiconscious stupor engendered by unconscious thoughts that had only just recently found a voice, Murph addressed the team. The formal announcement was not much of an announcement at all, for everyone had already heard the rumors and rumblings. But with the announcement came an old, familiar madness and resistance.

"What the hell is he thinking?" Danvers carped. "This is Boxcar's replacement? Is he for real?"

Others grumbled as well, not with the same pugilistic intent as Danvers, but out of fear and frustration and uncertainty. The room all at once became a cavernous tomb, filled with bodies that featured slumping shoulders and drooping heads. Murph, aware that most disorders of the mind and soul could be read clearly in the state one's physical affect, tried to assuage the unrest.

"Look, fellas, we are in a tight spot here. Losing Boxcar is a tremendous hit. I know that. And he would have been here today, if he were feeling better. I don't know. Maybe that would have helped. But with or without him, we have to get on with things. Sure, it may not be easy. I know that. But Lester here has agreed to help us out. And just as I stood before all of you last season, with Mickey, and asked for your confidence and patience and loyalty, I am asking again. Different is not the same as bad. I think we know that now. We are better than most people. We have proven that. So what I think is that we can make this work." The grumbling grew stronger and assumed a more definitive shape.

"I don't think this is good, Woody," Finster whispered. "It don't feel right. How can this possibly work?"

"Work?" Woody repeated. "How can it work? Simple. It can't. It won't work. Not now. Not ten years from now. Not ever. I'll bet anything it blows up right in Murph's face."

Others caught wind of Woody's rant and began grumbling again themselves—a low, insidious murmur that vibrated ominously off the concrete walls. Lester watched, along with Murph, as the room slowly morphed into a contagion of irrepressible anger and frustration. Lester, tender of heart but tough of constitution, felt the animosity but stood tall, equally ready for acceptance or a full-fledged attack. He smiled faintly, strangely, and buried his sweaty hands deep in his pockets. Then he spoke.

"I would, uh, just like to say that I ain't here to take no one's place. No, sir. I play ball too. Know what it means to be loyal to teammates. Hell, I ain't Raymond—uh, Boxcar. Never claimed to be. But he ain't me neither. I'm just a guy—like all of you here— who wants to play ball. I play hard and I will play hard for you too." Lester's voice strained with trepidation. His eyes, glassy now with emotion, sagged a bit as they scanned the patchwork of wooden faces that had all but dismissed anything he had to say. Murph sighed quietly. He knew that talk was cheap. In order to quell any misgivings, the group would just have to see for themselves how talented Lester was. The proof, as Matheson said, would be in the pudding.

"Okay, fellas," he interjected, disrupting the uncomfortable silence. "I guess that's it. If nobody has anything else, I'll see you all on the field."

The group filed out in a tempestuous wind of petulance and swearing. Murph cringed. All of his life had been made up, it seemed, of moments like these. Opportunities that glimmered with hope, only to detonate in a blaze of failure. Would this be yet another conflagration? His mind struggled with the dismal labyrinth of doubt.

"I thought you said you was *all* on my side, Mr. Murphy?" Lester asked before following the others out. "Sure don't sound that way to me."

Murph scowled, half maddened by the dissension that was just beginning to brew. "They will be, Lester," he said. "Don't you worry, son. Trust me, they will be."

THE DEBUT

It did not take long for the turbid waters of unrest to bubble to the surface. Nobody said anything to Murph or Matheson or anyone else after that afternoon when Murph dropped the bomb on all of them, but their actions told the story. Lester had expected a little razing and the usual high jinks germane to being the "new guy." Hell, it happened in the Negro Leagues as well. He could recall his first day with the Bears, when his baseball pants, jersey, and all of his work clothes mysteriously disappeared while he was showering after practice. He returned to his locker, mindful that he was expected at a team meeting, only to find that all of his stuff was gone. All he had in his tiny stall was an old T-shirt, two sizes too small, and a torn pair of pink women's shorts. He was mortified, but couldn't help but chuckle when he recalled sometime later the ribbing he took when he entered the room.

"Damn, Lester, you's sure one fine looking dandy. Purtry as a picture." All the guys hooted and hollered and pushed him around a bit, but it was all harmless fun. They all laughed about it. There was nothing funny, however, about what was happening now.

How could there be? How do you laugh about a locker full of manure, with a note attached that read *stinky shit for a stinky piece of shit.* Or a burlap dummy, fashioned in your likeness, hanging from a backstop by a hangman's knot. No, there was nothing funny about any of it. But here he was. He had given Murph his promise, and anchored it with expressions of unwavering gratitude. But promises and anchors weigh heavy some times, and Lester Sledge found himself in the unenviable position of showing appreciation for something that was, for the most part, offensive and painful. All of the enmity began to chip away at the young catcher's resolve. Only Mickey, whose constant questioning of the others at every turn as to why Lester's arrival had created such a stir, invoking impassioned admonitions and clear directives for the boy to shut both his eyes and mouth, offered any real support.

"Don't be sad, Lester," he told him. "Mickey thinks you're a swell player." The boy was drawn to Lester by some ineffable kinship. He was remembering the time last season when Danvers and some of the others nailed his cleats to the floor, causing him to freak out so badly that he almost ran out of the room and never came back. He wanted to explain it to Lester, to tell him that somehow it would be alright, but his lips just could not form the words germinating in his mind. "We'll play baseball tomorrow, Lester. Yeah. Tomorrow. You'll play baseball tomorrow and show 'em you're a swell baseball player."

Lester's eyes sank. He wanted to smile, but couldn't.

The following evening was one peculiar to Borchert Field. Despite all of the buzz about Lester's arrival, everything was mute and calm. The sky, although streaked with a pink hue that was inching its way across the horizon, seemed fixed, a painting whose slick canvas had dried and set prematurely. Perhaps the headline that morning had altered the face of things irreparably.

NEGRO LEAGUE CATCHER TO REPLACE BREW
CREW'S BOXCAR TONIGHT

The turnstiles still clicked, but not with the vigor and frequency of previous nights. Sure, there were those whose devotion to Mickey and the Brew Crew could not be swayed, no matter what the town scuttlebutt was. Others came as well, for different reasons. Some bought a ticket to the spectacle out of a perverse curiosity, driven by a galling need to know what was going to transpire, while another group showed up with the intention of using the tiny ballpark as a platform from which they could espouse their bigotry and hatred. But despite those factions in attendance that night, many seats remained noticeably unoccupied, something that drew the ire of Dennison, particularly since the match-up featured the hometown Brewers once again against the arch rival Rangers of Spokane.

As the yawning horizon swallowed the sinking sun, the Brewers took the field to a curious amalgam of cheers and jeers. The intimate ballpark, which just minutes before had appeared muted by some diaphanous cover that sealed the happenings as if they were transpiring in some tiny fishbowl, had suddenly erupted into a frenetic frenzy.

Naturally, Mickey's disciples were well represented, lead by the wild animation of the Baby Bazooka Brigade, who were chanting Mickey's name and had come to worship with their signature army helmets and battle fatigues. Mickey's Minions were also there, waving a bed sheet turned banner featuring a giant red number eight fashioned from the artful placement of two hearts on top of each other and the loving words *Go Mickey Go!* painted underneath. They too made their voices heard. But the raucous exuberance was soon drowned out by another chant, one that slithered up from the shadows in the seats behind home plate and stole insidiously across the entire field of play: *"Go home black boy! Go home black boy! Go home black boy!"*

Lester, who had only just squatted down to receive Mickey's

warm up tosses, heard the venomous cry and felt more than anything, even more than fear and sadness, a feral hatred that had all at once risen from some unknown depth tied to his years of suffering. His face was stolid, even stony, behind his mask. He pounded his glove and thought about his mama. How her poise and equanimity always seemed to bridge the abyss which constantly lay before her.

"It's not enough to be as good as them, Lester," she always preached every time he questioned what he perceived to be her spiritless acquiescence. "We has got to be better."

He never understood that part of her, or how playing the role of the obsequious dog could ever result in anything good. It frustrated him more than anything. But it was this moral resiliency that he clung to that day—the same moral resiliency that squelched his demoniac notion to race into the stands behind him and start swinging.

Murph watched the detached, impassive affectations of his new catcher and prayed he wouldn't crumble. Things had never seemed so desperate. McNally was watching too, but his prayers were darker.

"Would you listen to all that yelling?" he gloated devilishly. "Murph has really done it this time. He's done for. They'll run him, and his two-bit circus, right out of town."

The crowd eventually settled in as Mickey delivered his first pitch, a blazing fastball that missed high and outside. Kiki Delaney, the Rangers' leadoff man and premier table setter in the league, banged his spikes with the barrel of his bat and inched closer to the plate, exaggerating his crouch deliberately in an attempt to shrink the strike zone even further. The transparent stratagem worked, as the second offering missed upstairs again for ball two. The crowd voiced its displeasure, certain that Delaney had duped the umpire by ducking under the pitch.

"Come on, ump!" they screamed in frustration. "Get in the game! That ball's right there!"

Mickey got the ball back and sighed heavily. Then he peered in at Lester, who again pounded his glove before setting up on the inner half of the plate. Mickey rolled his arms, rocked back, lifted his leg and fired once more, a four-seam bullet that sped toward the plate and exploded into Lester's glove.

"Ball three," the umpire called.

Murph's spirit sagged. It was not the start he had hoped for.

"Okay now, Mick," he called out from the top step of the dugout. "Nice and easy now. No worries. Just find the zone."

Mickey shrugged his shoulders. He appeared to be somewhat unnerved. His eyes glazed a bit, then wandered into the stands behind the plate, filtering through a nefarious patchwork of angry faces all yelling at both him and Lester. It was a lot for him to manage at one time. He found himself drawn back into the old habits of his mind, and had just begun to recite the first line from the now all too familiar poem, when Murph motioned to Pee Wee at short to come in and talk to the rattled hurler.

"Hey, Mick," Pee Wee said, patting him on the shoulder. "What's up?" The agitated pitcher shook his head and frowned. It all seemed to him absolutely strange and awful.

"Mickey does not understand, Pee Wee."

"What Mick? What don't you understand?"

"Those people," he answered, pointing his glove in the direction of the intrusion. "They are angry. They are angry at Lester. Why? Why are they angry? Lester did not do nothin' to them. Lester is just catching the ball."

Pee Wee heard Mickey's protest with his own senses ablaze and struggled to find anything to say that would assuage the ugliness. "I, uh, don't know Mick," he explained. "But hey, don't sweat it.

They're probably not angry at Lester. And even if they were, if you start throwing strikes, everyone will start smiling again." He trotted back to his position, happy to be relieved finally of the burden of putting into words something both loathsome and inexplicable.

Mickey toed the rubber and prepared for his next delivery, his eyes fixed on the surly crowd. He paused oddly just before winding up, overwhelmed by the pressing necessity of choosing one direction over the other. He floundered, as always, with the space that these decisions afforded. He felt as he often did in these situations—victimized, a prisoner to all that blew in his face and at his back. He tried to center his thoughts, and almost managed to push the specter of ugliness aside and focus on the game. But no matter how hard he tried, he just could not remove his gaze from the sordidness.

"Ball four," the umpire shouted. "Take your base." The crowd groaned as Delaney scampered down the first base line clapping his hands.

Some were more vocal about their feelings.

"How do you expect him to pitch to a yard ape!" one man shouted. "Murphy, you bum! You're a bum! Washed up has-been! Get him out of there!"

Murph and Matheson watched helplessly from the bench as the Rangers' second place hitter stepped to the plate. A small cloud passed before the pale moon. Mickey tugged nervously at the bill of his cap and got into the stretch position, digging his foot feverishly into the hole just in front of the rubber.

"Hold 'em close, Mick," Murph yelled excitedly, aware of Delaney's penchant for stealing on the first pitch. "He's gonna test you guys."

Delaney heard the warning and laughed before inching his way off the bag. He had led the league in swiped bases each of the last two seasons. Made even the most prolific backstops look inept with his impeccable timing and blinding speed. Did Murph really think this ragtag duo had a prayer? He continued to inch toward his goal, so that by the time the batter had finished cocking his bat and setting his feet in the box, the brazen Delaney had jumped out to a huge lead. He was clapping his hands and jawing at both Mickey and Lester. Mickey peered in at Lester's signs. He heard the bluster but was too mired in the routine of his pitch preparation to offer any real resistance.

Lester, however, read the storm in Delaney's eyes like a seasoned sailor and rose slightly from his crouch while working the fingers on his throwing hand involuntarily as if fingering the trigger of a loaded revolver. He knew exactly what Delaney was thinking. It was the same thing all the Rangers were thinking. Run on the new guy.

The Rangers' sparkplug broke for second just as Mickey lifted his leg and released the ball home. It was a good pitch, strong and true, one that just missed the outside corner. But nobody was very interested in that. All eyes were on Delaney, who was already halfway to his intended destination

The crowd held its breath and the tiny cloud released the moon, bathing the players in a dazzling light, just as Lester's bare hand reached into his glove and pulled the ball back by his ear. Then he released a dart that traveled swiftly, no more than three feet off the ground, right to the inside corner of the bag. Delaney never saw it coming. Just heard the pop of Pee Wee's glove then and lay there, after sliding into the waiting tag, mired in incredulous defeat.

"Yer out!" A smattering of applause rose tentatively from the bi-partisan crowd. Most felt it easier to deny themselves the natural impulse to cheer for the home team rather than incurring any wrath or reproach from those in attendance who felt something unnatural was transpiring right before their eyes.

"Aw heck, he just got lucky, Kiki," McNally chirped as his speed-ster malingered off the field and into the dugout. "That ain't noth-ing. We'll get him next time."

With the count 1–0 to the second place hitter, Mickey steadied himself and adjusted his feet on the rubber, trying to remedy his wildness. His mind wandered for a moment, with small splashes of last year's first meeting against the Rangers washing up against the fragile walls of his mind. Even though he came all this way, and had proven time and again that he belonged, it sort of felt the same to him. Maybe it was all of the hysteria surrounding Lester. The air was so heavy with discord, and Mickey found it hard to breathe. Of course it could have been the venomous, penetrating stare of Lefty Rogers, Mickey's ex-teammate turned nemesis, that had the boy flustered. Or it might have been Mickey, just being Mickey. Whatever it was, it had crept out to the mound, seized him, and would not let go. The boy threw three more pitches, and missed the strike zone each time, giving the Rangers their second consecutive base on balls.

Murph cursed his rotten luck once more before considering calling for a pitch out. He was certain, as was Lester, that McNal-ly believed Delaney being gunned down was a fluke and that he would push the envelope with the new catcher. He whispered the idea in Matheson's ear, but soon abandoned the plan when Mathe-son mentioned something about "old dogs and new tricks." The old coot was probably right. Mickey was having enough trouble hitting his spots. Why make it any worse.

Instead, Murph opted for the more obvious, conventional ap-proach. "Okay now, Lester," he called emphatically from the dug-out. "On your toes. If he goes, shoot 'em down."

Lester heard the call to arms but was already there. He had only met Chip McNally less than an hour ago but knew all about him.

Had seen his kind his whole life. His lack of respect was an transparent as the winking stars pressed against the now clear night sky.

The Rangers' third batter, Johnny Forester, gave a quick look at McNally before stepping in. Lester pounded his glove again and encouraged Mickey to relax. Then he placed one finger down between his legs and set himself up just off the outside edge of home plate. The runner at first got his sign, and danced off the bag. Finster, who was holding him on with great urgency, readied himself for a possible pickoff throw. "Watch him," he yelled wildly. "He's gonna go."

Mickey took his sign from Lester, came set and exhaled deeply. He spun the ball in his glove until his fingers settled neatly across the seams. Then he lifted his leg, reared back and fired. It was another fastball that missed upstairs, but this time Lester was thankful for the blunder, for he was up and out of his crouch almost instantly. The ball was in and out of his glove and speeding toward second in one deft motion. It was a perfect toss, splitting the air with the speed and faithful trajectory of an arrow destined for a bull's eye. In fact, the throw was so masterful, so perfect, that it arrived at the bag a good two seconds before the runner. The most difficult part of the play belonged to Pee Wee, who awaited the arrival of the would-be base stealer awkwardly, not knowing what to do with the inordinate amount of time he had been afforded to apply the tag, something he eventually did as the dejected runner pulled up, head hung and shoulders sagged, in silent abdication.

The crowd was still. Nobody said anything, but it was clear what was ruminating. In the excitement of the moment, with the moon's glow lighting Lester's silhouette like a Times Square billboard, the beleaguered catcher seemed to shed the skin of past subjugation and emerged, in the dazzling light, like a powerful pupa.

Murph applauded his catcher's efforts, then instructed him to make a trip out to the mound to settle Mickey. Lester moved, not with any poignancy or higher purpose, but with a palpable, dynamic exhilaration that was now pushing him along through the cool night air.

"Say, Mick," he said, flipping his mask to the top of his head. "What's going on kid? You sure didn't throw like this when *I* was facing you." Mickey stood, untouched by Lester's overture.

"Mickey had a pig Lester. A swell pig. Name was Oscar."

"Yeah, I know, Mick. I think you mentioned that once or twice."

"Was the biggest one on my farm," the boy continued. "Black and white. He were mine. My pig." Lester tried to see through the layer of torment that had clouded the boy's eyes.

"What about the game, Mick?" he asked. "You know, throwing strikes and all. We got a game to play here."

Mickey's gaze wandered perversely into the Ranger dugout. Lefty was in his head, bumping into other polluted images, like Clarence, The Bucket, the angry man in the stands behind home plate who kept yelling the word *coon* and the neatly colored rows of M & M's in his locker that had accidentally spilled into a random mess.

"Mickey can't think, Lester. It's all messy in my head. And loud. Too many things, crashing into each other. I can't make it stop."

"Say, I got an idea. Murph said you like numbers, and shapes and things. Right?"

"Yup. Numbers and shapes are neat. Love 'em. Nice and neat. And clean."

"Well, looky here then," Lester explained. "Think of my two knees as the bottom points of a big ole triangle. And my glove as the third one, right on top. See? Now all you's got to do is throw that ball into the triangle. That's all. Nothin' else. See? Forget Lefty, and the crowd, and everything else. Just you and the triangle. Okay? What do ya say?"

"Mickey likes circles and squares better, Lester," he said blankly. "What?"

"Circles are round. I like round. And squares are even. Triangles are—" McNally's carping over the inordinate length of Lester's visit drew the umpire out for a visit of his own.

"Let's go, fellas," he said dutifully. "Break it up. Let's play ball."

"Sure thing," Lester said. "We's done here anyhow." Then he slid his mask back over his face and followed the umpire back home, but not before turning back to Mickey to offer one more attempt.

"Draw me a triangle with that ball, Mick. That's all. One point at a time."

The Rangers' three man, usually a free swinger, was mindful that the first nine pitches had missed their mark. Consequently, he was taking all the way. With the bases clear once again, Mickey switched to the more familiar, comfortable windup. He peered in at Lester, who was still calling for good old number one. Mickey nodded his head, and despite the continued heckling from the Rangers' bench, managed to see the triangle. He smiled a half smile, rolled his arms, lifted his leg and fired.

"Steerike one!" was the call. Lester was pleased. He pumped his fist in the air before returning the ball.

"Atta boy, Mick," he shouted. "Draw that triangle." Mickey let go a long sigh of triumph. He stood calm now, transfixed on the imaginary points of his new target. His next delivery was equally true and effortless.

"That's two!" the umpire bellowed. The righting of the ship awakened some of the muted crowd, including Mickey's Minions and the Baby Bazooka Brigade, who, in unison, were chanting for the same result.

Strike him out! Strike him out! Strike him out!

Lester glanced up from his crouch at the batter, who was shaking his head. He had passed on a fastball at Lester's left knee for strike one. The second was taken as well, a fastball at the catcher's right knee. Lester smiled as he realized what Mickey was doing. Okay now, he laughed to himself. Let's finish drawing this thing.

Lester knew that the Rangers' slugger would not pass again. And Mickey was coming right down the middle, wedded to the catcher's suggestion in the most literal sense. It was the perfect occasion for one of the big boy's classic benders.

The reborn hurler peered in again and saw Lester dangling two fingers. He nodded mechanically, rolled and rocked, and let fly what appeared to be a flat fastball headed right down Broadway. The batter's eyes swelled with anticipation. His front foot hitched and his hands strained against the impulse to attack immediately. This was it, he thought, wiggling his hips as he began his approach to the ball. A classic mistake, there for the taking.

As the tiny white sphere orbited into the hitting zone, the batter clenched his teeth and whipped his bat through violently, only to discover, a split second too late, that the ball had betrayed its original path, diving unexpectedly beneath the raging barrel, landing safely in the patient pocket of Lester's glove.

"Yer out!"

Lefty Rogers took the hill for the Rangers in the bottom half of the first frame, and had immediate success, fanning both Pee Wee and Arky Fries with little difficulty.

Rogers was always touted as a live arm with deadly accuracy. But on this night, he was particularly sharp. God, how he hated Murph for all that he had done to him. Never gave him a chance. Not really anyway. And then there was Mickey. The freaky fireballer who stole his job, then laid him up in the hospitable for weeks, almost ending his career for good. The recollection sharpened his antipathy. They were all, every last one of them, albatrosses. All of the past turmoil and misfortune, coupled with the painful loss on opening day just a couple of weeks prior, burned in effigy before his eyes and stoked his competitive fires like never before. Lefty was particularly juiced to face Woody Danvers again, the one guy who had claimed from the beginning to dislike Mickey as much as he did, only to betray their unholy alliance in the end. In Lefty's mind, he was made out to be the fall guy. It was the same Woody Danvers who took him yard on opening day, dashing his hopes for a much needed victory—one he had hoped to stick up all their asses.

Danvers stepped to the plate with a strut and swagger indicative of one who was leading the league early in the season in all of the major offensive categories. He was locked in. Had hit safely in each of the team's first fifteen games, including eight homers and eighteen RBI. Facing Lefty again imbued him with the same fantastic anger and competitive pangs that stood just sixty feet, six inches away.

Their first meeting that night would prove most uneventful, as Danvers lined the first pitch he saw into the corner for any easy double. It burned the mercurial pitcher that he had lost the confrontation, but he was glad he had kept him in the yard. It was only one hit. Just one hit. He managed to shrug it off, his focus riveted to the larger prize.

Clem Finster was next. He had never before batted cleanup, but Boxcar's absence had necessitated some line-up shuffling. Murph had toyed with the idea of penciling Lester in that spot, but decided that the pressure of playing his first game before an agitated home crowd was more than enough for him to handle.

Lefty smiled when Finster stepped in, reveling in the mismatch. Finster was a decent hitter, but by no means a four man. Ordinarily, a runner in scoring position and the cleanup hitter at the plate would require a little chicanery. Nibble a corner here. Bounce a curveball in the dirt. Something like that. That was the beauty of having an open base. But Finster's anemic run production, coupled with the nervous look pasted to his face, made it all moot. Lefty went right after him, sending him back to the bench and ending the inning with just three pitches. Good morning. Good afternoon. Good night.

Mickey bounded out of the home dugout for the top of the second and made quick work of the middle of the Rangers' order, ringing up all three batters on just eleven pitches. The doubt and fear that had clouded his eyes previously were erased by the ease with which he was mowing down the opposition. Whatever was plaguing the enigmatic phenom at the start of the game had disappeared as mysteriously as it had arrived.

With the game knotted in what was shaping up to be a good old-fashioned pitcher's duel, Lester led things off in the home half of the second. The announcement of his name by the public address system engendered quite a mélange of reactions from the crowd. Lester had said he was ready for this. He had assured Murph it was no big deal. But truth be told, he never could have anticipated such a fervor, such unrest, all because he was black.

Standing there, banging his spikes with the end of his bat as he prepared to step into the box, he felt he was just like everyone else. Practiced the same way. Dressed the same way. Even had some of the same superstitions as the rest of them. In some ways he was more like them than they were. But as his eyes scanned the kaleidoscope of cutting faces watching his every move, he knew he was anything but the same.

Some of it made sense. Like the chant of WE WANT BOXCAR that rose up the instant he stepped out of the dugout. He knew what Boxcar meant to these people. And how upset they were that he had been taken from them. He was a big boy. He could take it.

But some of the other antics troubled him, deep to his core. There were the signs, each fashioned with bigotry and vitriol. **Go Home Black Boy** one read. Another was not as polite in its request. **No Blacks Allowed.** They were troubling indeed, but he could look the other way. The mordant words raining down all around him, however, just seemed to hang in the air indefinitely, like mist on his face. *Yard ape, coon,* and *porch monkey* were sentiments not easily wiped away. Still, Lester dug in, firm of purpose. His face was tight, and his whole body bristled with a fierce, surging pressure that had begun deep within his gut and spread to his legs, arms and hands. With his bat roiling in silent defiance, the newest addition to the Brewers' lineup narrowed his gaze on Lefty as the southpaw rocked back and fired.

Lester followed the ball as it sliced through the air and cut across the inner part of the plate, handcuffing him before he was able to extend his arms and get the bat head out in front. His whole body seemed to sag a little.

"Strike one! On the corner."

Lefty smirked behind his glove and the legion of malcontents who had set up camp all around Borchert Field continued to fire invectives, this time louder and with greater ferocity. Lester stepped out and breathed heavily, his heart slamming against the walls of his chest. He tried like hell to calm himself. *Easy now, Lester. Nice and easy.* He maintained this constant stream of inner commentary, cajoling his burgeoning fear into believing that everything would be okay. That the next pitch would be his.

Lefty had other thoughts. He saw Lester's crumbling mien and smelled that fear. There ran through his head a profound, dark, wordless conviction that beckoned for immediate satisfaction. *Do him now,* it seemed to suggest. *Right now.*

Lester stepped back in the box, this time seemingly impervious to the wrathful cries and epithets peppering the field. His bat was still and his mind in a much better place as Lefty released the next pitch, a heater that seared right through the middle of the hitting zone and toward the inner half of the dish. It was exactly where Lefty wanted it. Knee high, middle in. Enticing enough to offer at, but bereft of any real value for the hitter. Yes, it would have been the perfect pitch had Lester not dropped the bat head just as the ball danced across the plate, golfing it high and deep into the blackening night.

The explosion was thunderous, and the flight of the white wafer against the dark sky nothing short of majestic. It seemed to climb higher and higher, a real moon shot, its ascension finally halted when it appeared to clip an errant star that had inadvertently crossed its path. Then, and only then, did the ball, amidst a coterie of glowing splinters, land somewhere unknown, far beyond the left field fence.

"Great Caesar's ghost," Matheson mumbled to Murph. "Did you see that?"

"I sure did, Farley. I sure did." He folded his arms and smiled. "I sure did. And something tells me it's only the beginning."

A deafening hush slipped across the crowd. Everyone was speechless. By all estimations, it was the furthest ball ever hit out of Borchert Field. The only audible sounds came by way of a few whispers here and there, all conjecturing about just how far the ball had really traveled.

Lefty regrouped and recovered easily enough, shaking off the sting of the monstrous blow to retire Jimmy Llamas, Buck Faber, and Amos Ruffings with barely a whimper. Mickey matched the southpaw's dominance, striking out the side in each of the next two frames, sending the dubious crowd, who was still reeling over Lester's improbable debut, into a dizzying fit of unbridled emotion.

With the moon glowing now directly overhead in a dozing sky, and the score still just 1–0 courtesy of Lester's Herculean blast, the young man whose name was on every person's lips that night led off again in the home half of the fifth. The announcement of his spot in the order was greeted once again with some more of the same rancor, only this time, the volume was decidedly less. Lefty pounded the ball in his pocket as Lester dug in. Besides Danver's scorching double and the mistake to the Brewer catcher in his first at bat, Lefty had been perfect all night. He was painting the black with his hard stuff and had his hook diving out of the strike zone. But he knew, as he took his sign from the catcher, that there was no margin for error. Down one run already, and with Mickey throwing aspirin tablets past virtually every Ranger hitter, he had to hold the Brewer offense at bay if he had any chance of procuring a victory.

The crafty southpaw got ahead early in the count with a sweeping curveball that nicked the outside corner. The second offering, a two-seam fastball, was equally crafty and well executed, placing Lester in an 0–2 hole. Lefty was pleased with his work. Though stoic in his demeanor as he prepared to finish the job, his aloof silence belied the fabulous thoughts unfurling in his head.

Despite the pitcher's count, Lester was fairly calm as well. The success he had enjoyed earlier that evening provided a modicum of self assurance, enough so that when Lefty hung the next curveball around the letters, Lester did not jump at it. Rather, most of his weight remained on his back foot, and his hands lingered by his ear long enough, allowing him to crush the mistake over the centerfield wall. The ball jumped out of the ballpark in the blink of an eye. Lefty never even turned around. Just hung his head. Lester did not admire his handiwork either. He put his head down as well, and began circling the bases, oblivious to the wake of wondering stares and ignited imaginations streaming out behind him.

Mickey made the two runs stand up. His combination of blazing fastballs and physics-defying breaking stuff completely stymied the Ranger offense. By the time it was all over, he had wracked up thirteen strikeouts while surrendering just three hits.

The team was all smiles after the game. It was always good to beat the Rangers. Twice in less than a month was pure ecstasy. Mickey was subjected to his usual post-game hoopla courtesy of the local sportswriters, but all he could talk about was Lester.

"What do ya think about the game tonight, Mick?"

"I liked it," he answered. "Lester Sledge is a good player."

"What about all those strikeouts, Mickey? Did the first two walks get you angry?"

"Mickey isn't angry, sir. I'm happy. My friend Lester is fun to watch. He hits the ball really far. Really far." There was a collective frustration that passed between all of those awaiting something suitable to print.

"Don't you have anything to say about your pitching? I mean, you were great tonight."

"It was fun."

"That's it, Mickey? Fun? Can you give us something else?" Mickey paused only long enough to scratch an itch behind his right ear.

"We're going to eat now. Me and Lester, Murph. At Rosie's. Then we're gonna feed my rabbits. I like Rosie's. I think Mickey is going to have—" The crew began packing up and was all but gone before Mickey could even finish his thought.

Lester was not without conversation himself. Murph hugged the slugger immediately following the game and thanked him for his heroic efforts, and after all of the press had grown tired of the disordered volleying with Mickey, a few of them made their way over to his locker to tap what had potential to be a noteworthy story.

Lester even got what he believed to be one or two gratuitous nods of approval as the players filed into the locker room. But it was the exchange with Danvers that stayed with him. "You know, it ain't so easy boy?" the third baseman said. "Ain't always gonna be like this."

"I know," Lester replied. "Never said it was. Just glad I could help."

"Ain't always gonna have reporters buzzing round you. Look at me. Two more knocks tonight. Leading the league in hitting. And I barely got a second look." Lester's head hurt a little and his mouth was horribly dry. "I wouldn't get all crazy now, celebrating and all," Danvers continued. "This ain't the Negro leagues. It's a little harder here than it is in black ball."

Lester drew a long breath and released it slowly. "I know that."

"And Boxcar? You know, Boxcar will be back soon. So all this hullabaloo ain't worth nothin' more than a wooden nickel."

Lester's brow lowered and his gaze moved across the empty eyes of his suddenly voluble teammate. "You played a good game too, Mr. Danvers. And I'm glad the team won. But if that's all, I am going to grab some grub with Mickey and Murph over at Rosie's. I hear she ain't so particular about that whole Jim Crow thing. Then I reckon we'll go back to Murph's place and hit the hay. Start getting ready for tomorrow night's game."

Woody's tongue was seized by the candor. After an awkward silence that ended in neither a handshake nor a spoken goodnight, the two men parted ways. Although Murph did not suggest Rosie's as some sort of celebratory repast, he could not help but gush about his vision coming to fruition in such startling fashion.

"I knew it, kid," he beamed. "Just knew it. You were great, Lester. Both you guys. Man, with the way you and Danvers are hitting, and with Mickey's arm, we can't miss."

Lester felt the warmth of the words like a hand on his back while Mickey busied himself with a tiny dispenser of tooth picks.

"Ain't no big deal, Murph," the emotional catcher finally said. "It's me who owes you the thank you."

The three of them talked some more about the night, ate and drank, then talked some more. Murph and Lester recounted his two long balls and shared a laugh while trying to explain to Mickey why so many people at the ballpark were "yelling at Lester." It was all good. Everything vague and desultory had seemed to order itself, almost magically. And in some small way, as the minutes and words passed between them, each was just a little more reluctant to part with the substance of their imaginings. The quixotic banter continued on the ride home. Talk of the pennant? In early May? It was foolish, sure, but Murph could not help himself. Everything in his professional being cried out against such a capricious prophecy. He had been burned so many times before. But what had just transpired hours before at Borchert Field was that special.

Even the stars that still remained in the vaulted sky shone brighter as they drove the familiar stretch of Diamond Drive that lead to Murph's house.

"Now, I know I shouldn't say this," Murph began as they neared the final bend in the road, "because you never mess with success. But how do you feel, Mr. Sledge, about moving into the cleanup spot tomorrow night?"

Lester was touched. Truly. The last twenty-four hours had proven to be quite a whirlwind. He was thinking about what his mama would say, and struggling to collect his thoughts. His lips had all but formed the words when all three of them were seized by the unholy vision. It was awful. Mickey cried out in terror, a shrill, plaintive wail. Murph and Lester were simply speechless, their eyes suspended not in the flashing lights atop Sheriff Rosco's car, but in the storm of fiery embers leaping off the burning cross wedged in the center of Arthur Murphy's front yard.

MAY

Crosses continued to burn, and Boxcar's disease moved along the usual course, tantalizing him with transitory stretches of optimism and vitality now and again, only to shatter the improbable hope for recovery with relapses that enervated both his physical strength and emotional resolve. He was ornery and obstinate, and continued to refuse treatment. But when things seemed to turn a dark corner, he finally acquiesced to the idea of a doctor, even though it was to be of little consequence, for there was nothing to be done.

"We can always set you up in a good hospital, Box," Murph suggested during his last visit. The once animated catcher, whose body had always looked like it had been chiseled from stone, just sat there, exanimate, a shadow of his former self, mired in sorrow and self loathing.

"That won't be necessary, Murph," he said. "I'll get by."

Boxcar was true to his word; he did get by, but his struggle was eating away at Murph. He loved the fiery catcher like a son. They all did, especially Mickey, who Murph had shielded as best he could from what was beginning to look like certain tragedy. He shared his vision with Molly, and the news all but devastated her. She wanted to tell Mickey, but Murph had convinced her it was not the right time. She agreed, but the thought of Mickey's friend in such trouble weighed heavily upon her.

"I was in town today," Molly said a few days later, as all three of them sat down for dinner. "Ran into Dorothy Chambers. Seems her brother Thomas is real ill. Has two little ones at home. Sort of made me sad and all, especially with all of us doing so well here. Don't seem fair, that some should suffer more than others." She was talking more than usual, and her words were choppy and feverish, each running into the next.

"It's okay, Ma," Mickey said, folding his napkin neatly. "Don't be sad."

She sighed and took a quick forkful of creamed spinach. The severity of her expression worsened as she chewed. Her eyes became glassy and she looked as though she were going to explode until her thoughts once again came spilling out.

"I know we said that we were going to try and eat less beef, Arthur, on account of the price and all, but I have been wanting to try this brisquet recipe for weeks. The meat is so tender. Melts in your mouth. We have fresh apple pie for dessert after. The crust got a little burnt, but it's still good. Is it okay? Arthur, is it okay?" She was looking at him with such peculiar urgency. Tears began to emerge from her quivering lids.

"Yes, Molly, of course it is," he said.

"It sure is," Mickey blurted out. "Mickey loves beef. I do. All the fellas love it." He paused a moment and smiled, as a recent reminiscence flooded his consciousness. "Last week, after practice, we had a hamburger eating contest—at Pee Wee's place. Jimmy Llamas ate three, Finster had four, and Mickey had eight. First I had three, then I had a drink. Then I ate three more, but my stomach started to hurt, until I burped. I think it was all the soda I drank. Then I ate one more, and wanted to stop, but ate just one more after that, on account of seven being uneven and all. That didn't bother Pee Wee none. He only had one himself."

"That's great, Mick," Arthur said, chewing deliberately. "So you won, huh?"

"Yeah, Mickey won," the boy said with a strange note of resignation. "But that's only because Boxcar didn't have any. He always wins." Mickey watched as Molly brought her napkin to her mouth, dabbing her lips gently. Then she sighed again, this time louder, and brought the damp cloth to her eyes.

"Molly, please don't," Murph said. She would not look at him, but nodded. Then she began crying harder, as if somehow Murph's request had punctured her emotional reservoir.

"I'm sorry, Arthur," she said, getting up from the table. "I can't. I just can't. You'll have to finish without me."

Mickey was alarmed. His eyes began to well up too. "What did Mickey do?" he asked. "I'm sorry. Next time I wont eat so many hamburgers. I promise." There was an uncomfortable silence that settled between them, one that lasted a good while until Murph finally spoke.

"It's not you, Mick," Murph said. He looked away for a moment, as if trying to enlist strength and guidance from some imaginary source of inspiration. "It's Boxcar. Your mom's crying about Boxcar. He's not doing too well, Mick. I'm afraid I have something to tell you."

The other illness that had touched the entire town was yielding its own effects.

Despite Sheriff Rosco's investigation into the hate crime perpetrated that night at Murph's house, there seemed to be no answers.

"What do ya want me to say, Murph?" Rosco said days later. "Ain't nothin' that can be done."

The law man's flippancy drew Murph's ire. "So that's it? Huh? Some racist sons of bitches light up my house, right here in town, and nothing can be done? Is that what you're telling me, Rosco?"

"Ain't like last time. With Mickey. No one here really wants to help no black boy. I'm sorry to say it, but that's how it is."

The sheriff saw the violent contortions of Murph's face but paid them no mind. He just folded his arms and rolled the butt end of his cigar between his yellowing teeth. "Why don't you wise up, Arthur, eh? What's the sense? You's playing with fire here. Just go back to the way things was. You go back to the way things was, and I'm willing to bet all this ugliness will go away."

Rosco's indifference angered and frustrated Murph, but it sent Molly into orbit. All of the doubt and insecurity she had previously nourished about her son's welfare had risen once again to the surface. She thought about all of the beatings he'd taken at the hands of his tyrannical father, and about the attack he suffered last season outside The Bucket. She had not come this far, and sacrificed this much, to let Mickey play the victim once again.

"I told you, Arthur, from the very beginning, that the minute I don't like the looks of things, that's it." She slammed the pot she had just finished cleaning hard on the kitchen counter top. "He's done. Mickey is done."

He saw her, laboring beneath the weight of all things mountainous, her breath forced and audible, like a furious cloud of steam. "Relax, Molly. I'm upset too. But Mickey is in no danger. The issue is with Lester, and Rosco knows all about it. Look, it's unpleasant, sure. But Mickey is thriving, Molly. He's doing really well. He and Lester are the talk of the town. Besides, you said it was up to him. Remember? The boy hasn't said anything about quitting."

"Not in any danger? Unpleasant? Are you out of your mind? You are not thinking. We are *all* vulnerable now, Arthur. This time it was a cross. Next time maybe it will be a brick, or maybe bullets. You know what these people are like. Look, I like Lester, you know I do, but you have placed all of us in harm's way by bringing him into this house. And for what? To win a few lousy baseball games?"

They had never really fought before. It was not because Murph possessed some exaggerated sense of chivalry or obsequious compunction, but because he was mindful, at every turn, of the tumultuous marriage she and Clarence had had and never wanted to stir any of the old feelings. Most often, it was easy enough to acquiesce to her wishes, regardless of what his desires were. But his immediate fate, his very livelihood, were now tied to her latest request.

"Baseball games? Is that all you think this is? Sure, that's what started all of this. And it has worked out real fine. We are better than we have ever been. But do you know, Molly, what this opportunity has done for Lester? As a man? Do you know the hardship this boy has seen? Do you even have a clue as to how this sort of break through could change the beliefs and sensibilities of folks everywhere? And open doors for Lester and colored folks across the board? Now you tell me how that qualifies as not thinking. You tell me how that can be wrong."

"I'll tell you that, when you can tell *me* how I am supposed to explain to my son about racism, and lynchings, and bigotry and all of the other horrors I try to shield him from every day. Do you know what that feels like? Huh? Do you even have a clue about that? I feel for the colored folks too, Arthur. You know I do. But, Jesus, I have to worry about my boy. My charity must begin at home. I have to look out for my son. Because if I don't, nobody else will."

A sudden moodiness came over him. He sighed, and dug his hands into his hips.

"Nobody else, huh? Is that what you believe? Really? Is that what's been going on here the last year or so? I have opened my home to both you and Mickey. And you are welcome to stay as long as you like. Why? Cause I care. It's also the reason why last week, I made a phone call to Whitey Buzzo about Mickey. About the big club in Boston giving the kid a serious look. Listen, Molly. I know this ain't easy. I do. But baseball is all a kid like Mickey's got. This could be a home for him. Playing. Maybe coaching some day. Who knows. Baseball takes care of its own. So if you're worried about his future, you best think twice about taking from him the only thing he really has."

Molly stood stunned by Murph's pointed tone. Though she grasped what he was trying to impart, she remained, for the most part, crouched beneath the pall of the moment.

"I don't know, Arthur," she said tearfully. "It just doesn't feel right. I hear what you're saying. I do. Part of me knows you are probably right. God knows, you have been so far. But I'm tired of worrying. Tired, you hear? I just want to rest. I don't know if I can do this again."

He moved close to her, so that he could feel her hot breath against his face, then pulled her still closer, so that the furious rebellion of her heart beat against his own. He kissed her forehead, then took her trembling hand until, after some quivering, at last lay warm and inert in his.

"Please trust me, Molly," he whispered. "Trust me. Let things run their course. It will be okay."

The spell of the storm had broken. She was tired, and did not want to fight anymore. "I will try, Arthur," she said, sighing before wiping her eyes. "As best I can. I will try." She wiped her eyes again with the frayed end of her sleeve and stared into his eyes. "I promise. I will. Really. I mean it. But it is a lot to ask."

Later that day, Murph found himself defending his actions in a similar manner. There he was, once again, in Dennison's light-starved lair, staring across a littered desk at that churlish face that assumed all sorts of lurid implications in the artificial twilight cast by the two frosted bowls of Victorian glass hanging on the wall. Dennison was his typical petulant self, puffing on his cigar with such intense animation that it looked as though his head would explode.

"So you won the game, Mr. Murphy," he said, unrolling his newspaper before laying it flat on his desk "That's true. And an interesting game it was. But at what cost?"

"Come again?"

"The cost, Arthur. For the victory. Reduced attendance. All the unrest in the stands amongst those who actually came. The hate mail I am getting. The burning cross. Get my meaning?"

"Come on, Warren. Obviously you saw the paper this morning. Quite a headline: *Mickey and Negro Newbie Hammer Rangers* He's news, Warren. What's bad about that?"

A cloud of brooding anger hung on the owner's brow.

"Maybe you did not understand our first conversation, Arthur. Yes, you won. I love that. But I do not want all the bull that goes with it. Get me? I said that from the beginning."

"It will all pass, Warren. I told you that. Mickey's back, better than ever. Danvers is hot. The rest of the guys are playing well too. And, I'm telling you, dollars to donuts, this kid will win them over. Just give it time. Half the season, remember?"

An air of strained formality passed before them. Dennison glanced down at the headline once more and saw profitable visions lighted by Murph's plea.

"Look, I have another meeting this morning. I don't have time for this now. But you better hope you're right, Arthur," he said ominously before showing Murph to the door. "I'm not as patient as I used to be."

During the next two weeks, Mickey, Lester, and the rest of the

Brew Crew made quite a compelling argument for Murph's future employment as manager. Lester continued his torrid hitting, putting up home runs at a dizzying pace. He jacked another against the Colts, crushed a pair of dingers against the Sidewinders and Giants, and buried the Spartans with three mammoth blasts that landed, each one of them, on the sidewalk outside the ballpark. It seemed to matter little to him that there were still those who refused to accept a black man in a white man's league. Some of the hateful signs remained, and he received his fair share of heckling and harassment. But he played on, and began to win people over, including the local papers who, with the exception of when Mickey pitched, placed him in the morning headlines every day. Even Woody Danvers, who continued to lead the league in hitting with a .387 average and plenty of power of his own, could not crack the back page.

Perhaps it was journalism of the sensationalized variety. It *was* quite a story. Maybe it was just another chapter in the public's long standing love affair with the long ball. Or it just could have been the catchy moniker—(Sledge) Hammer inspired by the young man's last name. Whatever it was, Lester Sledge's name was in bold print every day and was becoming household conversation.

HAMMER NAILS COLTS BREW CREW
HAMMER POUNDS GIANTS
HAMMER BANGS THREE MORE AS BREWERS CRUSH SPARTANS

The headlines kept coming, and the talk continued to vibrate throughout the town. First it was the Baby Bazooka. Now the Hammer. Never before had Brewer baseball possessed such fervor and sex appeal. The baseball Gods sure seemed to be smiling on Borchert Field.

Not everything, however, was copasetic in Brewer Land. With the notable exception of Mickey, the pitching was really struggling.

Gabby Hooper, Rube Winkler and Butch Sanders all got pounded in consecutive starts. It was only the potent Brewer offensive attack, led by Lester, Danvers and a recently hot Clem Finster, that allowed the Brew Crew to actually win most of those games and open up a healthy lead in the standings. Murph, however, was not pleased with the pattern that had emerged.

"Alright, fellas," he said at a meeting of the staff after one of the games got away from them. "What the hell is going on?" The group just looked at one another, no one wanting to be the first to speak. "Well," Murph continued. "What is it? Enough of this bull. Let's hear it."

Sanders reddened under Murph's stare, but managed to fire the first shot. "We ain't so comfortable, Murph," he said. "You know, since Boxcar left and all."

Murph took off his cap and ran his hand through the thinning strands on top of his head. "Are you kidding me!" he thundered. "Is that what this is all about? Lester?"

Winkler spoke next. "I think what Sandy is trying to say is that we're all just used to Boxcar. You know, the way he calls the game, talks to us, all that crap."

Murph's blood raged and hammered at his temples. "And Lester is incapable of doing those things? Calling a game? Talking? He's of no use to you? Hell, the way I see it, with the damned carousel of runners you guys have been entertaining lately, you oughta thank your lucky stars he's back there. Seems to me he's bailed out all your asses on more than one occasion."

The pace of the conversation quickened with every comment. "What happens when Boxcar comes back, Murph?" Hopper asked next. "And what about Baker? He's been stuck on that bench, waiting for his opportunity. Honestly, the way I see it, we could all use a break from all the black/white bull we've had to put up with."

"So let me get this straight," Murph replied. "You want me to sit the best homerun hitter in the league. Bench him. Is that right? The same guy who has thrown out all but two base runners. The same guy who just happens to be one of the major reasons why we are in first place. All because you girl scouts are all tired of a little inconvenience. Is that what I'm hearing? Well, you know what? You know what I say to that? You go screw yourselves. All of you. You hear? Especially you, Sanders. You can't get a goddamned out if your mama's life depended on it. Bunch of pampered candy ass-es. I will only say this one more time. Boxcar is not coming back. I'll make it official at our next team meeting. And Baker? Baker ain't fit to carry Lester's jock. Lester is our catcher. Period. He will be behind the plate tomorrow, and the next day, and the day after that. He will be behind that plate until I say he's not. And when that happens, *I'll* be the one who decides who takes his place. You get that through your thick skulls. Now, I have work to do. That's it. If you still feel like crying about this, I suggest all of you talk to Mickey, and see how it is that he has no problem throwing to a black man."

In a different part of town, tensions were also high. Quinton Harrington was upset as well. And Chip McNally was feeling the brunt of his wrath. The bar stool Harrington occupied at Wally's Tavern became a pulpit from which he espoused his displeasure over McNally's current struggles.

"You realize that you trail the Brewers by four games, Chip," he said, slapping a rolled up newspaper in his open palm. "Four games. To a team led by a retard and a jungle bunny." McNally's thoughts were killing him. Couldn't get away from them. Sure it was eating him alive that Murph was getting the better of him. But what was he to do?

"I know we ain't off to the kind of start you had hoped for, Mr.

Harrington, but we ain't playing that bad. Take away those two close ones we dropped to Murph and we're right in it."

"Those two you dropped to Murph are the ones that bother me most, Chip. And I should think you'd feel the same way."

"I want to win just as bad as you do sir," he continued. "Especially against that rat bastard Murph."

"Well, what do you plan to do about it?"

"I don't reckon anything different from what I've been doing. We will start winning games. I know we will. We deserve better than our results show. A lot better. Lefty has been fantastic. The defense is solid. We are not playing that bad. We just need to get the sticks going. That's all. No worries, boss."

Quinton hesitated only a fraction of a moment, then licked his lips and smiled. "I am not worried, Chip," he said, nodding his head thoughtfully. "Why should I be worried? But you? Now there's a different story. Yes, sir. If I were you, with the way things are going, I'd be pissing myself."

MIDSEASON

Some weeks passed, but not much changed. Mickey was still brilliant, posting a staggering 11–1 record, and Lester continued his assault on the pitcher's in the league, racking up twenty-two homeruns by the midway point. Despite the improved play of the Rangers, who had won twenty-one of their last twenty-five games, the Brewers still had a two-game lead in the early race for the pennant.

One noticeable difference, however, was observable in the Brewer clubhouse. Lester had begun to grow on his teammates, including some of those who were not particularly enamored with the star catcher when he first arrived. Sure, there were still the occasional pranks at the expense of the new guy. Flour in the cleats. Cap in the toilet. And of course the old standard lineament in the jock strap. But it was all harmless high jinks. All of them had really started to gel. It was only a matter of time, Murph said, delighting in the veracity of his earlier prediction.

"Baseball guys gotta love other baseball guys."

Or, as Matheson put it in his own inimitable fashion, "these birds of a feather have finally flocked together."

It was easy to see how both men were right. Lester made it

impossible for some of them not to like him. Like Pee Wee Mc-
Ginty. It was late in a game against the Giants. The Brewers had
just battled back from a five-run deficit to take a one-run lead, and
needed just one more out to seal the deal. The Giants' third place
hitter smashed a scorcher that just ate up Pee Wee, ricocheting off
the inside half of his foot before scooting through his legs and into
left field. McGinty hung his head as the cleanup hitter, who was
already 4-4 with six RBI, strode to the plate, licking his chops. The
tiny shortstop could barely breathe, stifled by the dreadful thought
that he had just opened the door to a potential disaster.

Rube Winkler was pissed off as well. He had come in during the
eighth inning to put out a fire and was on his way to a much needed
win when McGinty's blunder derailed the victory train. He walked
around the mound, mumbling to himself, before getting back on
the rubber to face the Giants' most potent threat.

Winkler came set a number of times, but threw over to first in
each instance, chasing the runner back to the bag. Then he stepped
off the rubber a couple of times, trying to bait the tying run into
tipping his hand. Both attempts were fruitless, yielding only a dirty
uniform top over at first and a swell of anxiety in Pee Wee, who was
dying under the uncompromising weight of anticipation.

When Winkler was satisfied that his stratagems and attempts at
deception had altered the base runner's lead as much as they could,
he delivered home. Pee Wee held his breath as the ball zipped toward the plate, then jumped off the eager bat of the hitter. It was a
long, arching fly ball that had plenty of distance but landed in the
stands some eight feet foul. Both Pee Wee and Winkler let loose
audible sighs of relief.

Lester recognized the impetuous gesticulations of the batter
as he awaited Winkler's next offering. With this is mind, the wily
catcher put down two fingers, hoping to disrupt the timing and bal-

ance of the Rangers' assassin. Winkler took the sign and nodded, came set at his waist, gave a quick look over at first, then broke off a curve ball that fell way short of its intended destination, bouncing in the dirt some three feet in front of home plate. The batter held his swing, but the runner, certain that the wild pitch was a free pass into scoring position, took off for second base.

Lester, however, had other ideas. With a deft, cat-like motion, he slid to his right and dropped to his knees, smothering the errant toss with his chest protector. Then he picked up the wayward ball and fired a bullet to Pee Wee, who applied the tag in plenty of time, squelching the rally and handing the Brewers a well earned victory.

Everyone rushed the mound, congratulating Winkler on his gutsy performance. Everyone except Pee Wee, who had raced in to home plate immediately following the tag to hand the ball to Lester.

"This belongs to you, friend," he said, handing him the ball. "And a little bit of me does as well. Thanks, man."

A few days later, Lester bailed out Arky Fries in a similar fashion and then won the heart of the flaky Jimmy Llamas when Lester stretched across home plate to corral his errant throw from shallow centerfield, then reached back across to tag out a runner trying to score. Despite the violent collision at home, one that was created by the botched toss, Lester held on and saved Llamas from a most embarrassing moment. Sure, the dopey Llamas trotted in cavalierly from the outfield, firing his imaginary six shooters and spitting through the gap in his two front teeth as if nothing unusual had happened, but the minute he got into the dugout, he placed his hand on Lester's shoulder and gave him a wink.

Some of the fans at Borchert Field had been bitten by the love bug as well. While there was still the fair share of dissenters who refused to accept Lester's presence, attendance increased once again, including one or two groups of mixed race who had embraced the nickname "Hammer" coined by the press and made it the focal point of their adulation, attending each home game in overalls and tool belts, from which they pulled toy hammers that they pounded the rails with each time Lester did something memorable. Borchert Field was alive like never before, rocking to the colorful antics of the fanatical groups inspired by its two heroes.

It wasn't all champagne and roses though. Despite all the good will, the ignorance and ugliness just would not go away. It was still present at the ballpark, in the ulcerous screams from disgruntled fans and those bigots who attended games only to spread their malice. It had surfaced in the many threatening letters Dennison and the organization received every day. And it found its way to Murph's doorstep on more than one occasion, taking the form of packages left clandestinely on his front porch. One contained a dead skunk. Another was filled with a dozen roses, each painted black, with a note attached that simply read *Black for Black—Watch Your Back.* Murph did well to hide these harbingers of hate from Molly, and from Lester as well. But he couldn't shield them from everything.

He was working at the kitchen table one evening, with a stack of lineup cards, stat sheets and his wire recorder, when he heard the knock at the door and then the squealing of tires. He leaped to his feet and raced out the front door, only to find that Lester had beaten him there.

"Let me have that, Lester," he said, motioning for the small box he held in his hands. "You don't need to see that." Lester edged over restlessly in Murph's direction, with the box, and the two locked eyes.

"I ain't gonna just bury my head, Murph," he said. "Ain't my way now."

The two of them sat uneasily on the porch, neither one of them saying a word. Both of their faces were appropriately solemn.

"You know, Lester, you don't have to open that," Murph finally said. He was suddenly very aware of Lester's emotional fragility. "We could always just throw it away."

They sat there a little longer, like distant planets from different galaxies. There was a world of difference between the two of them, more than just black and white. It was their approach to this ungodly mess, and the vision each clung to of life afterward, if and when the dust finally settled, that linked them. For all the differences, they seemed to find some sort of kinship amidst the sea of abomination that had swelled and threatened to drown them both.

"I means to open it," Lester said, pursuing the thought with painful application. "Ain't running from this, Murph. No way."

Murph watched quietly as Lester undid the twine stretched across the brown paper wrapping. The box felt damp, and there was a peculiar odor emanating from inside. With trembling fingers, he worked open the top panels of the cardboard parcel and peered into the tiny abyss. He did not move once he saw what was inside. He just sat there, with the mystery package on his lap, struggling with the crumbling difference between right and wrong. His eyes welled up and his mouth formed words that never made it passed his lips.

"What is it, Lester?" Murph asked. "What's wrong?"

Lester could not speak. A rush of stifling air had filled his lungs and was squeezing his chest unmercifully. He staggered to his feet, box still in hand, and shook his head. He stood now, leaning against the wood rail, trying to steady his trembling knees.

"Lester, is everything okay?"

There was no reply. Whatever had seized him would not let go. He passed the box to Murph, who was also swallowed by what he saw. He cringed and turned away.

Minutes later, Murph notified Sheriff Rosco, who, as he had done each of the previous times Murph had called, dismissed the incident as mischief before reminding him how easy it would be for him to put an end to all the aggravation.

"Mischief?" Murph fired back. "Mischief? You call that box that Lester got mischief?"

"Calm down, Murph," Rosco said.

"Like hell I will," Murph replied. "You've got a real problem here, Sheriff. And I want something done about it."

They talked some more about Lester and about recent klan activity and some of the other concerns Murph had for Mickey and Molly as well. Rosco listened, and told Murph about the different leads he and his office were following. He was calm, and appeared to have heard what Murph was saying. But in the end, Murph still saw him as nothing more than just a flippant jackass.

"I will look into it, Murph," he said. "But I told before. And I know you don't like it. But once the boy goes, all your troubles will follow."

Molly never found out what had happened, but all the guys on the team knew. Murph did not want to make a scene, and would have preferred to keep things quiet. But when he heard the rumblings, and all the conjecture spawn from misinformation and half-truths, he knew he had to address the team formally.

"Look, fellas," he said, agonizing through his thoughts. "We are certainly no strangers to adversity. God knows. And I'm sure this too shall pass. But there are a few things we need to get straight."

He spoke passionately first about Boxcar, whose health had taken a recent turn for the worse. "He will always be a Brewer guys, always be our captain, but he will not be returning."

Then he turned his focus to the other pressing issue at hand. With a stiff wind rattling the windows of the tiny locker room, Murph paced nervously. He was a man on a mission, a pensive wanderer in search of a remedy for his soul and for some sort of panacea for his impressionable club. "And it appears that some people still have a problem with our new catcher, boys," he said. "I'm here today to tell you that that's okay, because that's *their* problem, not ours. I know that all of you here recognize the value of Mr. Sledge's contributions the last few months, and that none of you would not even think of perpetuating any of this bull any more than need be. We are a baseball team, fellas. No, scratch that. We are a baseball family. One unit. One goal. We may not always love each other, and we certainly don't always understand each other, but we better goddamn support each other, and oppose with fury those who would try to keep us from our goal. That is how I feel. Right here, right now. And that is what I expect from all of you."

Murph had hoped his speech would have ignited a little more camaraderie, and that some of the others would have embraced Lester by now and opened up a little more, just to ease some of the anxiety the poor boy was feeling. But it seemed as though it was still too soon. Murph did, however, find solace in all of the time Lester was spending with Mickey. It was good for both of them. They had become inseparable, their relationship burgeoning well beyond the normal affinity between pitcher and catcher. Murph was not surprised; in many respects, they were one in the same. Two baseball prodigies, each imbued with anomalous talents almost incomprehensible, crashing against the rigid walls of societal convention. They had each been, their entire lives, on the outside looking in at a world that seemed to move on in spite of them. Each, in his own way, had dreamed, conjured a picture of the world the way he wished it could be. A world unfettered. It was beautiful, an exciting landscape of hope and possibility. But alas, like every dream, there comes an awakening. The ruthless reality that floods the chimerical chambers with the light of truth, expunging the vision forever, leaving in its wake only disappointment and shame. Now, for the first time, the distance between that dream and reality did not seem as far. They had both elicited attention and had been noticed. Appreciated. Even celebrated. It felt good now and again. It did. But the sudden spotlight, coupled with the residue of lingering resistance from those not yet ready for anything unconventional, only made the previous shame more acute.

The two of them had gotten into the habit of eating together after the games. Usually it was at Rosie's. But they had run into some trouble there the last few times there so they decided, one night after a victory over the Spartans, to alter their plans a bit. "Hey, you guys heading over to Rosie's, Mick?" Pee Wee asked as they undressed.

"No, Pee Wee," Mickey answered. "Me and Lester are going someplace else."

"What? No Rosie's?"

The boy was not sure how to answer.

"We figured we best be eating somewhere else for a while," Lester added. "We've caught some crap from some good old boys who have come to expect us there. Seems that somehow, they know our every move. So we gonna try the Road House over past Willets Bridge, down the Chestnut Ridge Road."

"Ain't that a little out of the way?" Pee Wee asked.

"I reckon that's what we need right now," Lester said, laughing. "Just wanna be left alone." He finished tying his shoes and grabbed his hat.

"Maybe I'll join ya's," Pee Wee said. "I ain't doing nothin' special myself."

A little while later, the three men walked into the out-of-the-way eatery. It wasn't much to speak of inside. The walls were bleached and threadbare, four wooden slabs that supported for the moment a water-stained ceiling that buckled from the weight of the damp rectangular panels. Their feet struggled across a tacky floor littered here and there with bread crusts and peanut shells, until they finally came to rest in the far corner, at a broken booth whose back had broken free from the wall, revealing two bolts that now stood, rusted and exposed, beneath a cloudy window.

"I hear they have some kickass chili," Pee Wee said, trying desperately to inject some levity into the abject circumstance.

"I sure hope so," Lester said, frowning at the pile of dirty dishes visible behind the counter. "I sure hope so."

The three of them sat down on the cracked red leather cushions and surveyed the menu in cursory fashion, especially Mickey, who had placed his down almost instantly in order to address the most recent thought blooming in his mind.

"Mickey is awful sorry about the way some folks is treating you, Lester," Mickey said.

"Thank you Mick. But it's okay. I'm alright. I'll be fine."

Lester felt the emptiness of the room and his tenuous place in the menacing world brim full of transitory hope and warmth.

"You know, Mickey had it kind of rough when he first arrived," Pee Wee commented. "I mean, not as bad as this, but it was tough."

"That right, Mick?" Lester asked. "Murph mentioned that only briefly. What'd they do to you anyway?"

"Aw, it weren't so bad. Called me some names. Played tricks on me sometimes. Then they beat me up some. It weren't so bad."

"How'd you handle all that, Mick?" Lester asked.

"Don't reckon I know," the boy replied. "Don't ever think about that none."

Pee Wee's mind alighted with a frivolous thought. "Well, *I* can help you with that one, Lester," he said. "But I don't think it's gonna do you much good."

He went on to explain how Mickey would sometimes "zone

out—enter a world that nobody else was privileged to. He described the rocking and glassy eyes, and of course, the robotic recitation of the poem by Walter de la Mare. "So you see," he continued, "all you have to do is learn that poem, and maybe you can shut out all the crap as well, Lester."

The bemused catcher smiled.

"Yeah, maybe I should try that. What do ya say, Mick? Will ya teach me?"

Lester and Pee Wee laughed, but Mickey was somewhere else, his gaze fastened on a small bowl with the name Lucky on the front that sat on the floor next to the counter. "Hey, Mick," Pee Wee said louder. "Do you think you could teach Lester here some lines from 'Silver'?"

The boy began to move his lips, but his eyes were still somewhere else. "I reckon so. My ma taught me. When I was a little boy. Real little. Said it was our special poem, and that it would take me to a special place, in my heart, every time I said it."

Lester wasn't laughing anymore. "Your ma, she sounds a lot like my mama," he said, a little tearful. "Full of love and sweet things to say. That sure is something special now. Man, how I miss that."

"Why, Lester?" Mickey asked, shifting his gaze from the floor to his friend.

"My mama passed on, Mickey, some time ago. Haven't heard her voice in years."

Pee Wee looked at Lester now, as if he was really seeing him for the first time. "I know the feeling myself. I lost my pa when I was just a little boy. I hear ya, Lester. No matter how long it is, the pain never really goes away."

Mickey found work for his nervous hands, fashioning different shapes from the toothpicks he had pulled from tiny dispenser on the table. But his mind was also restless, so he spoke as he created.

"Mama says you can still hear someone who's gone, cause they are in heaven. I don't reckon I know where that is. Somewhere in the clouds. I ain't never seen it though. But I drew a picture of it once. You can still hear them, Mama says, cause they still speak to you. Only I never heard no one say nothin' to me. Not even Oscar. He were my porker. My favorite porker. I talk to him every day, but never heard nothin'. Mama says I got's to believe for it to happen, but it's hard to believe something you ain't never seen. Or heard. I don't like them things. I believe in shooting stars and caterpillars changing into butterflies cause I seen them. Just last month I seen both. But I'm still waiting on Oscar." Lester and Pee Wee looked at each other and nodded, each moved by the trembling sense of innocence attached to the boy's words.

"Thanks, Mickey," Lester finally said. "I think your ma is right. I think we should all just keep listening."

They finished their food and continued talking as they walked outside. It was a cool night, and the crickets were plentiful and loud. Mickey has just finished commenting about how he loved to catch fireflies and put them in a jar when it happened.

Up the road, emerging from the darkness like stealthy apparitions haunting the clear night air, came five figures, cloaked in white from head to toe. They were wielding baseball bats and venomous threats that were only partly audible to the stunned trio.

"Oh, man, I don't like the looks of this," Pee Wee said.

Lester fixed his jaw and began rolling up his sleeves. "Take Mickey, McGinty," Lester ordered, "and the two of you scram. Hurry. Ain't your fight. Go now and get the sheriff."

Mickey was still thinking about heaven when he saw the five men in white and Lester and Pee Wee's curious reaction to them. It troubled him briefly, but he was more concerned with the unusual image for the moment.

"What are those people doing?" he asked. "It ain't Halloween."

"I told you, McGinty," Lester repeated loudly. "Get the hell out of here. Now!"

McGinty thought only for a second, then whispered something in Mickey's ear before rolling up his own sleeves. "We ain't going nowhere, Lester," he said. "Baseball family, remember?"

The moon dimmed capriciously behind a creeping cloud just as the horrible realization lit Mickey's unsuspecting mind. All at once the melodious song of the crickets and other night dwellers was muted now by Mickey's frantic rocking and poetic recitation and the guttural cries of the approaching mob.

"How's about a little night ball, jungle bunny?" one of the men mocked, pounding his open palm with the barrel of the bat he was carrying. "You game now?"

Lester took a step back, his face awash with fear, and stood uneasily between Pee Wee and Mickey. "Look, we don't want no trouble here. We's just on our way home."

"He doesn't want no trouble?" another repeated. "Did you boys hear that? Our monkey friend don't want no trouble. Ain't that precious. Well, I can understand that. Who wants trouble? But, sometimes, monkey boy, you get what you get. And for a monkey boy who's put on that uniform you's been wearing, parading around town like you's one of us, I'd say you done asked for it and plum forgot about it." The others laughed. "Now, we aims to oblige, and show you some good old-fashioned small town hospitality."

The two groups clashed like freight trains vying for the same stretch of track. Lester had just raised his fists, placed them before a tear-streaked face that flashed dimly in the pale moonlight, when two of the intruders swarmed with unrelenting malice on both sides of him, punching and kicking until the stunned Lester fell to the ground.

Mickey and Pee Wee were embroiled as well. Pee Wee tried desperately to ward off the attack, posturing and swinging frantically with all his might, but fell almost instantly, leaving a dazed Mickey to face the remaining threesome all by himself.

It appeared that the boy, who was rocking violently and crying, was no match for the venomous miscreants. He watched, in brooding horror, as the chaos began to unfold. "Slowly, silently, now the moon, Walks the night in her silver shoon…"

The three men laughed and ceased their assault momentarily, arrested by the catatonic recitation.

"Are you kidding me?" one of them said, slapping the side of his leg as he guffawed. "Nursery rhymes? This is way too easy"

Mickey continued to rock and recite each line with an amplified sense of urgency. "Hey, are you listening to this, Willard?" one of the men questioned. "What kind of stupid shit is this retard mumbling?"

The assailants closed in, bats whirling. But something was happening—something pure and unbridled. Somewhere deep within the recesses of Mickey's fractured memory, torrents of painful recollections rushed over the walls of reminiscence and rocked the boy. These turbulent waters splashed across his usual sensibility, taking with them any inhibitions before uniting at last in one stormy squall that filled his arms and hands with surging anger. He became incensed, a whirling dervish of frenetic fists and feet that hammered away at the group like a cyclone tearing apart a sleepy township. First one fell. Then another. The third went down as well. They all lay pressed to the earth for a moment, flaccid and stunned.

For a moment, there was silence. Mickey backed off and stared. The moonlight slanting through the wind—pinched branches above lit intermittently the bloodied faces and tattered clothing. It bothered him, but not as much as the low moan that suddenly rose from the pile, a plaintive hum that vibrated sinfully in the night air before morphing into a mumbled exchange between the fallen men. Then slowly, pitiably, they pulled themselves up languidly, one at a time, out of the battle induced stupor and readied themselves for another pass.

Mickey freaked. He saw now in full moonlight what he had done, and realized the ordeal was far from over. With freshets of fear and shame coursing through his body, he placed his hands over his ears and rocked and roared.

The unholy threesome heard the cry, saw the boy's twisted mien and thought better of their intentions. They scattered instantly like flies into the heavy darkness. Mickey followed their flight with steamy eyes, his elbows now dug firmly into his sides in a vain attempt to keep his beleaguered body from shaking. He had all but righted the tremors when the strangled cries of Lester and Pee Wee sounded the alarm again, and Mickey was, once more, a raging instrument of malediction.

The two remaining assailants continued. Pee Wee went down again, but Lester refused to submit. He stood hunched over, chin to chest, forearms locked in front of his face. He was staggering around like a punch drunk boxer about to kiss the canvas when he felt the iron grip of his assailants weaken. Then, just like that, he was free. He unlocked his forearms with guarded curiosity to discover the body of one of his attackers completely sagged, melted into an exanimate heap of twisted limbs; the other was in the vice-like hands of Mickey.

Lester watched from a safe distance as the boy shook the robed villain with erupting vengeance. He pulled him one way, then the next. The violent jostling had all but rendered the man unconscious. Mickey was just about to finish the job, hammer him to the ground, when a fickle wind slipped under the hood of the scoundrel, lifting it just enough so that only Mickey's eyes could see inside. The face was pale and terror stricken. The face was also familiar. The boy froze. He could hardly breathe. It was as if someone had struck him in the head with a two-by-four. He just stood there, unable to utter a sound, his mind filled with discord. Anyone within one hundred feet of the boy would have sworn he heard the grating confusion—and that it came from inside Mickey's head. It was an awful sound. Something like metal on metal. The grinding of incongruous realities rubbing up against each other.

Pee Wee and Lester continued to watch, and were struck by the boy's sudden paralysis. They were just about to come closer, for fear that their friend was injured, when Mickey's head drooped and his eyes began to leak. Then, with a sinking heart, he released his victim, who crumpled to the ground momentarily before scampering off to join the others.

Murph was to be at a meeting with Dennison that next morning. It was that time of year already—midseason report. Time to face the music. This ritual of Dennison's was always an onerous experience, one replete with the self absorbed owner's haughty posturing and banal observations. Then there were the questions—a proliferation of calculated inquires designed to humiliate him on some level while reaffirming that smug bastard's own dominance. It was torture. And this year, there was an additional angst attached to the appointment, for the status of Murph's job was now twisting in the wind.

On the way to the ballpark, Murph stopped off at the sheriff's station in order to follow up on the report that Lester and the others had filed in the early morning hours.

"I'm sorry, Murph," Rosco said. "You know I am. But those boys of yours can't give me much. I got nothing to go on here. Hell, throw a white sheet over anyone in this town and you got a possible suspect. My hands are tied."

Things did not improve much one Murph arrived at the park. Dennison was standing behind his desk, holding a gray portfolio filled with attendance charts and game reports, when Murph arrived at his office. Wordless, the peevish owner crossed the floor to greet his manager, fanning the air with the stack of papers while nodding his head in cryptic fashion.

"Just been crunching the numbers, Murph," he said. "Interesting. Very Interesting." The two took their usual places—Murph on the bleached wood chair whose varnished seat and curious incline kept him sliding obsequiously toward the owner's desk and Dennison, safely ensconced in his preposterously enormous burgundy leather chair, the spot from which he always preferred to espouse his inner workings.

"I have several things I want to discuss with you, Murph," he said, his voice laced with what sounded like tragic exactitude. "But, before we do that, I'd like to hear from you."

Murph was a little crestfallen and noticeably phlegmatic in his response to Dennison. He sat, his hands folded neatly on his lap in subtle defiance, saying nothing while staring at the ripple of lines that Father Time and the unforgiving sun had seared into the old man's forehead.

"Well, Mr. Murphy. I'm waiting. What have you got to say for yourself?"

Murph laughed somewhat grimly, then spoke. "What I think, Warren," he began, folding his arms and leaning his head to one side in thoughtful deliberation, "is that the play on the field speaks for itself."

Dennison smiled, his thoughts rising precipitously and overflowing like the swell of papers challenging the thin cardboard binding of his portfolio.

"I have all of that, Murph, right here," he said. "Numbers. Statistics. Projections. Charts and graphs. It's all here. I can see the value there. Believe me. But, I also know that those things only tell part of the story."

Dennison walked backed to his desk, sighed purposefully, and pulled from the top drawer a stack of letters addressed to Lester in care of the team. "Do you know what these are, Mr. Murphy?" he asked. "Hmm? Allow me."

He undid the shoelace holding the envelopes together, pulled and opened the first, then began to read aloud.

Dear Mr. Sledge,

Ain't nothin' more sickening than a jigaboo that don't know his place. You best watch yourself boy. Hear? Nobody wants you here and nobody will cry none when they find your black jungle bunny ass hanging in the woods. You better know I'm watching you and your jigaboo loving friends.

Murph shook his head, his mind flushing faintly into frustration. "Don't give me this crap, Warren," Murph said. "I know all about that. Ain't anything new. Lester has already shown me a hundred others, just like it."

"And what about all the other stuff, Murph?" Dennison persisted. "Huh? Is that all 'nothing new' as well?"

Murph felt the approaching crisis in Dennison's words. "Look, Warren, things have not been easy. And I guess I should have told you about some of the other things that have happened. Yes, it's not always pleasant. I hear you. But you know what? Look at us. Would you just look at us? We are a pretty good damned baseball team. Despite all of this horse crap—the letters, the threats—we have played through and have come out on top. Think about that. We are halfway through the season, and sitting on top. You can't argue with that."

"I'm aware of the numbers, Murph. I am."

"And have you seen the newspapers? Have you really thought about this? Here we are, with the best freakin' pitcher on the planet, and the league's leading hitter, and we are getting all the ink. I think Lester has started to really win people over. It's news, Warren. And good news. He's fascinating to talk about. Now what could be bad about that?"

"I know all that, Murph. And it's —"

"Stop right there," Murph ordered, reading the old man's expression. "We had a deal, Warren! Jesus Christ!"

"All of that is good, Murph. But there's a little something called opportunity cost. You know, weighing that good against the bad. And I've done that. Now, that being said, I called you here today —"

"I know exactly why you called me here today. Bull. That's what it is."

"I called you here today," Dennison continued, "to tell you I am fairly satisfied with what you have done. I am. And I don't suppose I could justify to the people letting you go. Not now anyway. However, if we are to continue as is, I need some of this to go away. It's gotta stop. It's bad press. You need to find a way to keep this boy out of trouble. Out of the public eye."

Murph wrinkled his nose and shook his head. "Wait. Are you saying what I think you're saying? Continue? As we are?"

"Now don't go breaking your arm patting yourself on the back, Arthur," Dennison replied. "And don't be making any party plans either. You ain't out of the woods yet. Not by a long shot. You've got a lot of work to do before you can lift up any glasses."

Murph shook his head again as his insecurities took their final breaths. "Work is fine," he said. "Work I can handle."

That night, Murph celebrated the news with Molly. They ate steak and drank wine by candlelight, and Molly played the clarinet for him afterward while he sipped his brandy. Then, under a sleek velvet sky adorned with a thousand glinting diamonds, they walked in the cool night air, arm in arm, listening to the crickets and reveling in the happiness they continued to find together. Their feet were light and moved in unison, displacing dead thistles and loose gravel with every step. Murph was quiet. She watched, with fascination, the moon's reflection in his eyes and tried, at every turn, to gauge his mood. He said nothing, however. Just filled his lungs and stared transfixed at the myriad constellations peeking through the gathering clouds that had lingered curiously in front of the moon for a moment before continuing their nightly pilgrimage.

"Mr. Murphy, you are a million miles away tonight," Molly said, her lashes fluttering. "What in the world are you thinking about?"

He took a few more steps with her, still reticent, then finally alighted, bringing his hand from his side to her cheek. "It's beautiful out here, Molly," he said, staring out into the tide of darkness at a star ensconced in a purplish hue. "Sort of makes you believe that everything in the universe is right—just the way it should be. All we need to do is just stop and look."

Molly smiled as the crickets continued to blow their tiny kazoos. "I agree, Arthur," she said, squeezing his hand. "It's a perfect night." Her reply brought about in Murph a swift return of thought to issues of a more earthly nature.

"It *is* perfect, Molly. I've been thinking that it's all perfect. All of it. Including right now, which seems the perfect moment for us to do what only seems good and natural."

He looked at her softly and tucked the errant strands of hair hanging in her eyes behind her ears. For a while, they said nothing. Just stood, face to face, locked in a sort of visual embrace. The air was still, the only movement coming from a handful of desultory fireflies sprinkled across a dark canvas, tiny drops of soft light that glowed intermittently as they embarked on their nocturnal odyssey.

"I'm thinking that it's about time I made an honest woman out of you, Molly," he finally said, kneeling on bended knee. "You know, make this whole thing official."

Molly's eyes dilated. She sighed deeply, as if his words had forced all of the air from her lungs, and turned her head. It was not what she was expecting. She was finally legally free from Clarence, and this afforded her considerable peace, but she still suffered from the indelible residue of their tumultuous union. So much of it, she thought, was rooted in all the years she spent in silent subjugation. Clarence was a ruthless martinet. Volatile. Self-serving. Abusive. He had stripped her of every last shred of self worth and dignity. His dominion was so inexorable, so unrelenting, that she marveled at how she had even survived. It began almost the very minute they were wed. That night, at the farm, under the auspices of matrimonial consummation, he climbed on top of her, his rancid breath strong, and told her not to move.

She shuddered at the recollection and swore she would never again subject herself to such incarceration.

Yet part of her also remembered how it was she came to recognize the evils to which she had grown so numb. He was standing next to her. Arthur Murphy was no Clarence. Far from it. From the very first time they met, he was warm and attentive. She never felt more liberated than when she was with him. And then there was Mickey. The boy had really blossomed in Murph's care. There was no denying that. With the moon melting down the backside of the distant oaks, she struggled with the opposing forces. It was a lot to consider. This protracted pause, an awkward silence that swelled all around them was interminable—certainly long enough to fill Murph's head with the dreadful thought that he had misspoken. He stood there, foot tapping, wishing he could recapture his words, certain he had jumped the gun. He had just closed his eyes in cloying humiliation when he felt her lips press softly against his. It was unlike any other kiss they had shared. There was something ethereal, ineffably electric about it. As if her entire lifetime had been communicated to him through her soft, wet lips. He had never felt closer to her.

"I love you, Arthur," she said softly, holding his face in her hands.

"It's going to all work out," he assured her. " It will. The time will have to be right, but I love you, Molly. I love you too."

JUNE SWOON

Murph continued to ride the swell of good fortune. He never smiled so much. His happiness was indomitable, had taken off like the company of field sparrow that skimmed low and playfully over the flowering meadow just beyond the artificial boundaries of his modest lot. He was intoxicated with blithesome promise, and his joyous mien could not be tamed. Even Matheson's trite admonitions could not dampen his spirits.

"Don't go counting your chickens, son," the old timer warned him. "Things are good, sure, but Fate's a fickle shrew. One day, everything's coming up roses, and you're riding high, and the next, misery is all around you, like a mad woman's piss."

Murph paid him no mind. It was all good. Glorious even. His burgeoning career. This relationship with Molly which had blossomed into a beautiful flower. What had he done to all of a sudden become worthy of such bliss? He could not fathom an answer. The world just seem to burst into a spinning wheel of brilliant color. Even things he had observed a thousand times before had come to life. And it wasn't just those large, unmistakable things that were now imbued with this ferocious vitality, like the grass at Borchert Field or the towering oaks surrounding his home. No, it was everywhere. Even in the most rudimentary things, like the morning air, now crisp and redolent, and the pattern of the tiny leaves on the elderberry bushes just outside his bedroom window, which had morphed into tiny canvasses of marvel. But amidst all the euphoria, he was still galled by the problems with Lester, frustrated like a willful child eager to set in place the final piece of a jigsaw puzzle.

"Look, about what happened that night, Lester," Murph said, as he and Mickey sat around on the porch showing Lester some pictures from last season. "Did anyone see you guys leave, or say something to you?"

"No, no way. We even switched up our routine, just to get away from all of it. I don't get it. It's like someone followed us, or knew somehow where to find us."

Lester's words rattled something loose inside Murph.

"Yeah, it does seems a little strange," he said raising his eyebrows. "The whole thing just ain't right. Things don't seem to add up. Not at all."

"You don't know something?" Lester asked. "Do ya, Murph?"

Murph began to speak, as though something had suddenly occurred to him, but he kept himself in hand and said nothing more.

Mickey sat, tapping his foot nervously against the leg of his chair. The conversation had ignited a spark in his mind as well. He had said nothing about the attack that night. Until now.

"Why do those men wear white hoods, Murph?" he asked.

"Those men are bad, Mickey. Bad apples."

"All of them?"

"Every last one."

"I thought that bad men always wore black. Like in them movies, with John Wayne."

"Well, this here is a special kind of bad man, Mickey. Ain't no rhyme or reason to what they do. They're just plain bad."

"All of them?"

"Yup. All of them." Mickey's eyes tightened and seemed to fix themselves on something distant.

"Can there be one who isn't bad?"

"I don't reckon that's possible, Mick," Lester said, reading the boy's face carefully. "Haven't met one yet who didn't have the devil in his eye." Murph watched as Mickey fidgeted, his back hunched unnaturally.

"Something on your mind you want to talk about, Mick?" Murph asked. The boy chewed at his fingers.

"Nope." Mickey don't want to talk about nothing."

"You sure now?"

He looked away before answering. "Yup. Mickey is sure."

"Look, I know this is hard to understand, Mickey. Hell, I don't even get most of it. But people are funny sometimes. But not everyone. There are plenty of good people out there too. The trick is knowing who the good ones are and who are the ones you need to steer clear of."

The boy's voice rattled, as if something were lodged in his throat. "Some people are mean. I reckon that's why I'd rather be with Duncan and Daphney and the rest of the animals. Ain't no bad ones there."

The wave of prosperity on which Murph had ridden gleefully for months eventually fell. It was to be expected he told himself. Just the natural ordering of the universe. With the exception of his plans with Molly, everything seemed to turn to crap. The latest news about Boxcar was not good. Dennison was on his ass and no matter how hard he tried, he just could not shield Lester from the festering odium. The letters and packages and violent affronts kept coming. It was maddening. The more successful Lester was on the field, and the more hearts he won, the worse it got. Murph did not know what to do.

To make matters worse, the Brewers hit their first rough patch of the season during that same stretch. They dropped four straight and were spiraling out of control. Murph was beside himself. Dennison's edict was clear: win or you're out. His face grew a shade paler as he recalled the conviction with which those words had been said.

Just the thought of his recent success—now ephemeral and as certain as a fist full of sand—was enough to light the fuse of utter panic. It was this desperation that lead to an emergency meeting following their last failure.

"Listen, fellas. I'm done screaming. Now I don't know what the hell is going on here. I'll be damned if I can make any sense of any of it. All I know is that we are in trouble, boys. Real trouble. Our lead is dwindling. And it doesn't appear to be getting any better."

There was something melancholic and urgent in his voice that accented the contours of his sunken face and fleeting eyes.

"Now I don't know if any of this matters to you guys. Or if you have anything left inside of you. Any part of you, no matter how small, that wants to fight for your own well being and self respect. If you do, and I know that some of you do, I am asking for you to call on it. Now. We need it now. It cannot wait any longer. And if for some reason none of this means a hill of beans to you, and I'm asking too much, then do it for *me*. Because I gotta be honest with all of you. If we don't right this ship, I'll be gone. Dennison's had my head on the block for months now, and he's getting itchy. And I have to say, I've grown sort of attached to your ugly mugs, and I'm not quite ready to give that up. So please. Let's do this thing. We cannot afford any more setbacks. And we need everyone to contribute. We cannot do this without everyone in this room."

Many of the players felt Murph's words and sat around afterward, exchanging heartfelt confessions and promises of future exploits of heroism and bravado. Some said nothing.

However, despite their manager's impassioned plea, and a roiling recrimination that burned inside almost every man's belly, they still could not do anything right. They dropped four more games, each more frustrating than the one before. On Monday, they lost to the Colts. The bats were good enough to win, banging out fifteen hits and ten runs, but Butch Sanders was awful. He struggled all game with his command, walking seven batters and yielding four round trippers, and in the process, squandered three different leads. Murph suddenly felt afflicted with an uncompromising demon.

"What the hell is he doing out there?" he bawled. "Jesus Christ. Is he even trying?"

"Certainly is a queer duck," Matheson commented. "Never struggled like this before."

"Yeah, he's got it in his head that he can't pitch to Lester. Some bull about communication and comfort level."

"Well, you can't just leave him out there," Matheson continued. "Jesus, I know you don't feel like butting the bull off the bridge, but someone's gotta talk to him."

"I wish I could, Farley. I do. I have tried before, several times, but he's not having any of it."

"Bah," the old man grunted. "If wishes were horses, beggars would ride. I'll talk to him. I got plenty to say."

Murph's feelings raced back and forth between anger and action.

"No, Farley," he said. "No. I got a better idea. When he comes in, I'll have Mickey do it. Maybe it'll make some sense coming from another pitcher. Especially if it's Mickey."

The two of them watched from the top step of the dugout as Sanders continued to struggle. With two outs, he walked the Colts' two and three hitters on eight straight breaking balls in the dirt and then fell behind the cleanup hitter, 2–0. Lester shouted some encouraging words from behind the plate, and implored Sanders to heed the signs he was being given, but the intractable pitcher just looked past him, as if he hadn't heard a thing. He stood on the mound, full of piss and vinegar, and let go his next offering, a feckless fastball right down the middle of the plate. The Colts' slugger jumped all over it, mashing the baseball into the gap in left centerfield. The little white missile scorched the grass as it skidded toward the wall. It was destined for extra bases, and most certainly would have scored two, had Jimmy Llamas not gotten such a great jump on the ball, cutting it off with a deft backhand and then firing a strike to Arky Fries at second to nip the batter just as he slid into the bag. Llamas was thrilled, and began firing his imaginary six shooters all over Borchert Field as he jogged in from his position. It gave the fans something to cheer about, but the furrowed lines on Murph's face told the real story. "Sanders, sit your ass on the bench and don't move. You're done."

Murph stormed to the other side of the dugout and sat himself down next to Mickey. The boy was busy fingering a brand new baseball.

"Say, Mick, I need you to do something for me," Murph said, tapping Mickey on the knee. The boy did not stir. He could hear Murph talking to him, but did nothing to acknowledge him. He just sat there, chewing the inside of his cheek, examining the ball.

"One hundred eight," he finally said, spinning the ball in his hand.

"What?"

"One hundred eight." Murph shook his head and sighed.

"One hundred eight what, Mick?" he asked.

The boy tossed the baseball in his hand and smiled. "One hundred and eight red stitches. This ball has one hundred and eight."

Murph scratched his head with bewilderment. He sat there,

measuring what he was about to say, as Mickey remained suspended in his own web of thoughts. Murph was dying. A halo of misfortune spun around him and mocked his idleness. For a split second, he considered letting Matheson speak to Sanders. Maybe the old guy was right. Why would Sanders listen to Mickey? Then he remembered Matheson's inane ramblings and decided that his first choice was the lesser of two evils. "So Mick, I was thinking that—"

The boy began tossing the ball up again and caught it a few more times until another idea suddenly seized his imagination and catapulted him from his seat.

"Whoa there," Murph said, grabbing the boy before he took flight. "What's the hurry?" The boy motioned to the white bucket of balls resting against the dugout wall.

"Mickey's going to check the others."

"No, Mick. Not now. I have something you need to do for me." Murph explained to the boy the need for all the pitchers on the staff to be able to pitch to Lester. He complimented him for the way *he* worked with the catcher and suggested that his behavior was one that he wished the others would emulate.

"So you see, Mick, I was thinking that maybe you could talk to Sanders. You know, tell him how Lester has really helped you and all. I think he, and the others, just might listen. After all, nobody's had better results than you."

Mickey's face contorted, as if he had just placed something sour passed his lips. A dark voice sounded somewhere deep in his mind and a look of dull recollection glazed his eyes.

"Mickey, are you listening to me?" Murph asked, vexed by the boy's apparent indifference. "Did you hear what I said?"

Mickey stared straight ahead, and began chattering a partial repetition of his favorite poem.

"Mick, what's going on?" Murph persisted. "Come on. What's happening?"

"...a harvest mouse goes scampering by, with silver claws and a silver eye."

Murph's mouth tightened as if someone had pulled it shut with an invisible chord. "Come on, Mickey, we don't have time for this. Why are you doing this now? I need you to talk to Sanders. Stop messing around. Now. He's killing us and poisoning the rest of the staff."

The boy stood silent for a while looking down at his cleats.

"Mickey does not want to talk to Butch Sanders," he replied. "No. I do not want to."

"What do you mean you don't want to? Why the hell not?"

Mickey fell silent again.

"Why the hell not, Mick? Why won't you talk to him?"

"And moveless fish in the water gleam, by silver reeds in a silver stream."

Murph's frustration leaped wildly the following night. The Giants were in town, and brought with them an eight-game losing streak and the league's worst record.

Gabby Hooper got the ball and turned in a solid performance, scattering nine hits and allowing just four runs. But the Brewer offense sputtered, led by the anemic performance of their slumping cleanup hitter Woody Danvers. Danvers was flat out awful, stranding a staggering nine base runners in his first three at bats. He looked ghost-like, blundering through each inning ineffectually, a slave to the slump that had enervated his confidence and any vestige of his physical prowess.

Still reeling from the previous failures that night, he limped to the plate, carrying with him myriad misgivings and a chance for redemption. The bases were full of Brewers, and the crowd, still drenched in the thunderstorm of frustration that had washed away their voices for most of the night, began to stir, morphed into a striation of beleaguered souls united by the intoxicating idea that the script for some late inning heroics had all but been written.

The pitcher's first offering was true—a four-seam dart that split the plate knee high for a called first strike. Danvers bristled at the call, then stepped out of the box, rolling first his eyes and then his shoulders in a desperate attempt to shake himself from his offensive stupor. The next offering missed up and away, followed by an off speed delivery in the dirt. Both the buzz from the crowd and Danvers' confidence seemed to burgeon uncontrollably as the count shifted in the batter's favor. Even Matheson could not contain his enthusiasm.

"All right, Woody!" he screamed, the vein in his right temple straining against his leathery skin. "Bases chucked. You got 'em now. He's gonna try to bell the cat. Be ready now. Here comes a fat one."

Matheson was right. After wiping the sweat from his brow and then fingering the rosin bag and firing it to the ground, the frustrated pitcher grooved a fastball dead center. It was a perfect pitch—just as if it had been placed on a tee. Danvers drank in the opportunity, guzzled the myriad visions of breathless glory attached to the albescent sphere as it spun right toward his happy zone. The bat met the ball just as it crossed the plate. The timing was perfect, producing a melodious *crack* that for an instant, catapulting every fanny out of its seat for a closer look. It sounded like victory. Sweet victory. But that sound was all they would get, because in his haste to expiate the night's previous failures, Woody Danvers had swung too hard. Way too hard. His whole body twisted in spasmodic pulsation. His front shoulder flew open prematurely, and the back one dipped below his hands, so much so that when he whipped the bat through the hitting zone, he only caught the underside of the ball and sent it soaring straight up in the air, like a toy rocket whose trajectory was harmless and predictable. It wasn't long before the catcher was camped under the towering pop, pounding his glove as the lifeless ball parachuted safely into the yawning pocket.

When the game was over, the reporters spilled through the clubhouse and into Danvers' locker like a clutter of spiders carrying venomous intent. Their assault was dogged and merciless.

"What happened to you, Woody?" one writer asked. "Good God, you went from a house on fire to a smoldering campfire at a Girl Scout cookout." Danvers flushed, and his eyes alighted. The next salvo was even more biting.

"So, Woody, how are you gonna sleep tonight, with those goat horns on your head?"

The tortured slugger rumbled like a volcano. His face contorted with jeering defiance, and from his narrowing lips came a sizzling sound, something shrill and inhuman that had risen up from a place deep within him, the place in everyone rarely touched by others, the place where all clouded memories and brooding insecurities reside quietly, peacefully, until roused from their slumber.

"You goddamned guys are unbelievable," he exploded, firing his cap to the floor. The force of the projectile set them all on their heels. "Unbelievable. For weeks now, nobody's been better. Nobody. Where were you then? Huh? At Lester's locker. That's where. Or somewhere else. It sure wasn't here. So, why now? Huh? Why? Why don't you go ask Lester why he couldn't get it done? How about Hooper? Was he brilliant tonight? Or Finster or McGinty or Jimmy Llamas? Why don't you go bother them? Huh? Go see if they'll listen to your bull because I'm done." Danvers was inconsolable. He just slammed his locker and stormed off. Refused to speak to any of the media for days afterward. Things were certainly amiss.

But of all the Brewers, Mickey was struggling the most. He just wasn't himself. More than ever, his thoughts were scattered and prickly. It could have been all the ugliness he had seen. He was still asking Murph about the "men in white hoods" and was relentless in his pursuit of an answer to what in his world was a simple question.

"Murph, why does Lester being dark matter? *We* like him. Why don't other folks?"

Murph frowned. A pall of loneliness and doom gradually stole over him. "I don't know, Mick," he answered, shaking his head erratically. "I told you before, a hundred times, it ain't easy to understand."

The weight of confusion was eating away at him. It showed. Then again, maybe the boy was just getting tired. He had logged a lot of innings and had performed at an almost superhuman level. It was a lot to ask of a kid who still was, in essence, just a farm boy. Of course, his troubles could have had something to do with the notes he began receiving in his locker every day, He did the same thing every time he got one—leaned up against his locker, limbs slack, eyes wide and curiously vacant, his lips parted from his teeth, quivering in silent alarm. His hands were also unsteady, and the tiny paper would shake violently as it dampened beneath his tremulous grip. And the words. Those words he read to himself, over and over, were like tiny daggers pressed slowly into his sides.

Forget what you saw boy, or someone will get hurt bad.

Each time it happened, he felt this unavailing shame, as if somehow he had done something wrong by seeing what he saw. And he saw it, over and over again. That face, ugly and mean, revealed to him and only him that night. It was awful. The desire to conceal his secret was mastering. Nobody could know about this. Nobody. So each time he got another note, he tore the dreaded paper into a thousand pieces, one small section at a time, and then sprinkled the remnants like confetti into the waste paper basket, all this while reciting catatonically his favorite poetic lines.

Murph saw the boy was floundering, but was powerless to put a name to it. He hoped quietly that whatever it was that was ailing his young ace would pass as cryptically and swiftly as it had come. But things only got worse.

Mickey got the ball in the first half of a twi-night double dip against the Giants. It was a perfect evening, attenuated by a resplendent, even sky tinged here and there with splashes of red and orange. Borchert Field was filled to capacity, something that had become customary each time Mickey took the hill, with legions of Mickey Tussler disciples, including of course the rabid coterie of worshippers from Mickey's Minions and the Baby Bazooka Brigade. They were always the most vocal and demonstrative, but their unbridled zeal had struck a chord with many of the less expressive fans, who, after observing the antics of these fanatics, began coming to the ballpark dressed from head to toe in Brewer garb while carrying placards and banners professing their unmitigated love for their favorite Brewer. Everything was right, Murph told himself, filling his lungs with the cool evening air. This would be the night that Mickey would return to form.

The game began uneventfully, with Mickey retiring the first three batters in order, each on a weak groundball to the right side of the infield. The Brewers went quietly in their half of first as well, and were back on the field before most of the crowd had time to grab a hot dog or arrest the thunder of the beer carts rolling through the stands.

The leadoff batter for the Giants, Johnny McCullers, began the top of the second frame with one of those classic at bats that seemed to go on in perpetuity. He had fallen behind 0–2 on two straight fastballs that shaved the outside corner, but battled back, fouling off the next two offerings before demonstrating a keen eye on the next two pitches, which both missed just off that same corner. With the count now even, McCullers really went to work, spoiling the next five fastballs with a quick, defensive flick of the wrists, spraying the crowd with a shower of souvenirs. Mickey continued to fire, and McCullers answered the bell every time, fouling each one into the stands. The dance went on for several more pitches, until the umpire, having depleted his supply of baseballs, called time so that he could reload his pockets.

McCullers stepped out, and banged his cleats with the barrel of his bat. His arms were tired, but the determination still burned. He exhaled loudly, rolled his shoulders, and dug in once again. Mickey was up for the challenge as well, drawing strength and energy from the 15,000 strong who were standing and chanting in unison his name.

Mickey received a new ball from the umpire and spun it in his hand, searching for just the right grip. Then he took his sign from Lester. Another fastball, this time up and in. A little chin music. Something high and hard, designed to get into the stubborn batter's kitchen. McCullers had been leaning over the plate the entire at bat, trying desperately to protect the outer half. He was definitely vulnerable inside. A well placed heater would most certainly saw him off at the hands and end the interminable battle right then and there.

Lester kept one finger flush against his inner thigh until Mickey nodded; then he set the target just inches from McCuller's belt buckle. As the determined batter whirled his bat overhead, Mickey rocked back, extended his front leg and fired a dart that blistered the air en route to Lester's yawning pocket. McCullers, who had been expecting something away, froze instantly, his arms locking up like seized gears in an overworked machine, just as the ball exploded through the strike zone.

"Ball three," the umpire shouted. "Inside."

The Giant's bench roared its approval, reveling in the valiant battle their comrade was waging against his formidable opponent, while Murph broke out of his silence with cries of torment.

"Oh, for Christ sake!" he thundered. "Come on, ump. You're squeezing him now. That plate's got two sides. Holy crap. Open your eyes. You're missing a pretty damn good game here."

A torrent of boos rained down all across Borchert Field as the crowd began to voice its displeasure as well. Mickey, unphased by the raucous milieu, took the return toss from Lester and prepared for his next delivery. He licked his lips, blew out a cleansing breath, and adjusted the buckle on his belt, pulling it sharply to the left, then back a tad to the right, so that it lay in the center of his waist. Then he lined up his feet in their customary position, three inches from the right edge of the rubber. Standing there, looking at Lester's index and middle finger dangling furtively in between the crafty catcher's legs, Mickey was thinking that the air was cooler than usual. And that his stomach felt full, like maybe he had eaten too many biscuits and gravy at the pre-game meal. His eye marked the antics of two pigeons just beyond the grandstand, tussling over the discarded remnants of a hot dog bun. He smiled. He thought of Silas Harper, and the coop of pigeons the old man had at his place just down the road from the old farm where Mickey had grown up.

"These are special birds, Mick," he always told him, placing one in the boy's hands so that he could examine the creature up close. "Messenger pigeons. Trained 'em myself. Can carry a message a hundred miles. Yes sireee. Amazing birds."

Mickey smiled at the reminiscence, and somewhere, in the region of his mind reserved only for those thoughts that possessed the power to warm his fractured heart, he considered that maybe these Borchert Field pigeons weren't Borchert Field pigeons at all.

Maybe, just maybe, they belonged to Silas Harper, and had flown all the way from Indiana with a message. For him. His smile grew wider. He had just stepped off the rubber and began his quest to catch a better look when the sound of Murph's voice shook him from his momentary musing.

"Come on now, Mick. Concentrate now. Go get him. No letting up. Go right after him, kid."

Mickey refocused, steadying himself once again on the still pristine white stripe. With Lester's target now his primary focus, he placed his hands together, rolled his arms in inimitable fashion, and broke off a 12–6 bender that dove through the strike zone so sharply, so stealthily, that by the time McCullers had taken his hack, the ball was gone, leaving only the cool, vacant air as fodder for his eager bat.

"Steeerike three!" the umpire cried, ringing up McCullers with a histrionic flare that delighted the expectant crowd. Their boy had won the battle. The roars of approval were fleeting, however, replaced by gasps of incredulity and disappointment once everyone saw McCullers scampering down the line toward first base and Lester, who had let the brilliant pitch slip through the five hole, chasing the ball all the way to the wall behind home plate. By the time the dejected catcher retrieved his blunder, McCullers was standing safely on the first base bag.

Lester had been brilliant all year defensively. Nobody in the league was better. He had performed flawlessly for the entire season, making all the routine plays when called upon and turning in some highlight reel material as well. But there were still some malcontents, a sect of myopic trouble stirrers who refused to accept the presence of a black man on a white man's diamond, who came to the ballpark, just waiting for a moment like this to spew their venom.

"That's what you get when you let a negro do a man's job," one of the more vitriolic members of this unholy faction screamed from the seats behind home plate.

"Hey, boy, don't you have some things to shovel, or some shoes that need shining? Hmm? Are you listening to me, boy? Maybe I ought to come down there and slap that fat head of yours, teach you not to go messing up the game the way you do."

Lester looked up at the rabid miscreant, his eyes heavy and gray, then turned and began walking back to home plate.

"Don't you turn your back on me, boy. Ain't you listening? Huh? Is you stupid too? Can't you talk? Maybe that's your problem. You're just a big, dumb coon who don't know no better. That's why maybe you need to be taught—and I'm a mighty good teacher, boy—that there ain't no place for no dirty, stinkin' monkeys on a baseball field. That's right. Are you listening, boy?"

Lester was more than halfway back to home plate when he stopped suddenly. His face, now moist with perspiration, was hard and strained, and his nostrils flared, sending forth into the cool night air, with every breath, two barely perceptible lines of volcanic respiration. He knew that he should have just kept walking, like his mama would want him to, but something inside broke loose and was insisting to be heard.

He had just turned to face the reprobate once again when the strangled cries of another arrested his advance.

"Lester Sledge ain't stupid, Mister," Mickey shouted, walking in from his position on the mound toward the angry man's seat. "He's right smart. And he's my friend. My friend. You stop saying those bad words to him. He's my friend. Mickey thinks that…"

Lester turned yet again, this time placing himself strategically between an unhinged Mickey and his intended destination. The boy continued to scream at the man while trying to get closer, despite Lester's bear hug and reassuring whispers that everything was okay. The entire Brewers' bench emptied. Mickey's unexpected display enraged the man even further.

"Are you talking to me?" he fired back, finger pointed in Mickey's direction. "Ain't this rich. This is just priceless. Man alive. Now I done seen everything. A damn retard defending a stupid, good for nothing coon. What a circus. Sit down, retard, before you get hurt too."

Murph and the others got in between the war of words, and someone was just about to summon security when the natural order of things took over. It hadn't been more than a second or two after the words left the man's mouth that he was besieged by an impromptu assembly of Brew Crew vigilantes who, having taken umbrage at the pejorative remarks launched at their favorite son, leapt from their seats, subdued the villain and began dragging him, with a good deal of difficulty, toward the exit.

"Let me go! Take your friggin' hands off me!" he screamed, struggling to break free. "What's wrong with you people?" The man continued to struggle, his invectives becoming less and less audible as the group of men dragged him further and further from the field. He continued to rant about the white race, and injustice, and the old world order, but nobody was listening. Nobody, except Mickey, who heard the final words of the man's diatribe loud and clear. "I'll get you! You hear? Your black ass is mine. You hear me? I will get you."

The words were shrill and hateful and rattled the boy, brought him back instantly to that violent memory of not too long ago. And to those horrible little notes that just kept coming, day after day.

Mickey tried to go on. He got back on the mound and continued to pitch. But his mind was somewhere else. Somewhere dark and menacing, a place he'd only just discovered. A place he scarcely understood. He walked the next batter he faced on four straight pitches. That was followed by a sharp single up the middle, a booming double off the top of the left field wall, and a bases clearing triple that was smoked down the right field line. In a blink of an eye, the Brewers were trailing 4–0.

Lester called time and made a trip out to the mound at Murph's behest. Mickey was reeling, and spoke frantically to Lester with a back draft of fear and uncertainty washing over him.

"Mickey doesn't understand why people call you names, Lester Sledge," he began. "And why they want to hurt you. Mickey is trying to help Lester. Honest. I am. But I'm afraid. Mickey is a little scared."

Lester sighed and searched for words carefully, as if negotiating an unfamiliar room in the dark.

"Hey, no worries, Mick," he said, patting the boy on the shoulder. "Come on now. You're one of my best friends. And you are helping. Just by being with me. That guy, and the others like him? Don't pay them no mind. Ain't nothing worth troubling yourself with. My mama used to say, 'the empty drum always makes the loudest noise.' That's all they are. Empty drums. Ain't nothing fer either one of us to worry about."

Mickey was still, silenced by some internal affliction that he could not permit to the surface.

"Hey, Mick, ya hearing me? Come on now. You got's a game to pitch. Just do your thing, and stop thinking 'bout me."

More animated now, Lester returned to his position behind the plate, continuing his attempts to buoy Mickey's sagging spirits. The boy was listening, but the unyielding specter of impending horror was an uncompromising master. He couldn't do anything right. He hit one batter, then another. Two more Giants reached base via base on balls followed by a colossal drive that cleared the center field wall by a good twenty-five feet. "The wheels are coming off, for

Christ sake," Matheson carped. "Go and get him, Murph. Cripe, we're down by ten runs and it's only the second inning. The fat lady's getting ready to sing and we haven't even had one dance."

After the game, Murph sat in the shadows of his office, line score in one hand, a tumbler of Jack Daniels in the other. 19–2. One of the worst beatings he had ever taken as a manager. His shoulders slumped so heavily with weighty thoughts that it appeared he would topple forward and break right though the desk top at any moment. How did it get so crazy? Christ, it all seemed so perfect. That day at the mill. Lester and Mickey. The battery that was going to take the league by storm. Maybe that was his mistake, thinking it was only about baseball. That some sort of Darwinian principle would rule the day, and Lester's baseball prowess would render all of them masters of their little universe. He gulped his whiskey and grimaced, realizing now that he had forgotten about some little environmental struggles, things that skewed the parameters of competition, like ignorance, bigotry and hatred. Yeah, he had not taken those into account. Not fully anyway. Now he found himself in quite a mess; found himself drifting, being pushed inexorably by a merciless tide toward a rock laden jetty. The only thing in question now was when the horrific crash would happen. He felt defeated, but maintained still a little desire to paddle. To try and alter the collision course one last time.

He needed Mickey to be Mickey again. Yes. That was it. He needed Mickey back. Somehow, some way, he had to figure out how to make Mickey okay with this whole thing with Lester. And he desperately needed to find a way to make the boy talk.

Something was amiss. Yes, that was it. Mickey was the answer here. He was the one that made everything go. It had gone on long enough—all this mystery and unspoken truth of things. He poured himself another shot and threw it down. It is enough, he repeated, returning the tumbler to the desk top with a vengeance. The time has come. No more.

JULY

Things for Murph went from bad to worse. Although he and Molly were moving forward with their plans, Dennison was pressing him again with threats to his professional future. Moreover, Boxcar continued to grow sicker by the day, and Lester, in the wake of all the violence and hatred, decided that he had had enough and that he would be going back to the mill and his former team.

"Come on, Lester," Murph pleaded. "I know it's been bad. I do. But please. Leaving? Come on, this is where you belong. You're really making believers out of some very influential baseball guys. You're gonna leave now, when you are right there? Besides, I need you. *We* need you."

Lester's throat was thick with fear and confusion.

"It ain't so easy, Murph," he explained. "I just ain't happy. It's too much. It is. And I ain't really doing you no favors either. Look at all the trouble I caused you too. It's best this way.

"Lester, are you kidding me?" Murph said. "Trouble? The trouble ain't your fault. You didn't cause anything. Well, except a whole bunch of victories for us. Did you forget all of that?"

"I know all that, Murph. I know. But I just can't no more. I'm sorry. I am. I just ain't comfortable no more. You don't know what it's like. It's all I can think about. Can't eat. Can't sleep. Ain't no good to no one this way."

Murph leaned forward, his face strained, and placed his hand on Lester's shoulder.

"Listen, it'll get better, Les. I promise. I will be talking to the sheriff, and I got some ideas about how we can help too. And, what's more important, you can't just let them win. These ignorant, bigoted bastards. If you quit now, you're giving in. That's just what they want."

Lester grinned painfully and shook his head.

"I know you mean well and all," he said. "But it's funny. White folks is always brave with a black man's hide. You've been great to me, really, Murph. But you don't get it. I ain't wanted here. Not enough anyway. And that's the way it is. I don't like it none either. I ain't white. And it's a white man's world. That's it. But I also ain't stupid. I know I best be going for a while—just till things die down a bit. Got a cousin who's got some room for me for a spell."

Despite several more passionate protestations for Murph, Lester Sledge packed his bags and said his goodbyes, leaving the Brew Crew with a gaping hole in their lineup and the very palpable, very haunting feeling that their playoff chances left that day with their disillusioned catcher.

It was a devastating blow to the organization. The team suffered greatly in Lester's absence, losing a string of consecutive games, rendering them in the onerous position of having to chase their nemesis, the Rangers. They were upset, yes, and probably would have gone into the tank completely had it not been for the other distractions swirling around them.

They had bigger issues at hand. The entire Brewer family attended two very different services at St. Catherine's Roman Catholic Church within a month's time. The first was a somber occasion, to honor the passing of their fallen comrade, Boxcar, who had lost his valiant battle with cancer just when it looked as though he was going to beat it.

Scores of Brewer faithful turned out that hazy July morning to pay tribute to one of their favorite personalities and to thank him for the many breathtaking moments he had provided for them over the years. It was a touching ceremony, with many of the worshippers, most dressed in Brewer regalia sporting Boxcar's number 15, lined up shoulder to shoulder along the sides of the church pews, while others who sought entrance to the tiny church but were thwarted by the timeliness of those before them crammed themselves into the vestibule, trying desperately to secure a spot from where they could listen as several of Boxcar's teammates eulogized their late captain. Murph spoke first, extolling Boxcar's inimitable presence on the field, and his unwavering commitment to the fight, no matter what the score.

"He was a true warrior," Murph explained tearfully. "And the best captain a manger could ever ask for."

Pee Wee took the podium next, followed by Danvers, Finster, and Gabby Hooper.

Each man recalled anecdotally the marvelous duality that Raymond "Boxcar" Miller possessed—"priest and parole officer" Hooper mused—and the indelible influence he had had on all of their lives, both on and off the diamond. Their heartfelt reminiscences stretched the emotional boundaries of those listening that day, bringing them to tears one minute and making them laugh out loud the very next.

The most poignant words, however, belonged to Mickey, who read with a slight nausea and the unsteady inflection of a wounded animal a simple tribute to his teammate.

"Boxcar were my friend," he began, pausing to wipe his welling eyes. "Mickey liked Boxcar. He taught me how to—how to—how to do things, like throw a curveball and how to put my stirrups on so they don't fall down during the game. Mickey liked Boxcar. And Boxcar liked me too."

He paused before saying his final words.

"Boxcar is catching in heaven now."

The second gathering was just as serious but far more festive, a celebration of the long awaited union of Arthur Murphy and his new bride, the lovely Molly Tussler. A happier couple this world has yet to see. They descended the church steps arm in arm under a cloudless evening sky tinged here and there with a rosy hue, their smiles as wide and hopeful as the brilliant horizon, and proceeded to promenade, with hunched shoulders and lowered heads, through a makeshift canopy of Louisville Sluggers fashioned from the steady and dutiful arms of the entire Brewer team, thirteen on each side. It was a glorious day, and a welcome respite from the daily grind of baseball life. It was also wonderful seeing Lester again. Murph was so pleased, as were most of the guys, that his former catcher had accepted the invitation and was willing to, at least for the day, set everything else aside.

"Hey, now ain't you a sight for sore eyes?" Murph gushed, wrapping his arms around Lester the moment he saw him. "Christ, we have really missed you."

Lester nodded and smiled.

"Yeah, I miss you guys too."

"So how are you, Les?" Murph continued. "Things okay?"

"Yeah, things are okay I guess. You know how it is. How 'bout you?"

Murph cringed. For a man just married, he was certainly out of sorts. His words had recently become more and more candid, free from the safety of the trash can dreams that had suddenly yielded to the painful recognition that things were not as he had hoped they would be.

"Well, I'd like to say the same," he lamented, "but I can't. It's been brutal. Absolutely brutal. What can I say? The newspapers don't lie."

Murph took Lester aside and proceeded to chronicle the misery that had attenuated the last few games his beleaguered team had played. There was the anemic effort against the Sidewinders, where fifteen Brewers K'd, resulting in a shameful 12–0 drubbing. That lackluster effort was followed by a heartbreaking defeat at the hands of the Mudcats. Leading by one run in the bottom of the ninth, and with runners on second and third and just one more out to secure, Hooper fanned the last Mudcat on a wicked slider. The ball bounced in the dirt and careened off an inexperienced Hobey Baker's shin guards. The opportunistic batter took off for first just as the nervous catcher re-grouped, picking up the ball and cocking hid arm in the direction of the intended out. It all appeared harmless—just another routine 2–3 put out. But, despite having plenty of time to complete the play, Baker sailed the ball over Finster's head. The ball skipped off the outfield grass and rolled elusively into the right field corner, allowing both the tying and winning run to score. That contest was followed by a pitiful performance against the Spartans, in a game that saw the home town Brew Crew squander a 12–1 lead, punctuated by back-to-back-to-back homeruns in the visitors half of the eighth inning. The Brewers were certainly reeling, but they had yet to hit bottom. That came the very next night, against none other than McNally's Rangers. They had actually played a fairly crisp game, with the pitching and defense coming together to hold a potent Ranger attack to just three runs. The problem, though, was that the Brewers had left thirteen men on base and only managed to score three runs themselves, something that came back to bite them in the last inning.

With one out in the Rangers' half of the ninth, and Blaine Richardson on second and Kiki Delaney on first, Bart Williams hit a tailor-made double play ball to Pee Wee, who scooped up the one hopper and shovel a perfect feed to Arky Fries at the bag. Fries handled the exchange cleanly, but the ball got stuck momentarily in the webbing of his glove, delaying the relay long enough to allow Delaney the chance to come in with spikes flying.

"So what happened?" Lester asked. "No double play?"

"It was much worse than that," Murph replied. He continued to explain how Fries, with the ball still in his glove, pounced on Delaney, wrestling him to the ground with an explosion of fury and frustration that had never been seen before.

"No way," Lester mused. "No way. Are you telling me that Mc-Ginty took it to Delaney?"

"Oh yeah," Murph said. "He beat him good too. Only problem was that while McGinty was getting his rocks off, the winning run came around to score."

Some days passed. Murph found himself utterly depressed about his team's performance. He was equally plagued by the growing difficulty with Mickey's unusual behavior and the situation with Lester. It was driving him mad. He had embraced the attitude of a fledgling boxer measuring his opponent in the early rounds, determined to strike the face of the problem but uncertain as to how to proceed.

"I just can't put my finger on it," he complained to Matheson after entering the latest set of stats into his wire recorder. "I smell a rat here. Things just do not add up, but I'll be damned if I know what I can do about it."

He folded his hands tightly and placed them on his desk. Matheson, who had been looking through some old team photos and prattling on about the good old days, stopped his maudlin jaunt and sat down in from of his beleaguered manager.

"You smell a rat you say?" the old man grumbled. "I know rats. Been 'round 'em my whole life. Rats is easy. With rats—and I know this from experience, Murph—there's only one thing you *can* do."

The sententious geyser crossed his arms and leaned back in his chair.

"I always found that if you want to catch a rat, you need a rat trap—something foul, and mighty stinky."

Murph jotted a note to himself, smiled oddly, then came back at Matheson once again. "Okay Farls, now what about Baker? Do we go with him again? He's killing us back there."

The old man shrugged. "I reckon I don't know."

"Well, I'm open to any ideas you may have. What do you think?"

"What choice do we have, Murph? I mean Jesus. It ain't like we have anybody else."

Murph paused, as if he were about to reveal another approach, when from the open doorway came another voice, calm and unexpected, stealing the moment.

"Maybe I could help. I mean, it's been a little while, but I have done a little catching before."

Murph's eyes widened. At first he couldn't believe it. It wasn't until he heard the voice a second time and saw the bag on the floor in front of him that he let himself go. He looked at him motionlessly, staring into the light pouring in through the office door behind the welcome figure. Those massive hands. That bulging chest and passionate eyes.

"Well if that don't beat all," Murph finally said, grinning from ear to ear. "Now how long have you been standing out there, Mr. Sledge?"

Lester smiled, a big toothy smile, pulled his cap from his trouser pocket and placed it on his head.

"Long enough," he said. Murph shook his head, folded his arms and chuckled.

"So what brings you back, Les?" he asked. "Come to see the wedding photos?"

Lester just stood, much less animated now, as if he were being pulled back and forth across an invisible line in a tug of war.

"Naw, ain't much for that sort of thing now," he said, looking around sheepishly. "But, I have been thinking about what you said the other day. Made old Lester feel a little guilty about leaving. So, if I still have a place here, I think that maybe I will give things another try."

The next morning, with his thoughts swirling like flakes of snow in the first minutes of a blizzard, Murph phoned Sheriff Rosco and requested that he bring his car by the house three hours before the start of the game against the Senators. Lester was beside him when he hung up the phone, and followed him to the kitchen table where the two men sat uneasily for a while, sipping coffee and exchanging thoughts in hushed tones until they parted ways for the moment.

The day wore on in its usual fashion, with Murph embroiled in his pre-game ritual of line-up permeations, Lester reading his bible in the sitting room, and Mickey out back with Molly where together, they tended to the rabbit cages. Around 2:45 that afternoon, just as Murph and Lester sat down to discuss game plans, they heard the sound of tires on gravel just outside the kitchen window. Rosco was a little early.

"So what's this all about?" he asked, pushing his ten-gallon hat up off his brow with one finger. "Ain't nobody hurt I hope."

He was looking down curiously at the floor, at the two dusty bags of catcher's equipment propped against Lester's leg.

"No, Rosco, no one's hurt," Murph replied. "But I was thinking that you might be able to help us keep it that way."

"I'm not sure I follow, Arthur."

"Look, you know what's been going on with Lester, Rosco. It ain't no secret. Hell, I've called you at least a half dozen times myself over the last two months. But it's like you said. It's almost impossible to get to the bottom of it. Right? I mean, it's not like anyone is coming forward with any information."

"I still don't know what you're getting at, Murph," Rosco repeated, wrinkling his nose.

"Well, we think that maybe someone's going to try to hurt Lester again. Especially since he's back and all. Could be worse this time. I'm thinking it could happen today, on the way to the game. So, I—uh, we—were hoping that you would do us the service of driving Lester to the field. In your car. I'll follow behind, with Mickey. It's just a precaution. That's all."

The sheriff said nothing for a minute. A dark matrix of confusion washed across his face as he stood, arms folded and foot tapping, weighing the request.

"Well, I certainly don't want to make this a habit now, Arthur," he said peremptorily. "I got a whole damn town to look out for. Can't be doing personal favors for anyone that asks. But, I suppose this one time wouldn't hurt. Besides, it'll give me and Lester a chance to chat—get to know each other a little better." The Sheriff flashed a crooked grin and slapped Lester gently on the back.

"Super," Murph exclaimed. "We'll be ready in a flash."

The four men walked out to the car together. The sun was burning hot in a high sky, with the only relief coming from an occasional breeze. Murph and Mickey loaded their gear into Murph's car while Lester prepared to do the same with Rosco.

"Why don't you give me them bags, boy," Rosco said, extending his hand. "We'll put 'em in the trunk."

Lester stood, biting his lips, his eyes wide and distant.

"Just take the big one," he said, clutching the other tightly to his chest. "This one here is special. Has my gloves in it. I always keeps it with me."

"Suit yourself. But you best climb in the back with it. I don't want no dirt getting all over the front of my car."

Lester sat quietly, his bag flat on his lap, staring hypnotically as the bucolic landscape rolled away just outside his window. The gilly flowers were beautiful, a magical blanket of purple and white splashed across a field of weeping pines. He was thinking of his mom, and how she loved this time of year. "Hot July brings cooling showers, apricots and gilly flowers," she always sang when the calendar approached her favorite month. God, she loved those flowers. He could still hear so vividly her humming over the running water as she filled the old pickle jars she had collected with fragrant bouquets of freshly cut purples, pinks, and whites.

"You see, Lester," she explained, surveying the austere condition of their dwelling. "There's always a way to light up even the darkest room."

That was her. Always searching for the silver lining. He missed her.

"So, Lester," the sheriff began, as if suddenly bored by the silence. "These white folks gave you a pretty bad time?"

"Yes, sir, Sheriff. Ain't been easy."

"Well, then you won't mind me asking why the heck you came back here."

Lester took a while to answer.

"I was ready to just walk away, ya know? I knows what people think of me. Some of ya anyway. And I might a just stayed away, if it hadn't been for the guys. I miss the fellas. Mickey. Pee Wee. And Murph. That's one true white man. And I miss the baseball. Ain't the same in the Negro League. So I says to myself, after Murph's wedding, do you want to take the chance? Sure enough, my answer was that darn easy. So, here I am."

Rosco sighed.

"Well, it's like I told Murph. Don't have to be that way. You could always stop what you're doing, and go back to that Negro Leagues. When you stop and consider what you may be facing here, you might find it more to your liking."

"That's what I used to think too, 'cept I ain't doing nothing Sheriff," he answered. I'm just playing baseball. Baseball. A game. Ain't no crime in that."

Rosco laughed.

"Looky here. Why don't we just cut the horse crap, boy," he said, catching Lester's gaze in the rear view mirror.

Lester was surprised by the sheriff's sudden candor.

"You know that you don't belong here, and that these good old-fashioned white folk ain't gonna rest till you're gone. So what's the sense of it, huh? Ain't we all suffered enough?"

Realizing the true sentiment implied by Rosco's comments, Lester had the impulse to lash out, to tell this prattling bigot just what he'd like to do to him, but he remembered what Murph had told him and restrained himself before any invectives could pass his lips.

"I don't reckon I know how any of *you* have suffered," he said. "Looks to me like y'all doing okay. I'm the one's been put out."

Rosco checked his mirror again for Murph's car then shook his head and sighed.

"Goddammit, boy, you must be one stupid coon, you know that?

Now, I'm gonna say this, just one more time. And if you go repeating what I say, I'll deny it, and then I'll come after you myself. I'm telling you to pack up your shit and get the hell out of town. If you leave, I'll make sure nobody touches you. I can do that. And nobody has to know we talked. But if you're gonna be the same old pig-headed negro that don't know his place, well then, boy, I'm afraid you're in for more trouble—a lot worse—and something tells me I won't be around to help you when they wrap that rope 'round your neck and hang you from the highest limb in town."

Lester felt a steady throbbing at his temples and his throat burned. Waves of fury pulsated through his blood, igniting his eyes and heart and the rest of his body before finally settling in his hands, which had already begun curling into fists.

"Now that don't seem mighty fair, Sheriff," Lester said through clenched teeth, forcing his hands open before resting them on either side of his bag. "I'm just a ballplayer. That's all."

"It may not be fair, boy," Rosco replied, biting the tip off a new cigar, "but that's the law of the land in these parts. Always has been. Always will be. Now, you just use your head, boy. Go play your game, and in the morning, I trust you'll do the right thing."

Lester played the game, just as Rosco said. And what a game it was. He was never better. Everything he did was swift and effortless. In the top half of the first, he scooped a ball that was in the dirt, and from his knees, gunned down a would be base stealer by a good four feet. He followed that with a long two-run homer in the home half of the frame and added an extra base hit in each of the next three at bats as well. His stellar play electrified the crowd, who spent the majority of the contest on its feet, chanting the words "*Sledge Hammer*" while striking the air with clenched fists in celebratory pantomime. By the time the final out was recorded, Lester's stat line read as follows: 4-4, homerun, 2 doubles, triple and 8 RBI. He was also credited with 4 scored runs, 3 put outs, and 3 assists by virtue of the 3 base runners he cut down. All in all, it was quite a performance.

The most important statistic, however, was the "W" that the struggling Brew Crew earned, snapping a prolonged malaise that had all but decimated their chances of post-season play.

"Man, you were something else today, Lester," Murph said on their way home, shaking his head in glorious disbelief.

"Yeah, it felt pretty good today."

"Pretty good? Are you joking? You were a one-man wrecking crew."

Lester's self-effacing countenance erupted uncharacteristically into another toothy grin.

"Yeah, I *was* something, wasn't I? I guess I was motivated today for some reason."

Murph was dizzy with relief.

"Maybe Rosco should drive you to the games all the time," he said winking.

Lester laughed.

"Yeah, right. When pigs fly."

"So tell me now. Did he say what I thought he would say? Or something like it?"

"Uh huh."

"Just like I said," Murph exclaimed.

"Well, not exactly. But close enough. He expects me to leave tomorrow morning. First thing."

"Is that what he said?" Murph asked.

"Yup." Lester motioned with his eyes to the back seat, where Mickey sat, and put a finger to his lips. "I'll fill you in on all the rest once we get home."

Rosco received a call from Murph at eight o'clock the next morning just as the sun had pushed through what appeared to be a red-orange canvas through a bank of clouds loitering on the horizon. He was at the house by nine.

"Of course I'll escort Lester out of town," he said gaily. "Why, it's the least I can do for the kid, after all he's been through." Murph exchanged a quick look with Lester, then shifted his attention to the sheriff.

"That's not exactly why we asked you here," he said, reaching inside Lester's bag and removing the wire recorder which had been resting on top. Rosco scrutinized the machine, his mind floating vaguely on the intent of such a display.

"What's that?" Rosco asked, shrugging his shoulders. "This is why you asked me here? To show me some gizmo?"

"Not exactly." Murph responded. "We have something that we think you should hear."

Rosco stood moodily beside Murph and Lester as Murph hit the middle button on the machine.

"Goddammit, boy, you must be one stupid coon, you know that? Now, I'm gonna say this, just one more time. And if you go repeating what I say, I'll deny it, and then I'll come after you myself. I'm telling you to pack up your shit and get the hell out of town. If you leave, I'll make sure nobody touches you. I can do that. And nobody has to know we talked. But if you're gonna be the same old pig-headed negro that don't know his place, well then, boy, I'm afraid you're in for more trouble—a lot worse—and something tells me I won't be around to help you when they wrap that rope 'round your neck and hang you from the highest limb in town."

"I think I can stop it there," Murph said, his emotions in full control. "You get the idea." Rosco was standing dispiritedly, arms folded.

FRANK NAPPI

"That's clever. Real clever. But it don't mean a hill of crap, Arthur. No sir. Not a hill of crap. And I got a good mind, as is my right, to confiscate that machine there. Looks mighty similar to one that was reported stolen recently."

"You can take the machine if you want," Murph said sharply. "Wouldn't make no difference. The message has been saved somewhere else. You know, in the unlikely event that some unscrupulous person should try to tamper with it."

Rosco plunged his restless hands into his pockets and busied himself with some loose change.

"What are you trying to pull here, Arthur?" he asked, leaning forward as if to suggest some sort of physical threat. "Are you feeling okay?"

He laughed nervously. The two men stood for a moment staring at each other.

"It's really quite simple," Murph said. "You give us the names of those good old boys under the hoods, or I'll turn this whole thing, recording and all, over to the FBI, and blow the lid clear off this friggin' stink hole."

The sheriff stood awkwardly now, as if the room were moving beneath his feet and he were losing his balance. His face grew a shade paler, and his breath, quick and erratic, was all at once audible. Murph pulled out a chair and motioned for his guest to sit. Then, in the revealing glow of the morning light, Rosco began to speak, his blood burning beneath his skin as he struggled mightily with the acute discomfort that accompanies a man upon the sudden realization that he is suddenly suspended inviolably in the tendrils of fickle machinations.

THE BEST LAID PLANS

Married life agreed with Murph. He had never felt so grounded, so much a part of the universe. It never occurred to him it could be like this. Sure, he had had relationships before. But those were all, in retrospect, superficial dalliances that served only to fulfill transitory desires. It never lasted. This was different. Much different. His soul was directing his thoughts now, as if all of Molly's warmth and tenderness had filled his body and had become, through some celestial transformation, a salubrious energy and virility that was now guiding him through the rigor of every day.

The eight-game home stand provided a wonderful glimpse into what life would be like for them, if and when Murph should hang up his cleats for the very last time.

"Hello there, Mrs. Murphy," he said each time he came back home, a smile burgeoning behind a bouquet of freshly cut flowers. "What would you like to do?"

She always blushed and giggled like a school girl when he asked her that.

"I do not know, kind sir. What did you have in mind?"

It was good. The calendar indicated that the Brewers were scheduled for a night game, so Murph and Molly spent the first part of their day together, working in the garden or sitting on the porch, sharing lemonade and stories that neither one of them had ever heard before.

"Did I ever tell you about the time we were in Cleveland, with Whitey Burgess and the farmer's daughter he went skinny dipping with?"

"No," Molly said. "But from the look on your face, it sounds like a good one."

Murph took off his hat and began twisting it in his hands, as if the motion were somehow wringing out the details of the distant reminiscence.

"Whitey was a real ladies' man. Golden hair, broad shoulders, million dollar smile. He had it all going. So we're in this small town for a double header, and the night before, Whitey meets this beautiful girl—I think Eva was her name. Anyway, she agrees to sneak out and meet him at the lake that night, for a moonlit swim, and he tells me and Bump Livingston to come too, cause her old man apparently was a loose cannon. Used to follow her whenever she left the house, shot gun and all. Whitey wanted us to stand guard while he made time with this girl."

The laughter bathed both of them in a playful glow.

"So you guys went?" she asked. "Just like that?"

"Let me finish now. Somewhere between him asking and us actually going, we came up with the idea that it would be funny to teach old Whitey a lesson. He was always shooting his mouth off about how he was scoring all the time with the ladies. So Bump, he borrows a shot gun and some overalls and a hat. And about twenty minutes into Whitey's little escapade, Bump, dressed as this crazed farmer, starts hollering 'where's my little girl' and firing bullets into the air. Well Whitey, as soon as he hears all the ruckus, ducks his head down real low, just above the water, trying to stay out of the moonlight. He was terrified. It was priceless. Then, just to really put the fear of God into him, Bump starts screaming at me. 'I see you there. I'll learn ya to mess with my little girl.' With that, he fires another shot, well over my head, but I drop to the ground like a sack of potatoes, and lie there, still as a log."

"Oh no, you're kidding," Molly said, her hands flush to her cheeks. "He must have been dying. Then what happened?"

Murph, now fully immersed in the reminiscence, could barely get the words out he was laughing so hard.

"Whitey, he sees me go down, and he lets out a shriek that could have woke the dead. Then he jumps out of the water and starts running, buck naked, out to the road, waving his arms and screaming for help. Must have been there a good five minutes before me and Buck come up behind him and finally let him off."

"That *is* funny," she said laughing. "But there's one thing I don't understand. Didn't Eva know it wasn't her father? Why didn't she tell Whitey?"

"That's the beauty of the story," Murph explained. "She knew all the time. Not only was she beautiful and spirited, she also had a great sense of humor."

Molly's cheerful laughter dimmed and gave way to more meaningful discourse.

"I'm learning an awful lot about you lately, Arthur Murphy," she said.

"Is that right? You think you know me now, do ya?"

"No, not totally. But I have learned some other things about your past, Arthur," she said smiling.

"Yeah? And how's that?"

"Farley told me. He sure knows a lot about you."

"Aw, you can't believe everything that old geezer says," Murph said. "He ain't all there." She understood that Murph was private about a lot of his past, but she felt as though she wanted to know him better—to see him for what he used to be as well as what he was now.

"Well, he told me that they used to call you the next Ty Cobb," she said. "That's certainly very exciting." She batted her lashes and nuzzled his neck.

"Is that all he said?" he asked.

"Well, that, and that Chip McNally was the one who caused your injury."

Murph wiggled uncomfortably. Molly lifted her head off his shoulder.

"Come on, Arthur. Don't get all crazy now. It's okay. Don't be angry or anything. I'm glad he told me. I thought McNally was just a jerk. And that's why you hate him. Now all this bad blood with the Rangers makes sense to me."

Murph ran his finger methodically across the side of his sweating glass, drawing tiny circles in the condensation.

"I don't talk about that anymore," Murph said. "At least I haven't. It's a part of my life that I have been trying to forget. That's why losing the pennant to that bastard on the very last day of the season last year—especially without Mickey—was such a tough nut to swallow."

"What about this year? I mean, does it still matter as much?"

"Sure it matters. It always matters, Molly. And we're only five games behind. I know, in my heart, that we can right the ship if we can just settle this whole thing with Lester." Molly's eyes flickered in the bright afternoon light.

"And are you going to tell me what is happening with that Arthur?" she asked frowning. "I *would* like to know what is going on here."

"You know what I told you, Molly. I'd rather keep you out of it as long as possible. For your own safety. All you need to know right now is that Sheriff Rosco will be helping us put this thing to rest the day after tomorrow. Once it's all over, I'll tell you everything."

It was not the answer she wanted, but she let the issue go, taking his hand in hers while directing the conversation elsewhere, to a place that had them laughing and smiling once again.

The evenings they spent together were even better. When nightfall would deepen and extend its grip across the landscape, they would stroll through the valley of shadows, hand in hand, swinging their arms rhythmically without saying a word. They walked as if one, guided by the sheen of the glinting stars swimming atop the distant conifers, a dreamy jaunt through the grassy enclaves where patches of pink and blue wildflowers glowed ceremoniously beneath an electric moon. Molly was a long way from the austere routine of Clarence and Tussler farm. There were many times she felt breathless, like her happiness was all just a dream, a fleeting ecstasy waiting to be spoiled by the light of waking. It made her hold on to him even tighter. And Murph—he finally knew what it felt like to really love a woman. To tingle with this strange but rapturous energy that had enveloped him, filled his heart until this molten desire spilled over into all his thoughts, even the unconscious ones, leaving him breathless as well. This communion was bigger than either of them.

Everything was right. Mickey was feeling better too. Just the mention by Murph that the whole ordeal with Lester would be over the next day had him back on the mound and in the zone. He disposed of the first three Cub batters with just nine pitches, fanning each one on blistering fastballs that popped Lester's glove like it had before.

Mickey's Minions were out in full force again, energized by their hero's return to form. They had come to the park prepared to witness something special, and celebrated their portentous vision with the hanging of three stuffed bears from a railing just below their seats. Pee Wee laughed as he stepped to the plate to leadoff the home half of the first, pausing long enough for the last bear to be hung in place.

"Your fans really know how to celebrate, McGinty," the umpire muttered from behind his mask. "Ain't never seen anything like it."

Pee Wee tapped his cleats with his bat and winked.

"Yeah. They're something alright. I just hope they brought enough of those things."

The Brewers, in typical fashion, fed off the energy created by Mickey's domination. Pee Wee roped a single up the middle on the first pitch he saw. Then, with the count 2–1, Arky Fries shortened up and executed a perfect hit and run, slapping the ball through the vacated area on the right side of the infield, sending Pee Wee all the way around to third. The Cubs pitcher squatted on the mound and hung his head. He hadn't even broken a sweat and the Brewers were already threatening.

Danvers was next. He had cooled off considerably after his torrid start, going just 9 for his last 44, but he had a few good at bats of late and was showing signs of breaking out of his prolonged slump. He stepped to the plate brimming with optimism, savoring the unenviable predicament the Cubs hurler had created for himself. *He is going to come right after me*, Danvers thought to himself. Probably try to induce a ground ball with breaking stuff and get out of the inning with minimal damage. It was this part of the game he loved most. The cat and mouse. Every situation was fraught with so many different scenarios. Only the very best hitters stayed one step ahead. With that thought in mind, the wily Danvers inched forward in the batter's box, hoping to catch the hook before it had time to break away from him.

As the ball approached the hitting zone, Danver's eyes lit up like a child's on Christmas morning. There it was, just as he thought. Curveball. A flat delivery that sort of spun harmlessly as it came closer and closer. Helicopters they called them. Cripple pitches. They were made to order. The only danger was being too eager. Lunging at the inviting offering before it was time. Then you get *yourself* out, and curse your impetuousness all the way back to the dugout. Danvers knew all that. Knew just how to keep his hands back long enough, even when his front foot was restless and his weight shifted prematurely, so that he could still drive the ball with authority somewhere.

So Danvers, as if following some preordained script, did just that. His foot came down hard as his body strained toward the ball, but his hands remained locked and loaded, firing through the hitting zone just as the spinning sphere danced across the plate. Danvers hit it on the screws, and sent a frozen rope into the left center-field gap, scoring both runners. By the time the ball was corralled and thrown back into the infield, Danvers was all smiles, celebrating on the third base bag with a stand-up triple.

The hits kept coming. Lester followed Danvers' triple with a long homerun to left, Clem Finster, Jimmy Llamas, Buck Faber and Dutch McBride all singled consecutively, and Amos Ruffings, who had not hit a round tripper in more than a month, highlighted the barrage with a long, arching big fly that cleared the centerfield fence with plenty of room to spare. The Brew Crew had batted around en route to the most prolific inning in their history; by the time all was said and done, they had hammered out 18 hits and plated 17 runs.

Mickey returned to the mound some forty-five minutes later as sharp as he was when he left. He set down the Cubs one, two, three again, notching three more strikeouts and sending an already intoxicated crowd into a dizzying state of delirium.

"When was the last time you saw this place like this?" Matheson said, flashing a toothless smile. "I told ya. Grab the bull by the onions, and everything else falls in place."

"Yup, sure is nice," Murph replied. "Smells a little like pennant fever."

The Brewers' bats cooled off as the game went on, tallying just five more hits over the next seven innings. With a 17-run lead, and Mickey mowing down the opposition, there was no urgency in the Brewer dugout. Even the crowd was eager for their hometown heroes to make quick work of their at bats, for they were now fully enraptured with Mickey's assault on the Cub hitters. He had never looked so dominating.

By the top of the seventh, Mickey had already matched the team record for strikeouts in a game—16, previously held by Wyatt Thorton. The Brewer die hards were well aware of the history in the making and were loving every second of it. They were on their feet, chanting and cheering and of course, hanging stuffed bears, one after the other, fully immersed in the rapture of the moment until they discovered, to their horror and disappointment, that they were fresh out.

"Not to worry," the leader of the fanatical group proclaimed, holding up a few brown paper bags and a piece of charcoal he requisitioned from the barbeque pit.

"We will just have to draw our own."

As the sun crossed the sky over Borchert Field in usual fashion, Mickey kept rolling. Despite an infield dribbler that died just before it reached the bare hand of Woody Danvers, breaking up the no-hit bid, the boy remained undaunted. He fanned five more Cubbies to finish with an incomprehensible 21 strikeouts, obliterating the old mark while giving the hometown crowd the thrill of a lifetime and visions of a late season run at the pennant. With just five games to make up in six weeks, things were certainly looking up.

Chip McNally was not as enthused. He saw the steady approach of Murph and the surging Brewers as though he were viewing it from the rear view mirror of his car. His eyes were fixed on the road which lay before him, but every so often he would sneak furtive glances at a newspaper or linger briefly around a radio while the sports report was being given, only to turn his attention once again to that which lay immediately in front of him. Today, that was a meeting with Sheriff John Rosco.

"One hand washes the other, remember, John?" he asked.

The sheriff tapped his foot impatiently.

"Enough with the games, Chip. What's the problem?"

"The problem is that black boy and the rest of Arthur Murphy's crew. I'm getting some heat from upstairs. I was hoping that you could help me with that. You did say you were going to help me, right?"

Rosco stood uneasily outside McNally's house, staring at the broken wood fence that circled the property and the pile of pickets propped up here and there against the tangle of weeds just below.

"I'm sorry, Chip, but I done my best. Situation is what it is. It ain't as easy as we thought. My hands are tied."

"Your hands are tied? Since when? You run everything 'round here. How can your hands be tied?"

"Look, Chip, I've been thinking. Who am I to stop this kid from playing? Maybe we all over-reacted about this. Besides, I'm feeling mighty bad about taking favors from you in exchange for all this nonsense. Ain't right. And I aim to fix it."

McNally could almost see the dark shadow fall across Rosco's face. Blood flared up inside the desperate manager. He stood now, in a fit of bubbling rage, showing his teeth.

"John Rosco? A sudden attack of morality? Please. Who the hell are you kidding anyway? You, of all people! You feel bad about something? Please. You are one of the dirtiest bastards around here. Don't hand me your crap. I know you, John Rosco. Don't you forget that. I know a lot about you."

Rosco's eyes continued to roam, traveling now to the tiny dirt road that led from the unhinged gate in front of the property through the row of Sycamores, to the barn and silo out back.

"So you know me, Chip," he said, his gaze still off in the distance. "Okay. You know me. What's that supposed to mean?"

"That means you need to help me. Now. Now John. You promised me. We had a deal"

"Just leave it be for now, Chip. Leave it alone. Let it lie. I got you covered. I'm gonna need time. That's all I can say."

Meanwhile, the Brewers' juggernaut continued to roll. They won another game the following night. It was another convincing victory that had everyone thinking about the post-season. After the impressive display, Dennison summoned Murph to his office.

"Well, that was quite a performance tonight, Mr. Murphy," Dennison said, his face shrouded behind a viscous cloud of cigar smoke. "Quite a performance indeed."

"Thank you, sir," Murph said uncomfortably. "I think we are finally on our way."

Warren Dennison was pale, more so than usual. When the smoke cleared, Murph noticed a row of tiny beads of perspiration that had settled just above his tightened lip. Despite the amiable salutation just moments before, Dennison seemed disturbed, his mind pregnant with an unavailing agitation.

"Well now, one victory surely does not a season make," he went on, tapping the colorless ashes on the end of his cigar into a glass tray. "And I am still very unhappy, Arthur, with all of this black/white crap. You said it would go away. You said that everyone would—how did you put it—'get used to the idea of a black man playing for us.' Isn't that what you said? Huh? Well, it's damn near the end of the season, and it ain't no better now, is it?" The surly owner shook his head and made a clicking noise with his tongue. "I don't think I can have this anymore, Mr. Murphy. I am out of patience."

Murph withstood the surging insolence bubbling deep inside him and spoke calmly. "It is taken care of," he said, drying his damp palms on the front of his trousers. "Uh, at least it will be by tomorrow. I do not want to—I cannot say too much right now. But trust me, Warren—the sheriff is going to help all of us put thing to rest once and for all."

Dennison sat stoically, eyes tired and fixed on a point somewhere beyond Murph, his head propped up by one hand while the fingers on the other drummed the littered desktop. "It better be put to rest, Arthur. Tomorrow, or you and I will be having a different kind of conversation."

Later that night, as he lay quietly next to Molly, listening to her rhythmic breathing, Murph was besieged by a senseless, ineffable dread. It startled him, took his breath away. What was this feeling of profound trouble that rushed against his soul with such ferocity that it caused him to sit up, to fight against this pall of unknown catastrophe that had enveloped his senses, invaded his body, and poisoned his thoughts? Surely things would be okay. They had to be. He had thought of everything. Done everything right. His plan was brilliant, and executed to perfection. Yet despite the obvious, he remained, for the rest of that night, caught somewhere between waking and sleep, suspended in the tumult of fitful dreams—caught in crisis to which he could not attach a name.

He awoke early next morning to the sound of a ringing telephone. It was Dennison. Murph's heart sank when he heard the voice. It was as if the foreboding hours of the night had taken shape before him.

"Arthur, get here early today. We have to talk. And it can't wait."

"But I have that meeting in a little while," Murph replied. "I don't know how long I'll be."

"Go to your meeting," he said. "Just get here," the impatient owner continued. "Get here as fast as you can."

Later that morning, the scheduled meeting took place. Murph, a gentleman from the Federal Bureau of Investigation, Lester, and Mickey gathered together in Murph's office and, with the redolence of anger and fear all around them, spoke about Lester and the events of the past few months.

From under the fain't glow of lamp light, Mickey emerged as the focal point. He sat uneasily, eyes round with daunting expectation, his feet tapping uncontrollably. He was chewing at his fingernails and speaking feverishly under his breath. "Couched in his kennel, like a log, with paws of silver sleeps the dog."

The others exchanged uncomfortable glances, uncertain as to which one of them should take the lead. It was only after the gray-suited gentleman whispered something in Murph's ear did the silence finally cease.

"Mickey, there's nothing to worry about," Murph began. "Mr. Billings here is going to help us. All of us. But please. You need to talk. Now. I know you are holding onto something that we need to know. You have to talk to us. Tell us now. What do you know about what has happened to Lester these last few weeks? Do you know who did some of those things to him?"

The boy was unphased by Murph's plea. He continued to sit with an ardor of turmoil pasted to his face.

"Look, uh, Mickey, I don't want to scare you are anything," Billings said, removing his glasses and placing them gently in his shirt pocket. "We're not really too sure that Lester is safe. And maybe even you, or Murph. You follow?"

Mickey's lower lip extended out, and his eyes shot around the room.

"Mickey's not really in tune with that sort of stuff," Murph interjected. "He's simple when it comes to figuring things like that."

"Okay, let me try this another way." The man paused before trying again. "Mickey, do you love Arthur here?"

"Yes, sir," Mickey answered. "Mickey loves Arthur Murphy just like he were my own Pa."

"What about Lester? Do you like Lester too?"

"Sure thing. Lester Sledge is a swell fella. I'm always saying that. I said it yesterday. Yesterday, after practice, we—"

"Okay, son," Billings interrupted. "I understand. And I want you to know that this is your chance to help these two gentlemen who you are so fond of. You can really help me to protect them. And you. All you need to do is tell me everything you know."

Mickey sat sullenly as lurid images filtered through his mind like some twisted newsreel. He held his stomach in protest against a slight nausea and shut his eyes. His face glistened with perspiration. He sat for some time, locked inside himself, rocking nervously while the others just waited, heads hung in lifeless exasperation, on his response. He was really struggling. Waves of menacing thoughts crashed against the walls of his imagination with wild simplicity, and the boy continued to sit paralyzed for many minutes, joining the others in their silent vigil.

"But they will hurt Mickey," he blurted out unexpectedly, choking back a swell of tears. "And the team will lose. We will lose if we have any more trouble. Murph said so. I don't want Murph to go."

Billings was speechless, not sure what to make of the sudden outburst. But that was Mickey. He was often stricken with fear, and the impalpable uncertainty of its meaning and his own inability to place a label on it. It was during these moments when the boy usually disappeared completely, retreated inside himself to a place only he knew.

"You don't have to worry about that, Mick," Murph said, leaning forward and placing his hand on the boy's quivering knee. "All of us here—me, you, Lester, and Mr. Billings—we will all be fine once you help us get the men who are doing this. No worries. It will all go away once you tell us what you know."

They watched him, battered and frightened, laboring with scenes of polluted waters illuminated now, once again. He moved languidly, his breathing heavy and erratic, until the words finally came—words that split the still air like a trumpet blast that had all of them shaking their heads for several minutes until the room was quiet once again.

AUGUST 4, 1949

Chip McNally knew all about the private struggles of his arch rival and smelled blood in the water. The fractious relationship between Murph and Dennison was well chronicled, and McNally reveled at the thought of being the instrument behind Murph's ousting.

The Rangers blew into town to kick off an eight-game home stand clinging to a four-game lead over the recently resurgent Brewers. Murph labored a little over who should get the ball, but after only minor deliberation, he decided to go with Butch Sanders. Sanders was fresh and had looked pretty good in his last outing against the Bears. Besides, Murph had more pressing matters to worry about.

The Brewers took the field under a swollen moon that glowed ominously behind an oppressive summer haze. The temperature had reached a scalding 98 degrees earlier that afternoon and the onset of nightfall had provided very little relief. The players ran to their positions with sweat stained shirts and steaming brows, eager to play the inning and get back to the dugout, where buckets of cool water and freshly chipped ice awaited their return.

Kiki Delaney ignited the Ranger attack in usual fashion, laying down a beautiful bunt that flirted with the third base foul line, only to come to rest in front of a frustrated Woody Danvers.

"Son of a bitch," Danvers carped, hands on his hips. "I could've swore that sucker was going foul."

Sanders's next delivery saw Delaney take off for second while the next Rangers' table setter slapped the ball the opposite way, exploiting the hole on the right side of the infield left by Arky Fries after he vacated his normal position to cover the bag. Delaney never broke stride, and by the time Buck Faber had thrown the ball back in, the Rangers were sitting pretty, with runners on the corners and nobody out.

"Oh, holy crap," Murph griped to Matheson. "Once, just once, do you think we could get out of the first damned inning untouched? I mean, Jesus Christ. Is that too much to ask?"

Matheson worked the inside of his cheek with his wrinkled fingers and removed a wad of chew, adding it to the pile beneath the bench where he sat.

"Yup. Sanders is stiffer than a billy goat. They're all over him like ducks on a June bug."

Murph shrugged and sighed.

"I'm telling ya, Farley, I think I should just hang 'em up. I'm getting too old for this. It's all wrong. All of it. Hell, I gave it my best shot. Nobody can say I didn't try, right? So what's the harm if I walk away? Huh? Just retire to Molly and my little farm."

He rolled his eyes as Sanders walked the next batter, loading the bases.

"That may happen, Murph, but there ain't no use in hasty action. And it ain't worth a plugged nickel sitting around here like a bump on a pickle just waiting for misfortune to launch her rockets. If you're going to go down, well then by cracky, go down swinging. Try something. Holy Hannah, try anything. And when the season is over, let them chips fall as they will."

The Rangers continued to pound Sanders, spraying well-struck balls all over the yard. Two dingers, a couple of triples, four consecutive doubles and a salvo of singles had all the Brewer fielders wilting, matinee idols turned to melting clay in the oppressive August air. They barely had enough life left to limp off the field when, forty-one minutes after the first pitch was delivered, the final out of the inning was recorded.

"All right, you guys," Murph encouraged, with Matheson's words resonating in his head like a gong. "We've been down ten before." He removed his cap and used his sleeve to dab the beading sweat on his forehead. "Let's go now. There's a lot of baseball left to play."

The Brewers took their hacks in the bottom half of the first frame, but their bats were just as limp and feckless. Pee Wee waved at three straight breaking balls, Arky Fries went down looking on a pipe fastball, and Woody Danvers nearly screwed himself into the steaming ground when the Rangers' hurler dropped a wicked 2–2 hammer on him.

"This is not good, Farley," Murph said shaking his head. "Not good at all."

The sun continued to beat down mercilessly on the beleaguered Brew Crew. In the steady dissolution germane to late summer, and with visible relinquishment, each Brewer capitulated, one by one, to the Rangers' ruthless onslaught. Sanders left the game in a huff after the second inning, having surrendered fourteen runs, and was replaced by Packey Reynolds, Murph's best mop-up guy. The move was ineffectual, and produced a similar effect as gasoline being added to a fire. Reynolds was hit even harder, and failed to retire any of the first six batters he faced. His whole body sagged as he stood on the mound. Then the other eight guys on the field surrendered as well. A routine grounder to Arky Fries skipped through the wickets. Clem Finster dropped a routine pop, Jimmy Llamas lost a can of corn in the sun, and Woody Danvers collided with Pee Wee as both men tried to execute a run down that would have put a temporary end to the comedy of errors. They were in hot water the rest of the afternoon. When all was said and done, the Brewers had committed nine errors, allowed twenty-two hits, and had watched with painful attention as twenty-nine Rangers crossed home plate.

It was the most lopsided defeat in team history.

But the score was not the most difficult pill for Murph to swallow that afternoon. That was part of the game. Sometimes you ended up on the wrong side of a laugher. It came with the territory. The score he could handle. But the smug, inflammatory postgame comments from McNally? That was a different story. That was intolerable. He wished he could stop hearing the acerbic banter, or at least stop listening. He wanted nothing more than to think about himself, and his team, and where they were going. Christ, he needed to figure it all out. But McNally would not go away. His words kept resonating in Murph's mind like the clatter of cymbals clashing.

"Look on the bright side, old-timer," McNally said on his way past the Brewers' dugout after the final out was recorded. "It won't hurt as much as last year. You remember, losing on the last day? Naw, this is much better. Give ya a few weeks now to get used to the idea." Then the surly bane of Murph's existence cackled smugly and jogged away.

Murph stayed. Not because he wanted to, but because Dennison had asked to see him again. This too had become tedious. How many friggin' meetings did they have to have? How many damned times did Dennison have to remind him that his job was hanging in the balance?

With the horizon just about to swallow the drooping sun, Murph shuffled toward his destination, sinking too into an uncompromising apathy. *What's the point?* he thought to himself. Was there any point to any of it? This ghost of misfortune was relentless, and more alive than he was. "The fight is all you have," he always said. He believed it too. But as he stood outside Dennison's door, full of unimaginable fear and uncertainty, he shuddered when he considered the course a man's life would take once that was gone as well.

BAKER'S WOODS

Trailing the Rangers by a full five games with just twenty-five contests left to play, Murph decided to give the entire team the day off. He hoped that a little "R and R" would mitigate the tension under which they were all struggling and restore some of the vigor and resiliency needed to tackle the stretch run. All of them had been pressing, with each individual failure engendering a collective stupor and malaise that had enervated the entire group.

"Listen, fellas," he announced to the group as they sat sullenly by their lockers. "As Matheson would say, 'Ain't no use in beating a dead horse.' We've had quite a tough time of late. Real tough." He paused deliberately, his head throbbing as if there was something else trapped inside his head that was struggling to find the light, then folded his arms and squatted on his heels so that his eyes were now even with theirs. "I think we could all use a day off. Just to relax. I want all of you to do something you enjoy. Listen to some music. Take a drive. Some of you may even want to join McGinty, Mickey, and Lester for some fishing down at McGinty's place. Just do something to take your damned minds off baseball for a while. Then come back tomorrow ready to play ball for the next three weeks."

Murph's idea was well received. Most of the guys decided to just hang around at home and kick back, but McGinty, Mickey, and Lester left on their fishing excursion the next day under a dubious afternoon sky stricken with intermittent cloud bursts that seemed to suggest a storm despite the prevailing sun. McGinty's place was not much to speak of—just a threadbare shack that provided a place to sit and shoot the bull after a day of fishing at the lake—but it was his haven, and he was always willing to share the solitude with anyone who could tolerate the austere accommodations.

Once at the lake, Pee Wee was the first to set up shop. He found an old log and sat momentarily, baiting his hook and musing about the last time he and his brother caught enough bass to feed a small village, then stood up and cast his line into the middle of the water. Satisfied with the distance and placement of his effort, he sat back down and watched hypnotically as a succession of rings unfurled across the water.

"Okay, boys, who's next?" he asked, pulling his cap down over his brow to shield his eyes from the lengthening glare. "Don't wait too long now. Won't be any fish left for either of you."

Mickey found a log of his own on which to rest. His eyes, now the color of the lake, passed over the water to a grassy knoll across the way, and fixed themselves on a row of bushes, heavy with ripened red berries. He imagined himself on the other side, darting from thicket to thicket, his shirt pulled away from his waist to form a basket of sorts where the delectable fruits would sit before being counted and consumed.

"Whatta ya say, Mick," Lester called, as his line joined Pee Wee's in the murky pool. "Ain't you fishing today?"

"Aw, I reckon that Mickey will just sit for a while," he replied, his gaze still somewhere off in the distance.

"That's all right, Mick," Pee Wee added. "Lester and I will catch enough fish for all of us to share."

Here and there, shadows continued to creep across the water as the day wore on. Neither Pee Wee nor Lester had gotten even a nibble and Mickey, who was still seated close by, had yet to bait a hook all afternoon.

"You know, I was thinking," Pee Wee said. "Seems like the three of us have an awful lot in common." He looked first in the direction of Lester, who raised his eyebrows and smiled incredulously, and then at Mickey. "I'm serious. We are really a lot alike."

"So you think you two boys are like me?" Lester asked.

"Yeah, I do. I think we are *all* the same," Pee Wee said. "All of us."

Lester shook his head and tugged on his line.

"Wanna know what I think, McGinty?" Lester paused and smiled oddly. " I think you've been out in the sun too long."

"Come on, Lester. You've gotta be kidding me. You can't see what I'm saying?"

Lester shook his head again and tightened his lips.

"Don't you be asking about something you don't really want to hear about, Pee Wee."

"I'm serious, Lester. Come on. You really don't see it?"

"You want to know what I see? Huh? Is that what you want? What I see, what I always see, is the same thing I seen since the day I got here. That is one black man in a white man's world. Your world. A world that keeps pissing all over me and damn near expects me to call it champagne. A world that pats me on the back with one hand and grabs me by the onions with the other. So while I'm much obliged to Mr. Murphy and to you and Mickey and some of the other white folks who have shown me kindness, don't you dare tell me, ever, that we are the same."

The two men struggled with feelings both sharp and twisted. They sat in silence, their eyes tracing the erratic movements of a

cloud of black flies hovering over the water. It was only the innocence of Mickey that rescued them from each other.

"Mickey thinks Lester is right," he said, shattering the silence
before walking over to join the conversation. "Lester Sledge is right,
Pee Wee. Lester is right. He is. I'm sorry."

"What?" Pee Wee asked. "What the hell are you talking about,
Mickey?"

"There, you see, even Mickey gets it, McGinty. It ain't that
hard."

There was a brief pause before Mickey spoke again.

"Mickey is very tall, Pee Wee is very small and Lester is right in
the middle."

Pee Wee did his best to hide his exasperation.

"That's not what I mean, Mickey. Look, if you would just—"

"Lester has very dark skin and dark hair, Mickey has tan skin and
light hair, and Pee Wee has white skin and only a little hair."

Lester laughed and sputtered a few "I told you so's" as Mickey
continued a constant stream of commentary enumerating the many
physical disparities between the threesome.

"Aw, cut the crap, Lester," Pee Wee protested. "You know what
I'm talking about. I know all that, Mickey. I know all those things
you're saying. I ain't blind."

"But you said that—"

"I know what I said, Mick," Pee Wee interrupted. "But what I
meant is that we, the three of us, are all misfits in our own way. Jesus, look at *me*. Is this the body of a grown man, let alone a baseball
player? Do you know the abuse I have taken—all the snide remarks
and practical jokes at my expense? I have had to fight for everything
I have, every step of the way. And it ain't over yet. And what about
young Mickey here. Is he any different than me? So he's a little
slow sometimes, and has a few quirky habits. Does that make him

bad? No, but it sure makes him different, just like being five foot five makes me different. Then there's you, Lester. Yeah, your skin is darker than ours. And your hair is curly and you don't always speak the way we do. Yeah, you're different too. Just like we are. Just like we are. Get it? Do you guys get it now? We are different, sure, but not from each other."

Lester's first reaction was a bit bizarre, his face reminiscent of a Salvador Dali-like portrait in which eyes were not windows to the soul but simply prisms through which nothing was readily discernable. He said nothing—just stared blankly with a look both unsettling and surreal.

"Look, I hear ya, Pee Wee," he finally said some time later. "I do. But ya'll got to remember one thing. *My* different puts my life on the line. Every day. I gots to worry every day. It ain't just teasing and razzing. Or even simple prejudice. I'm talking 'bout the fear of getting my neck stretched, just cause I'm a negro. See what *I'm* saying? Ain't nobody burning crosses on your lawn or threatening you every day cause you is short."

A half hour passed without a single word spoken. They still had not caught any fish and the sun had already begun its descent below the tree line. Evening was fast approaching, with the day's light waning in slanted oblongs through the distant pines.

Sitting there, they had sunk into a heavy awkwardness that, save for Mickey's humming, had eradicated any exchange of sound among them. Pee Wee sat, imagining ways in which he could articulate this feeling he was trying to convey, but the more he thought about it, the more detached he felt from the others. He fidgeted on his log, and tugged gently on his fishing line now and again. He decided to focus on the fish. The distraction, however, was formidable, and the ruminations continued. After several more minutes of beating himself up over what had come out all wrong, he promised himself he would just let it go. He had all abandoned any hope of finding just the right words when to his own surprise he was suddenly seized by the need to speak.

"Look, Lester, I ain't trying to say that we've had it as tough as you, although Mickey here can tell you a few stories that would straighten some of those curls. All I'm saying is that I think we understand each other because we all have had similar experiences. Ya know? I have to tell you, when Mickey came last year, I finally felt normal. Like my life wasn't so messed up. I could finally talk to someone who also knows what it's like to grow up different, and without a father."

"Mickey's got a daddy," Lester said. "He told me so himself."

"His daddy's alive, sure," Pee Wee commented. "But he ain't no father. Damn near killed the boy a few times with his own hands."

"That right, Mick?" Lester asked. "Yer daddy go beatin' ya all the time?"

Mickey inhaled a few breaths then spoke, nourished by the softness in Lester's voice. "He hit me pretty good, Lester Sledge. Sometimes two and three times a day. All on account of me being a retard."

Lester set his pole down gently. He heard, in his own heart, echoes of misfortune and suffering that pounded his chest like a factory machine. His face sagged and the dark circles under his lower lids enlarged like a dam about to burst.

"Well don't that beat all," he said, a profound sadness tolling over him. "I think, Pee Wee, that I may owe you an apology. Ain't we the sorry lot here."

"Ya think?" Pee Wee asked.

"I sure do. The midget, the retard, and the monkey boy. You is right. We don't belong here. None of us. But, Christ, I'd still trade places with either of you guys in a second, but glory be, I sees where you is going."

The walk back to the cabin under a blackening sky that was signaling the impending death of another day was cloying. Between their unsuccessful fishing and the heavy conversation, all three were having difficulty shaking the foggy, lingering state of uncertainty that had filled the corners of their minds. Once back inside, Pee Wee pursued some levity. He posed in front of the only cabinet in the cabin, and gestured like Maryanne, their favorite waitress at Rosie's, placing one hand on his hip and the other in the air, palm up, as if balancing an imaginary tray.

"Welcome to Pee Wee's, boys," he announced in his best female southern drawl. "I'm afraid we are plum out of fish, but there's plenty of today's special left."

The glow of the gas lamps inside revealed a burgeoning smile on Lester's face.

"And what, pray tell, would that be, little darling?" he asked, winking while rubbing his hands together feverishly.

Pee Wee curtsied, held up one finger to both Lester and Mickey, a tacit request for their patience, then turned to face the cabinet. The rusty hinges protested against Pee Wee's intrusion, but the grating sound was soon replaced by mock cheers and applause as he held in his hands, for all to see, the staple of their grand repast.

"Anyone for pork and beans?"

They sat around on wooden crates with metal plates balancing on their laps, each taking a turn talking about struggles they wished they could forget but could not. "Mickey pissed himself once," the youngest of the three shared. "I told him I had to go. I did. Told him, lots of times, till he hit me for talking. Just kept telling me to shut my trap and shuck the corn. Mickey tried to hold it. I did. Crossed my legs, like this here, and tried to forget. But I just couldn't hold it no more. Soaked my pants something good." Lester and Pee Wee chuckled.

"Is that the thing that bothers you the most, kid?" Lester asked. "A little pee pee on your leg?"

The two men chuckled again, laughed heartily until Mickey, who had waited for the impromptu hysteria to abate, continued the painful reminiscence.

"My pa, he was so angry. Mickey remembers, he could not even speak no more. Just took the basket of corn, dumped it on the ground, and started hitting me with it. On my hands, the back of my neck, all over. Said I was a dim-witted numbskull, dumber than a stump."

There was no more laughter. Only silence, a deflated hush, as if all the air in the room had been released at once. Discomfort ruled the minute. Pee Wee's old boots hurt his feet, and Lester's hands could no longer steady the plate on his lap. All of them were, all at once, uneasy with themselves.

"Gee, we're sorry, Mick," Pee Wee said. "Didn't mean nothing by laughing like that. It ain't funny. Not at all."

"Nothing funny 'bout getting whooped," Lester added. "No, sir. Don't suppose I'll ever forget my first one."

Lester paused momentarily, as if summoning some necessary strength from deep within, before recounting the tale. He explained how it was a stormy day, with jagged clouds that had darkened all at once and began dumping rain everywhere. His mother was due back from her day of cleaning houses but had yet to arrive. It was a good four miles on foot from the good part of town and with this sort of weather, it would take her that much longer. So Lester did what any ten-year-old boy who loves his mother would do. He went out to find her. He wandered aimlessly, trying to remember the route his mother always took, and hadn't gotten very far when he ran into three boys, not too much older than he, playing in the puddles that had just begun to form.

"Hey, boy," one of them shouted.

Lester pretended he did not hear.

"Hey, boy. Yo, you over there. Boy. Come here now. We want to talk to you."

The voice was now closer. Lester turned to face the request. A stiff wind blew the rain hard against his face as he dragged his feet on the wet asphalt.

"What do you think you're doing in this part of town?" another asked.

Lester hung his head.

"Answer us now, boy. Don't you know there ain't no colored folks around here?"

A dark shadow passed over Lester's heart.

"I'm just looking for my ma," he said.

"Your ma? Is that what you said?" the third boy asked. "Are you jiving us boy? Why would a colored woman be here? Huh?"

Lester shrank, shivering beneath the cold rain drops and the bluster of the tiny mob.

"I think I know what's happening here," the first boy said, smiling devilishly. "I think our colored friend here has forgot that he's a negro."

The empowered miscreant turned and faced his two cohorts.

"Now, what do you suppose we should do about that?"

In his dim, frightened state, Lester never saw it coming. His heart beat deep and powerful as two of the boys held him down while the third filled his hands with mud and began smearing it all over Lester's face. He could still remember the punching and kicking and the taste of dirt on his tongue.

"Said he were gonna learn me that I would always be black,"

Lester explained. "And that nothing were ever gonna change that."

He stopped and nodded deliberately. "I reckon that boy was right."

He paused again as he recalled the painful reminiscence.

"That's why I loves baseball so much. Only time in my life where I can hit back."

They broke a while from the heavy banter, trying to allay the pall of misfortune with some whimsical chatter, until a ruckus from outside burst upon them like a storm cloud. There was a conflagration of voices, hot and pugilistic, like the earth was turning itself inside out, and the smell of smoke was strong in their noses. For a brief moment, they looked at each other, frozen by the unexpected intrusion. Then through the clouded casements, Pee Wee saw, standing menacingly, six figures, vaunted apparitions cloaked in white, each brandishing eager sticks of fire.

"Jesus Christ. Not again."

Lester and Mickey both joined Pee Wee, who was now pale and tremulous, and all three stood uneasily watching the ugliness unfold.

"We'll burn it to the ground," one of the intruders shouted through his hood. "Let us have him."

Pee Wee stepped back hesitatingly from the window, unable to perceive the dire nature of things. His panic soared beyond the meager limits of his resolve.

"What now, Lester? Wha— What are we gonna do now? They'll kill us all."

Lester stood stone-faced, burning with anger and rage and shame. Though caught in the tumult of his own despair, he managed to engineer his emotions in such a way so that only clear, exacting words came from his tremulous lips.

"I suppose we'll just have to give 'em what they came for."

Nightfall had begun dropping its veil, and it was getting too dark to see.

Pee Wee and Mickey watched as Lester steeled himself before reaching for the doorknob. Pee Wee had brewing inside of him the idea that he should jump out in front of his teammates, and lead them all outside. It would be the noble thing to do. Besides, after they finished with Lester, there was no doubt they would have to silence all those who witnessed the atrocity. Why not go out fighting? A tremor of this bravado rose up inside the diminutive shortstop and he almost embraced it wholly. But then he checked himself methodically, like a sea captain examining his vessel before embarking on a journey through tempestuous waters, and all at once he was paralyzed again, only able to watch as his friend flung open the door to a night filled with terror.

It could not have been uglier. The minute Lester stepped outside, he was seized by the tentacles of the unholy mob. The fulmination was swift and lawless; all six assailants got a hand on Lester and together, the collective beast dragged the struggling catcher away from the house and toward the tree they had already selected. Lester's cries were high and frantic, like those of an animal being lead to slaughter, and his eyes were wet and rolled from side to side, as if he were looking for something. Pee Wee and Mickey watched motionlessly from the doorway, frozen in a nightmarish state in which there seemed to be nothing more than suspended animation, and the dreamlike suffocation that usually accompanies the terror germane to such subconscious paralysis. It was almost entirely dark now. The orange sky had all but dissolved, leaving all of the players in this sordid scene ensconced in a lurid, ever-darkening shroud. Pee Wee and Mickey continued to stand stiffly in that darkness, but everything else was in motion. A group of upstart crows, protesting over the burgeoning ruckus, dispersed wildly and crossed in front of the emerging moon, which had slid down just above the tree tops, and in doing so, now illuminated the silhouettes of busy legs and grasping hands. Things moved quickly. All around Lester was methodical, predatory movements, wild and heinous, which now mimicked the steady motion of jaws. When the rope was placed around Lester's neck, he said nothing. Didn't make a sound. Pee Wee and Mickey still looked on, now under the watchful eye of one of the reprobates who was wielding a metal pipe. Mickey's eyes flickered with a gray light, and the beads of sweat that had assembled almost instantly on his forehead and upper lip shone curiously in the wake of the blazing torches.

He felt a vague, familiar burning in his stomach, and the mannerisms that they had all come to dismiss as just idiosyncratic "mickeyisms" warped into something grotesque and alien. His face hardened and his posture became severe and robotic. His limbs were completely stiff; the only movements observable were the fain't rocking of his upper torso and his trembling lips, from which came forth the audible recitation of the familiar poem, "'Slowly, silently now the moon, Walks the night in her silver shoon…'"

The alteration of his deportment was alarming. But the change in him went deeper than that. Somewhere deep inside the most cavernous recesses of the boys memory, something broke loose, coursed through his body now wild and unfettered, and seized him. He appeared to be all at once a hollow shell.

When the group noticed the strange antics, there came forth a blast of corrupt laughter, followed by whooping and hollering as the loose end of the rope still tied to Lester soared skyward, then disappeared beyond a stodgy limb before returning back to the hands from whence it came. The thrower wrapped the end of the rope around his hand, tight coils that suggested he was just about ready to begin pulling, then looked up at the others with a demoniac grin. Then the diabolical incantation began.

"String him up! String him up! String him up!" they chanted, lost in a ridiculous swell of baseless malevolence. Their focus was sharp and all at once insatiable. They followed the impulse, blind apostles wedded to the mastering lust, in sinful concert. The savagery was deliciously wicked, and had all but begged for immediate satisfaction when a fragment of their attention caught some movement in the distance; it was soft at first, then grew louder and louder—closer and closer still. Reluctantly, they suspended their assault.

At first it sounded like an animal rustling in the brush, a wayward forest dweller, foraging for morsels to complete the evening's repast. Night had now come completely, with the moon throwing a peculiar spotlight on the unfolding drama. They all stood, hands tight and sweaty, as they looked from side to side in incredulous self pity while Murph and the entire Brewer team spilled out of the woods from the east, and a half dozen men in gray suits distended at the hip on one side by swollen holsters came from the west. The group in white hoods stood inanimate, their arms dangling dejectedly at their sides, as the cavalry swarmed all around Lester.

"What's happening, fellas?" Murph asked, hands on hips and his head titled ever so slightly. "A costume party—and nobody invited us?"

Then, in the orange light of the torches, Murph pushed passed the two executioners and went to Lester and removed the rope from around his neck.

"Man, Murph, you sure know how to make an entrance," he said sighing deeply. "What the hell kept ya?" Murph smiled and winked playfully.

"Now is that any way to show appreciation? I'm not that off. Besides, you know what they say now. Better late than never."

They both laughed, but the levity engendered by the exchange was fleeting. The reason for the assembly returned to Murph's consciousness with an unavailing wrath and impatience. He swallowed his temper, and with the scene dissolving slowly, motioned for one of the men in suits to join him. For a moment it appeared as though Murph may just abdicate all punishment and justice to the Feds. He stood unresponsive, as though incapable of action, until a surge of riotous rage rose up and rattled his lifeless limbs. "You piece of crap! How could you?" he said through clenched teeth, ripping the hood off the head of the man closest to Lester. "After all I've done for you?"

There was once again a peculiar silence, save for nightly song of the tree frogs, as everyone struggled with the disquieting sight before them. Especially Lester.

"Aw, no. That can't be. Sanders?" Lester said softly while shaking his head. "Sanders? Naw, that can't be. Can't be. He's one of us. I just helped him get on top of his curveball. Sanders? A racist? How about that. Old Lester was fooled again. And right under my nose the whole time. Now don't that just beat all."

As the Feds counted and cuffed each of the klansmen, Mickey and Pee Wee, ensconced in their idleness, finally came forward and rallied around Murph and Lester, their fears and private longings now simply thoughts of the past.

"You knew about this, Lester?" Pee Wee asked breathlessly. "I mean, that this was gonna happen? And you never let on?"

"Wasn't part of the plan, little man," Lester replied. "Besides, ain't like you knowing 'bout it would've changed nothing."

"Wouldn't have changed nothing? That's your answer? You almost got us all killed."

"Back off, Pee Wee," Murph said, placing his hand on the shortstop's shoulder. "*I* told Lester not to say anything. It was my idea. The whole thing. Nobody knew anything. It was for your own good."

Pee Wee shook his head, and noticed that Mickey was staring at him with unusual intentness. His jaw was tight and his eyes glowed, lit by the scattered thoughts burning behind them.

"*Mickey* knew," the boy said, the weighty secret leaping from his unburdened soul. Murph frowned. "About Sanders," the boy continued. "Mickey saw him, that night. The night Lester was almost beat up."

All around them the man-made glow from the torches mixed with the moonlight, bathing all of their faces in peculiar hues. Disturbed considerably by Mickey's announcement, both Pee Wee and Lester stood dumbfounded, brooding over the nature of what had been brought to light. The whole scene struck them oddly.

"This is unbelievable," Lester said thickly. "Mickey, you knew about Sanders, all this time, and didn't say nothing? Not anything? To no one?

"Well, Mickey didn't—"

All at once the boy who had endeared himself so easily to Lester was now somehow part of the ugliness of the world. Lester's head throbbed and his tongue burned.

"This is bullshit, Mickey!" he exploded. "Bullshit! I don't care how special you—"

"But I couldn't say nothing," he continued. "I was not allowed to. Murph said that we needed all of our arms. That we had to win games, Lester. I did not want to lose. And I were scared too. I just—"

"Shut up, Mickey!" the catcher bawled. "Just shut up! I do not want to hear any more—"

"Hey, *you* shut your mouth now, Lester," Murph said, stepping in between the two so that his figure could sufficiently conceal Lester from Mickey's vision. "What the hell's wrong with you?"

"Get away from me, Murph!" Lester screamed. "Enough. What

kind of bull is this? Do you know what my life has been like these past few months? And he knew? Left me in harm's way?"

Murph grabbed Lester by the shoulders and shook him steadily.

"This whole thing has not been easy for any of us—including *Mickey*. Do you know what is was like for this boy to carry that secret around with him? Do ya? He was damn near frightened out of his own skin. Could barely function. You've seen him. Has he been himself? Hell no! But even with all that, and all the other horse crap he's had to deal with, this boy who you are attacking still came to me. Told me everything. Everything. You hear? That's gutsy. And I'll tell you something else. Without him, this thing would still be going on right now."

Murph kicked at the dirt in front of him, and in the flickering light, he took notice of Lester's drooping profile, as the man struggled to release the words that needed to be said, while Mickey, with his thoughts raw and untamed, collided hard with the limitations of his sensibility.

SEPTEMBER

Chip McNally was miserable. He saw the tide turning against him, an undertow of inexorable energy that seemed to be pulling him further and further from his intended goal. With the arrest of Hooper and some of the others, and the subsequent success of a re-focused Brewers team, the Rangers' manager was reeling. Rosco, who was in the middle of a conversation with someone else, never saw him coming.

"This is how you have me covered?" he barked at the blemished law man. "You let this happen? Are you kidding me, John? Now what am I gonna do? That negro is gonna do his darnest now to stick it to me."

Rosco was unphased by McNally's harangue.

"Chip McNally, I'd like you to meet my friend, Victor Bryant. Vic here is in town for a little while. He's looking for some work."

"What? Are you listening to me, Rosco?"

"I am, Chip. But I'd like you to meet someone."

McNally surveyed Rosco's friend with a quick eye. He seemed like an okay guy—middle-aged, graying temples and big, dark eyes. Yup, a real regular Joe, except for his little finger, which sported a fancy, black onyx ring with a diamond in the shape of a baseball right in the center.

"Good to meet you, Vic," he said robotically.

"Nice to meet you too," the stranger replied.

With the introductions now complete, Rosco set his mind to disarming his visitor.

"Hey, Vic, would you excuse us a minute?" Rosco asked, pointing in the direction of his car. "If you wait for me over there, I shouldn't be more than a minute or two."

Once alone, Rosco and McNally began their heart-to-heart.

"I had no choice, Chip. I already told you that. It was either Sanders and the others, or me and you. Is that what you wanted? You wanted me to blow us up instead?"

"No, of course not, but now—"

"It's fine. Everything is fine."

"It's not fine. My ass is out there John. Quinton is calling for my job if I don't beat these guys and capture the pennant. I have no room for error here. And how do you know the others won't take us down with them?"

Rosco said nothing. McNally watched him while the sheriff stood, arms folded, eyes flat and expressionless. There was something indistinguishable yet definitive in his face. It was neither hope nor despair, or even anger.

"Look, have a little patience," he said, placing his hand on McNally's shoulder and guiding him back toward his car. "I know what I'm doing here. Trust me. You worry too much. Remember, I have my hands in more pockets than you know."

Here and there, a throng of bristling figures bathed in the dim twilight and fluorescent glow spilling from the towering light stanchions at Borchert Field rushed to their seats, eager to watch the impending contest against the Giants. The excitement in the stands floated and eddied from person to person, an ineffable energy that lit the inner fires of those Brewer faithful who had been rewarded for standing by their boys of summer even through what many predicated would be a season ending slump. The Brew Crew was streaking, winning four straight since the whole Butch Sanders debacle had been put to rest. Sure, there was still the occasional racial epithet tossed Lester's way, and not every fan was ready to embrace the idea of baseball integration, but for the most part, people had grown tired of all the contention and finger pointing and just wanted to enjoy some good old-fashioned hard ball.

Of all the Brewers, Mickey was the one who had flourished the most noticeably. He was on fire. In his previous start against the Sidewinders, he was never better. His fastball was exploding with such velocity that each offering appeared to the mesmerized crowd to be an aspirin tablet, a tiny blip of white that sliced the air each time with remarkable precision and accuracy. His curveball was equally impressive. Although he was still trying to master the new pitch, and could not always throw it for a strike, when he did find the zone, the ball broke with such power and deliberateness that it was virtually unhittable.

It didn't take the Giants very long to feel the young phenom's resurrected prowess. Through the deepening twilight, Mickey disposed of the first three Giants batters handily, fanning each on just three pitches.

"The best thing since little apples, eh Murph?" Matheson gushed, folding his arms while grinning from ear to ear. "Man oh man, we're back in business."

The crowd felt the swell of good fortune too. All around Borchert Field, talk of a stretch run punctuated just about every conversation. The Brewer faithful had been down this road before, as recently as last year, but somehow they knew, just knew, that this season's out-come would be different.

"It's our year, boys!" many of the most ardent fans screamed as their hometown heroes prepared for their first at bat. "Yes, sir, this is our year!"

Pee Wee wasted no time getting things started, dropping a beautiful bunt down the third base line. The ball hugged the narrow lane between the edge of the grass and the foul line, rolling along like a tiny white tumbleweed before coming to rest quietly in front of the helpless hands of the Giants' keeper of the hot corner. The crowd stamped its feet in approval, and roared even louder when Arky Fries punched a 2–2 fastball through the right side of the in-field, setting up first and third for the dangerous Woody Danvers. The Brewer third baseman strode to the plate, the wisps of his dark brown hair dancing about in the late summer breeze. His movements were deliberate yet easy. With his heart thumping insubordinately, and his mind tied to visions of something truly spectacular, he dug in at home, staring straight out at the pitcher with an almost mocking flicker in his eye.

The first pitch to the dangerous Danvers missed low and away. He stepped out briefly, banged his cleats, and smiled inside. Once back in the box, he steadied himself for the next offering. Up and in. The moon was now high and bright in the middle of the sky, and it bathed Danvers in a brilliant silver pool.

"Let's go now, Wood Man!" Murph shouted from the bench. "Hitter's count now. Get yours."

Danvers stood at the plate, wind-milling his bat with a determination and desire that stretched beyond all imaginable limits of both body and mind. He lived for these situations. The pitcher, now crippled by the count and the mounting trouble on the base paths, had no choice but to groove a fat fastball down the middle.

Danvers didn't miss it. The bat caught the ball square, sending the little white sphere soaring toward the diamond-dotted sky like a missile threatening to disrupt the beauty of nature's sparkling symmetry before disappearing into the night.

With the upstart Brew Crew leading 3–0, Mickey took the field for inning number two. He was just as sharp in the second frame, fanning all three hitters with little protest.

The crowd stood up and saluted their hero. Mickey, who a year later was still thinking about how odd it was for people to fuss so feverishly over something that came to him so naturally, trotted off the field in a maze-like incomprehension.

From that point forward, the game moved along at a rigorous clip. Both teams traded zeroes for the next several innings. Mickey remained sharp, but the Brewers' offense sputtered. After posting three runs in the first inning, the home team managed only two base runners over the next six frames, neither of which made it past first base. It was frustrating to watch, and would have been cause for real alarm had Mickey not been so indomitable.

The top of the ninth arrived quickly and without event. Mickey plunged zealously into all the hollering and fanfare that attenuated what looked like a sure victory, disposing of the Giants' leadoff hitter in routine fashion. Through the deepening darkness, punctuated now by intermittent flashbulbs, the Baby Bazooka reared back and attacked the next batter. The pitch was exactly like so many others that night, hard and true, and his delivery equally adroit. His accuracy, however, betrayed him momentarily—a blip in the typically flawless choreography. The offering missed its mark by a healthy margin, speeding off the plate and plunking the hitter square between the shoulder blades. The thud was deafening. The stunned batter fell to his knees in a heartbeat, as if he had just taken a bullet. The crowd fell silent, yielding now to its captured curiosity, as the fallen player remained on all fours for several minutes, wincing and gasping for air before finally staggering to his feet with the help of his manager and the umpire. Then slowly, and with discernible difficulty, he made his way down the first base line, his deliberate gait prolonging the tension attached to the moment.

"Hey, what kind of horse crap is that?" one the Giants screamed from the dugout. "Friggin' hayseed. Could've killed him. Just wait till we get a crack at your ass, freak show."

Mickey heard the invectives and was all at once uncomfortable under his uniform. He stood on the mound, inert and broken, while Murph and the others returned the verbal fire from their side of the field.

"The ball just got away, you idiots," Murph screamed. "Please. He's gonna throw at *him?* On purpose? When you guys can't even touch him?" He huffed loudly and shook his head. "Assholes."

Previews of retaliation filtered through the mind of the Giants' manager, setting the frustrated skipper ablaze with roiling anger.

"Just wait," he yelled to Murph, pointing his finger in the direction of the Brewers' bench. "Just you wait. There's still plenty of baseball to play this season. And I got a pretty good memory."

Mickey looked on with great concern. The vision of the moment adjusted itself, and he struggled with the residue of conflict. Despite support from his teammates and legions of adoring fans exhorting their hero to finish off the enemy, he could not reclaim his composure. Fearful and spellbound, he walked the next three batters, forcing in a run while moving the tying tally to second base. The game was slipping away.

"Time," Murph barked before making his way onto the field.

His steps were heavy and purposeful, and it seemed to those watching to take an eternity for him to join the meeting on the pitcher's mound.

"What's going on, Mick?" he asked, folding his arms tightly against his chest. "You okay?"

Mickey nodded inanimately. His eyes squinted hard against the glare from the distant lights visible just above Murph's shoulder.

"Don't go getting rabbit ears on me now, boy, ya hear? Ignore what those guys are saying. They're just trying to get under your skin. All part of the game. Hit batsman? Also part of the game. Okay? Can't be afraid to throw the ball now. Trust yourself, Mick. Come on. Give it your best here."

Mickey looked like he could shatter with a blink of his eye. He stood inertly, listening to Murph's gentle admonition while struggling with the shifting tide of tension.

"Murph's right, Mick," Lester said, patting the fretful pitcher on his back. "Relax, man. Nice and easy. Just hit the glove."

The stars seemed to move across the deep sky in desultory fashion, a bizarre display under which the young hurler labored. He watched, almost hypnotically, as the meeting dissolved, with each participant returning to his previous position. Mickey's lips, engaged now in the tragic monologue to which they had all grown accustomed, moved ever so slightly, and continued to do so for several seconds before the call of "play ball" shattered the stupor, leaving him to face the situation at hand.

With the bases full of Giants, and no margin for error, Petey Stewart, one of the Giants' best RBI guys, strode to the plate. Stewart was tall and lean, but had tremendous pop in his bat. He had finished in the American Association's top ten in extra base hits in each of the last three seasons. He could hit for average as well, hovering consistently around the .320 in each campaign. Mickey had bested him thus far, fanning him on a 2–2 curveball the first time up and retiring him the next two times on weak ground balls to Arky Fries at second. Now, with a chance to do some real damage,

Stewart looked stone-like. His face was still, a battle mask chiseled so artfully that he appeared almost sinister in the artificial shadows. Mickey winced a bit as his eyes caught the deep lines framing Stewart's jaw. It was awful. It was familiar. Standing there, he couldn't help but think of the ghastly scarecrow that Clarence would set up each season in the corn field just to the right of the barn. That face. That awful, menacing face. A stained burlap countenance featuring searing red eyes, bulging cheeks, and a twisted mouth stenciled so craftily that it appeared the makeshift sentinel was always just about to speak. Clarence knew how much it bothered Mickey, and on more than one occasion, the twisted farmer used the straw-stuffed demon as punishment when Mickey transgressed against his wishes.

"Come on now, boy," he would say with a perverse note of joy in his voice. "Time to pay a visit to old Mr. Bojangels. You may not listen to me, but he'll learn you proper."

As Stewart wind-milled his bat unmercifully, setting himself for Mickey's first delivery, the boy closed his eyes, trying desperately to clear the lens of his memory. Encouraged by Lester's continued prodding from behind the plate, Mickey managed to quiet, if only for the moment, the demons he had been fighting in torturous silence. His first pitch to the Giants' slugger was a seed that shaved the outer half of the plate for a called strike one. The next pitch was equally adroit, another fastball that tickled the inner half of the dish, tying a frustrated Stewart in knots.

"Atta boy, Mick," Lester yelled jubilantly from underneath his mask. "That's the old pepper. Keep chucking boy!"

Mickey peered in to Lester. The boy looked as though he was okay, like he was back in the zone. But Mr. Bojangels was still on his mind. So was Clarence.

The thoughts polluted his head. And when the Giants started

talking crap again from the dugout, lambasting the young hurler for plunking their leadoff man, he lost his grip entirely. Mickey felt, as he watched Lester place two fingers down in between his legs, that it was all wrong. That these men had falsely accused him of something for which he was truly sorry. The paradox haunted him. *How can I be sorry for something I did not do?* he wondered silently. He shuddered. It reminded him of the time Clarence exploded after discovering that the gate to the pig pen had been left open, resulting in the loss of one of farmer's prized porkers.

"What kind of numb skull are you anyway?" he thundered. "Why in tarnation didn't you close the damned gate, boy?"

Mickey fought the accusation feverishly in the mid morning heat.

"Mickey did close the gate. I did."

Clarence sighed loudly and shook his head. The two just stood for a moment, defined to each other now more than ever, by the searing sun and the burgeoning discomfort of the moment.

"Don't you hand me none of yer shit, boy!" the irascible farmer ranted. "You tell the truth now or so help me God you'll feel me."

Mickey cowered a bit and listened in horror as his Clarence kicked the dirt while continuing his harangue about the lost pig.

"I'm sorry, Pa. Mickey is sorry. Really. I miss Jasper too. But I, I didn't—"

"Damn right yer sorry. A sorry excuse for a boy is what you are. Don't know why I even bother with ya."

A soft starlight now fell like a gentle mist on the dozing face of the field. Red and white streamers festooned in the crisp air, and the smell of hot pretzels and nervous waiting permeated the tiny ballpark like a flurry of tiny flies. The crowd was growing restless, as was Stewart, who had been waiting on Mickey's next pitch for what seemed like an eternity.

"Come on, Mick," Lester called, pounding his glove, mindful of the boy's escalating paralysis. "0–2 now. Way ahead. Just like before. Nice and easy now. Just hit the glove."

Mickey steadied himself on the rubber, but the apparent calm belied the tumult of his mind. He thought about just stopping what he was doing and apologizing. Just hopping off the mound and explaining to all of them that the pitch just got away. Maybe that would make things right again. Surely they had to know that he would never hurt anyone intentionally. The word "sorry" always disarmed Clarence. Perhaps it would work with the Giants as well.

His mind, however, was cluttered, and his stomach was sick. The words would never come. *Pitch the ball instead*, he told himself. *Pitch the ball*. So he did. But much to Mickey's dismay, the delivery broke off the plate for a ball. He missed with his next offering as well, and appeared now to be floundering once again. He stood on the rubber, rocking back and forth in the cool night air, as a feeling of profound defeat tore through his body. He felt sick and thought for a moment that he'd much prefer to be sitting. His tongue was burning and his knees wobbled against each other. He probably would have just flopped to the ground and curled up right there had it not been for Lester's keen eye and timely words.

"Come on now, Mick," he called. "Hey, look at me. Remember what we always say. Let 'em hit it. Split the plate—right down the middle. That's all, baby. Right down the middle."

Mickey stood now, perfectly still, his mouth slightly contorted as he measured the words of his batterymate. He looked at Lester softly, and recognized the freedom that lay behind the catcher's gesture as he pounded his glove, imploring Mickey to throw the ball right over the plate. Mickey smiled a little, absorbed in the feeling that Lester had somehow made everything okay, then rocked back, kicked his leg in the air and fired.

The ball's trajectory was just as planned. It's flight was straight and true, a white blur that rocketed toward the batter who, in recognizing the desperation of the situation, was sitting dead red all the way.

The crack of the bat was significant, a thunderous blow that resonated throughout the entire park. All eyes watched dutifully as the little white sphere arched skyward and toward the centerfield wall, sending Jimmy Llamas into a full sprint. The quirky centerfielder ran with grave determination, his eyes dancing between the flight of the ball and the grim reality of the six-foot barricade that lay waiting for him should his jaunt take him one step too far.

Llamas, despite one or two ill-advised turns, kept his direction by the ball, like a night traveler following a Northern Star. His movements were for the most part awkward and spastic, and he almost fell once or twice in his fevered pursuit. But somehow, despite the improbability of such a feat, he snagged the prodigious blast with a remarkable over-the-shoulder catch.

The crowd, which had written the game off as yet another devastating loss once the ball had left the bat, roared its approval. Suddenly, they were back in business—snatched from the jaws of defeat by a sparkling defensive gem. What could have been a bases clearing extra base hit had been rehabilitated into a relatively harmless sacrifice fly, yielding just one run scored instead of the potential three. With the score now 3–2 in favor of the Brew Crew, Mickey readied himself for the final out. The sinister trumpets of fear were much quieter now, quelled by Llama's catch and the comforting fact that he was just one out away from escaping the jam.

"Right over the plate, Mick," Lester repeated.

Mickey, free now completely from the tremulous self pity, nodded dutifully. Standing there on the hill, with 14,000 people on their feet calling his name, Mickey could, in this moment, forget the previous agony and make it right.

The Giants sent to the plate a pinch hitter—Nate Buckley—a left-handed line drive hitter who had been sidelined for a week with a bruised right thumb. Buckley had been itching to grab a piece of the action all game, certain that despite his ailing hand, he could make a difference. The Giants skipper did not want to use him, but with his bench already depleted, he had no choice but to send the eager Buckley to the dish with a final chance to put the visitors ahead.

Mickey wasted no time with Buckley, burning a fastball right down the pipe for a called strike one. The second pitch, a slow curveball that grazed the outer half of the plate, was called a strike as well. Buckley shook his head in disgust and stepped out of the box. He banged his cleats hard with his bat and mumbled under his breath something about glasses and distinguishing asses from elbows.

Mickey received the ball back from Lester and got right back on the rubber.

With just one strike needed to secure a most uplifting victory, the crowd, in its frenzied anticipation, rose to its feet and roared. Mickey was ready. One pitch. One pitch and it was all over.

With the pandemonium building toward fevered crescendo, Mickey rolled his arms, kicked his leg, reared back and fired. The ball came out of his hand like a torpedo. It swam deftly through the tense air and sped inexorably toward the intended target. It was the perfect pitch. Buckley, who had been prematurely anesthetized by the crowd's frenzy, suddenly felt something inside of him stir, something like a current being turned on somewhere beneath his skin. The energy was hot and prickly, and flowed to his brain where it lit his imagination with rapturous thoughts before traveling to his arms and legs and fingers and toes, setting his entire body ablaze with unbridled determination.

For all those watching, everything at that moment seemed to creep all at once to a series of slow motion frames. The ball, which appeared to be spinning in slow motion, was true—a knee-high seed destined for Lester's yawning glove, which sat patiently behind Buckley on the inner half of the plate. It was the perfect pitch. Everyone knew it was the perfect pitch. A thin man with a mustache and eye glasses threw up his hands in premature exultation. A young blonde woman in a pretty blue dress laughed giddily and a row of impish children jumped up and down, screaming wildly about the power of their hometown hero.

The entire ballpark was rocking, was in full celebration mode when Buckley, despite the artful placement of the pitch, opened his hips and lashed the bat head through the hitting zone. The crack of the bat was mystifying, and fell across the bristling legions like a hollow darkness. Gone was the spark of buoyancy and the promise of merriment.

Just like that. Gone. It was surreal. It was dreadful.

The ball, upon being struck, leaped off the bat and sped past Mickey's glove with such force that the stunned hurler never had a chance to touch it. He could only turn helplessly and watch over his shoulder as the tiny white missile sped toward the middle of the diamond.

With the runners now in motion, and a desperate Jimmy Llamas charging in from centerfield, the unforeseen opportunity for the Giants to pull ahead overwhelmed the crowd, made them breathless. There were no more shouts of glory, no more visions of victory and all that followed. No. All of that was gone, replaced by an ominous momentary silence, an uncomfortable waiting for the proverbial axe to fall. They had all but hung their heads in abject disappointment, and some had already begun their familiar lamentations, when the ball, still in flight, struck the second base bag, diverting the intended course right to a stunned Arky Fries, who picked up the fortuitous carom and fired it to Finster. Game over. The tiny ballpark, awakened suddenly from its tomb, erupted in thunderous shouts and applause, creating a milieu of unbridled energy that did not subside for a good ten minutes after the final out was recorded.

The post-game euphoria in the locker room was equally enthralling. There were high fives, slaps on the backs and clinking of beer bottles. Players hugged and laughed and marveled out loud over the good fortune that had befallen them. Even the management was left scratching their heads.

"Holy crap, Farley," Murph said, unable to suppress his boy-like smile as he sat and talked about the game with his assistant. "That was huge! Unreal. Simply unreal. Have you ever seen anything like that before?"

Matheson laughed loudly. He shook his head, as though he were having some sort of seizure, then and stood up with profound vigor and purpose.

"Nope, can't say that I have, Murph. But it's good. Damn good. I seen this *sort* of thing before. You know, baseball miracles? And it's always the same. I'm telling ya, it's good. When the baseball Gods are smiling on you, ain't no mistakin' it."

STRETCH RUN

Despite a pitching rotation that was one starter short, and some residual fall out linked to the Sanders scandal, the Brewers made Matheson's prognostication stand up, going on a two-week tear that saw the resurgent Brew Crew peel off nine straight wins, catching the first place Rangers for a share of the penthouse while igniting a frenzied interest throughout the entire town.

This excitement fed off itself, morphing into a sort of willful paradise, a passionate, breathless longing for the impossible dream, an uncompromising fervor that captivated even the most dispassionate Milwaukee resident. The local butcher, bathed in this vicarious hue of the team's success, hung a large sign in his window extolling the recent exploits of the hometown heroes; many farmers, despite the daily rigors germane to tending fruitful cornfields, stripped their scarecrows of the usual flannel and denim in favor of full Brewers regalia; on every street corner, lampposts were tattooed with colorful fliers advertising the next five home dates at Borchert Field, and many of the municipal buildings closer to town decorated their doorways with Brewers flags and adorned their windows with an assortment of red and blue crepe paper streamers.

The fever was rampant.

Interest really peaked during four weeks of stellar baseball; now, after a rigorous schedule that began months ago, entrance to the playoffs came down to just one game. A one-game tie breaker—winner take all. Once again, Murph's Brew Crew would have to face McNally's Rangers on the final day of the regular season to determine their post-season fate.

In the wake of all the hoopla surrounding the Brewers incredible rise to prominence, Arthur Murphy became a wanted man—that is, a steady stream of people began showing up at his office and his home each day, all seeking an audience with the most popular guy in town. Some just wanted to be around the man, to share in the excitement that was by most estimations attributable to him. Others came by just to wish him luck, and to tell him how much his team's success meant to them personally, and of course there were a few visits from the token opportunists who happened by, seeking tickets or an autograph. Everyone wanted a piece of Murph. He must have accepted more than two dozen visits over a five-day period, most of a harmless nature, but none as strange as the one he received from Sheriff John Rosco.

"I hear you're a pretty popular fella these days, Arthur," Rosco began, his mouth thin and tight. "Sure is a great story. I'm happy for you. You have handled this whole Lester thing with a lot of poise. I have to say—I am very impressed."

Murph was silent for a moment.

"Well, thanks, John. That's mighty nice of you. Really. But somehow, I don't think you came all the way out here just to tell me how wonderful I am."

"Now, what kind of comment is that? Come on, Murph. Ain't we friends?"

Murph cringed over the insipid insincerity.

"Friends? No, John, we're not friends. My friends don't threaten the people I love."

Rosco grew moodily silent for a moment before finally answering.

"Are you still upset over that whole misunderstanding in the car with Lester?" Rosco asked. "Now I thought we were past that?"

Murph's eyes were distant. He seemed to be beyond the unscrupulous lawman.

"Okay, Murph, okay," he continued. "You win. I'm gonna level with you. I appreciate you not showing them G men the tape. I do. That could have really been a heap of trouble for me. And I'm still not quite sure *why* you didn't. Hell if I know too much of anything these days. Anyhow, I wanted to say thanks. And, I wanted to ask you for it—the tape. I mean, if you're not gonna use it, ain't no sense in you hanging onto to it, right?"

"I'm keeping the tape, John."

"Well, that don't make much sense now. Why would you—"

"Look, John," Murph said, shaking his head. "I'm a busy guy these days. You may have heard. I have a big game to prepare for. So if it's all the same to you, I think—"

"Funny you should mention that," Rosco said, laughing intently. "I just may be able to help you with that—or at least sweeten the pot a bit."

Murph struggled with an unpleasant feeling. A nagging tapping at the base of his skull that seemed to suggest that there was even more to Rosco than he had previously imagined.

"Well," the sheriff continued. "I hear that you've been poking around a little, inquiring about Chip McNally's alleged role in all of the monkey doings related to Lester. Makes sense. I'd be doing the same thing. But McNally's a pretty slippery fella, Murph. You know that. Ain't easy to catch a guy like that. Unless, of course, you've got a friend who may know something—someone, let's say, who's willing to help out a bit?"

"What is it that you want, John?" Murph asked, exasperated by the sheriff's circumlocution.

"Now, there you go again, hurting my feelings, Murph," he said. "I just want to help out. That's all. I can give you McNally—lock, stock, and barrel. He'll never be a thorn in your side again."

"Yes . . . and?"

"Here's what I'm thinking. A friendly wager. You beat McNally in the big game, you can keep the tape. And, as a bonus, I'll give you the scumbag. Fair and square. I'll testify and everything. You will never have to see his sorry ass again. Wouldn't that be grand?" Murph breathed deeply and folded his arms.

"And if I lose?"

"If you lose, you give me the tape, and we never talk about this again. We close the book on this nasty little chapter forever."

A puzzled came across Murph's face.

"Why not just make the exchange right now, John? You know, the tape for McNally? Why all the rabba dabba?"

Rosco pulled out a cigar, bit off the end, lit it and released a cloud of smoke over Murph's head.

"I'm a sportsman, Murph. Love the challenge, and the gamble. Keeps the blood flowing. Nothing like it. Besides, think about it. Should McNally win, ain't nobody gonna want to go after the guy. It'll look like sour grapes. Can't have that. Only a winner gets the sympathy of the people. That's just the way it goes."

Murph stiffened at first. Then he melted a little, a subtle thawing noticeable not even to the most astute observer. Rosco's idea was a little out there, but it had somehow reached out and wrapped itself around Murph's imagination nonetheless. It only took another few seconds for the hesitation to finally give birth to a decision.

"You know what, John? That's fine. It's fine. Nothing's gonna stop us this time. We're gonna win this damn thing anyway, so why not get both you and McNally off my back in the process? Right? Yeah. I like the sound of that. You got yourself a deal."

Murph reached out, and he and Rosco locked hands.

"Okay then. We have a deal." Rosco smiled.

"Yes, we have a deal. But I have to tell you, John. I still don't like you. And you should know something right now. If you step out of line here—if you do not live up to your end of the bargain, or if any other stuff happens, you're done. I mean it. If you screw with me, you will be one sorry son of a bitch."

PENNANT FEVER

As the hours before the final contest wore on, Murph grew more and more uneasy, with the indomitable fear of yet another season that would see him and his Brew Crew whimper into the off season without having finally made some meaningful memory for the Milwaukee faithful. He felt so miserable that he questioned whether or not he would even make it to the game—thought that perhaps at any minute, he would take one final breath, a painful attempt for just a little more air, before collapsing violently to the ground.

The enormity of the situation was overwhelming. Molly was there for him, her cheery buoyancy a constant source of comfort. Yet, despite her gentle ways, Murph struggled with the specter of fading hope, with the possibility that this could be the last game he would ever manage for the Brewers. Dennison's edict was clear.

"You know what you have to do, Arthur, right?" he had asked at the onset of their last closed door session. "I'm not kidding this time."

"I know, Warren," he said, struggling against pangs of sullen aggression. "I get it."

As a way of allaying his nervous energy, Murph summoned the entire team for an early meeting and subsequent practice the day before the showdown. He stood in front of them, with something camouflaged and disrupted brewing behind his eyes.

"I don't think I have to tell all of you what tomorrow means," he began, wiping the corners of his mouth with his forefinger and thumb. As he stood there, he recalled, in a blurred montage of images from his past, the fleeting glory that had whispered to him such false promise. There was the Rookie of the Year honor back in 1924; then there was the batting title the following season. He even hit the pennant clinching homerun later that year. Oh, what could have been had Fate only smiled upon him. It was another lifetime ago, sure, yet during moments like these, the sting was just as painful. "Tomorrow, we have a unique opportunity, fellas," he continued. "Redemption. Tomorrow is about redemption. About righting a wrong. I want you to remember last year. I want you to remember what it felt like to watch them celebrate, knowing that you were going home for the winter. I want you to picture that—every pitch, every out, every inning. Picture how that made you feel. Then I want you to look inside yourselves—really look inside yourselves—and imagine just how awful it would feel for that to happen to you, again. How it would stick in your craw, eat away at you, for the rest of your lives. Trust me, fellas, there are some things that you never forget. It will trail you like a ghost if Chip McNally and the Rangers get the best of you again tomorrow."

He picked up the baseball resting on the trainer's table and looked into it as if it were made of crystal.

"But, the opportunity for you to set things right—to claim what is rightfully yours—is priceless. Embrace that. Use that as the motivation to play your asses off. Play every out like your life depends on it. Like it's the last out you will ever play. Do that, because it will inspire you. Do that, because you owe it to yourselves. And to those fans who will be screaming for you. Do it, because for some of us, it may very well be the last hoorah."

Then, through a luminous morning mist that made each of them appear to be apparitions out for a senseless jaunt, they took the field in customary fashion, with the infielders spreading across the freshly turned dirt in preparation for box drills and the outfielders loping out toward the damp grass where they would spend the majority of the morning shagging flies. The pitchers and catchers did their own thing as well; jogged down the right field line, settled in the corner and began pairing up for some light throwing and tactical preparation for tomorrow's big contest.

"Mr. Murphy sure wants to win that game," Mickey said, as he and Lester began stretching their legs. "Yup. Mickey thinks Mr. Murphy is a good manager. He should win. He likes baseball more than anyone I know."

Lester smiled.

"Yeah, Mick, he does," he said, sitting on the grass.

He spread his legs out as far as they would go, until the formed a giant "V", then leaned forward with his fingers, reaching first for his left foot, then for the right. Mickey did the same.

"He sure does, Mick. But just liking the game ain't enough sometimes. You gotta prepare, work hard, and then the players, like us, we gotta perform. Do the things that everyone's expectin' us to do. Then old Murph got's a chance to bring home the prize."

He stopped for a minute to pull his legs into his body.

"And even then, if all that happens, there ain't no guarantees. Baseball's funny like that. You just never know."

Mickey's nerves tightened. He clenched his teeth and drew both hands together in a sudden tremor of realization.

"What if Mickey is no good tomorrow, Lester?" he asked, plowing through a snowstorm of unsettling thoughts. "What if they hit the ball, Lester? Or I can't throw hard enough?"

"Don't sweat it, Mick," Lester replied, his eyes wide and calm. "You're the best we got kid. Hell, you're the best anyone's got. Ain't no game without you."

Mickey's eyes were glassy in the morning glare. He was thinking about last year, and Lefty, and what had happened to Oscar that day, and how he had lost control, and wound up sitting in that dirty jail cell instead of pitching that day. God he missed Oscar. He was also remembering Murph's face after that game—how it looked like it was melting right off his head.

"But last year, Lester. Last year, Mickey wasn't there. Mickey let the team—"

"That was *last* year, kid," Lester said. "Last year is last year. Ain't nothin' to be done about that now. All you can do is go out there tomorrow and do like Murph said—give it everything you got. Somethin' tells me that if you can do that, we'll all be alright."

Mickey rose to his feet. He was still a little stiff, but his breathing was easier for the moment. He put on his glove, took the ball from Lester and watched almost hypnotically as his partner jogged a few steps away before settling directly across from him, some sixty feet away. Then, in the first warm rays of the ascending sun, the boy began tossing the baseball, ever mindful of the daunting test that awaited him.

JUDGMENT DAY

The evanescence of September twilight faded quickly into a deep night. The entire area surrounding Borchert Field lay shrouded in darkness save for the brilliant glow of a silver moon that shone through the weightless clouds hovering dreamily above the dozing hamlet and the emerging light beginning to hum from the towering light stanchions all around the stadium—splashes of artificial luminosity that lit the eager faces of the Brewer faithful as they poured through the turnstiles and made their way to their seats.

Murph had been in his office the entire day, fettered to his desk and the daunting prospects which lay ahead. He had come a long way in this game, had his fair share of both success and failure, with the latter emerging as the norm the past few years. Still, through it all, the game was all that mattered. Just being a part of it. Baseball was him. He *was* baseball. Now, after all these years, everything had been reduced to just nine innings; twenty-seven outs to determine his fate. Christ it was vexing. The sea of crumpled lineup cards strewn across the floor told the collective story of his torment.

"What's all the lollygagging about, young fella?" Matheson barked, clearing a path on the littered floor with his foot. "Come on now. Time's a-wasting. It's time to thump the tub."

"I just don't know, Farley," Murph said, shaking his head. "I don't know if I can stomach this. Don't know if I can do it."

"What are ya talking about, Murph?' the old man questioned.

"It ain't like before, Farley. This is really it. Dennison means business this time."

"Bah. Warren Dennison is a damned mooncalf. A real soft head. Don't know his ass from third base."

The tumult slowly rising outside from the impatient crowd reached Arthur's ears. He was weighing an image of a younger him, circling the bases, then crossing home plate with the pennant clinching run. The entire team was waiting for him, arms open, mouths frothing with celebratory juices. It was a moment he never forgot. That, and the conversation he had afterward with Otis Clayton, the man who had scouted him for the big league Braves.

"You've arrived, kid," he said, stuffing the end of his pipe with a pinch of tobacco. "And let me be the first to say it. You're the real deal. Five-tool player. One who is going to be one of the best to have ever put on a pair of spikes. Your future is as good as done."

It was all there that day, unfurling before him like a golden path to stardom and baseball immortality. Standing there now, he realized just how far he had fallen. Somehow, things just did not turn out the way he had always envisioned.

"I know, Farley, I know," he said, trying to jolt his face back into some semblance of sanity. "It's just that—ah, never mind. You're right. We got a game to play."

"That's the old pepper, Murphy boy," Matheson gushed. "Now let's go out there and give 'em hell."

The steady glare from the stadium lights painted the freshly manicured field with a luminous sheen, one that imbued the dirt and grass with a celestial quality. Murph climbed the dugout steps, gave a long look around and filled his lungs before placing one foot on the sacred ground, careful not to disrupt the freshly lain lines of lime as he made his way toward home plate for the pre-game ritual. McNally was already there, his mouth curling in a fain't but noticeable smile, as if to suggest that he somehow knew the outcome of the contest and was trying not to boast too early. He was always the same—always in character. Murph hated this man now more than ever.

"You guys sure are making this a habit," the umpire said as Murph arrived at the batters box. "Wouldn't be the final game of the season without a showdown between you two."

Murph forced a smile and handed the man in blue his lineup card. McNally was still wearing that stupid grin.

"Yup," the opposing skipper said, pulling his lineup card from his back pocket. "Every season ends the same way. You can count on that."

Murph fought against the throbbing in his temple.

"Don't be so sure of yourself, gimpy," he said, rubbing his hands together. "Things are a *little* different this time. You couldn't get to my pitcher this year."

McNally found himself propped up against the old truth and struggled momentarily with the feeling.

"Now, I told you I had nothing to do with that, Arthur," McNally said, laughing. "It hurts my feelings that you would suggest that I did. Was a terrible thing that Rogers did. A real shame. I actually want Tussler in the game. Wouldn't have it any other way. This way, when we beat you—and make no bones about it, we will beat you—there ain't no excuses to be had."

Murph, feeling like he wanted to place his hands around McNally's throat and squeeze, did what he usually did in circumstances such as these. It was the only way he knew.

"I wouldn't go popping any champagne corks just yet," he said before walking away.

Mickey led the Brewers onto the field to a chorus of raucous cheers. The tiny ballpark was in bloom. In every row, in every seat, in every corner where there was enough room to house a body, hope was ripening with a pulsating, breathless energy. All of the Brewers tingled with the energy flowing from the stands, as if somehow the standing-room-only crowd had found a way to transmit the emotional current to each of their hometown heroes.

Mickey felt his stomach churn. The excitement was awesome, and made him smile for the moment, but reminded him just how vital he was to the night's happenings. He scanned the crowd behind home plate quickly as he prepared to take his warm-up tosses. He saw Mr. Meyer, the butcher. In the row behind him, just to the left, was the man who fixed the leak in Murph's roof last fall. He was sitting next to Mrs. Kutner, the elementary school teacher, who was talking with Joan Ulanoff, a good friend of hers who had just arrived and hadn't even had time to sit. Mickey noticed that the man sitting directly behind her was laughing and using a handkerchief to clean the dust off her seat. It was Sheriff Rosco. And of course, there was Molly, sitting in her usual seat, watching her special boy perform at a level she was still unable to truly conceptualize. There were so many people there who he knew, and just as many, mostly men dressed in suits and fedoras, that he did not. And they were all holding rectangular pieces of cardboard, each with his name on it, spelled in such a way as to celebrate the young hurler's pitching prowess: GO MIC**K**EY! He had a fain't impulse to begin counting but Lester's impatient cry from behind the dish jolted him back to matters at hand. He began treating the eager crowd to a series of warm-ups that sounded something like a twenty-one gun salute.

The Rangers began their quest for back-to-back pennants with Kiki Delaney, the speedster who had had another productive year. Delaney lead the league again in all of the less glamorous offensive categories, infield hits, bunt singles, and stolen bases. He was their catalyst, the spark that ignited a fairly potent Ranger attack. Delaney stepped into the batters box, and Mickey prepared to unleash his first pitch, all while the rumbling ballpark prepared to erupt into complete bedlam. Every fan was on his feet, clapping, whistling, or stomping the high risers with fevered craving. Mickey was still nervous, but the frenetic atmosphere buoyed his resolve and he felt a familiar lift of his heart, just like the very first time he took the mound at Borchert Field.

It was nice to hear his name, and all the applause. He was thinking that he wanted to talk to all of the nice people who had come to cheer for him, perhaps thank them, maybe have them over to the house, where he could show them his rabbits, and the new pen he had built for them, when the immediacy of the moment took over, causing him to roll his arms in customary fashion, kick his leg, and fire the evening's opening salvo.

The pitch was deft and true, a fastball so fast, so explosive, that it was only heard, not seen.

"Steerike one!" the umpire called, as the ball popped Lester's glove.

Upon hearing the thunderous explosion, and the subsequent judgment, the crowd roared even louder than before. The Brewers' bench was just as pleased.

"Atta boy, Mick," they called to him. "Atta boy. All you now. Go get 'em."

Mickey's next delivery was just as impressive—a four-seam heater that blasted into Delaney's kitchen, shattering his bat into a thousand pieces. The overmatched speedster just stood there forlorn, with only the remnants of what formerly was his favorite piece of lumber in his hand, like a little boy whose balloon had just been popped. Murph and Matheson looked at each other and smiled.

"It's a beautiful thing, Murph," Matheson said, tugging excitedly on the peak of his cap while motioning to the Rangers' dugout. "Look at all of 'em over there. Sweatin' like a bunch of whores in church."

Delaney's shoulders sagged. He walked back to the bench, grabbed another bat, and slipped back into the box, but everyone knew, including Delaney himself, that it was pointless. The fear flickering in his eyes revealed itself to all, and shone more brightly when Mickey rolled his arms once more and dropped a wicked 0–2 hammer on the paralyzed Delaney, buckling his knees as if the frightened batter had been cut down at the ankles by a buzz saw.

"Strike three, yer out!"

The frenzied crowd erupted once more, stomping its feet while waving the promotional GO MICKEY! placards that had been distributed prior to the game. It was just the sort of start everyone in Brewer Land had hoped for.

Mickey seemed fueled by the enthusiasm raining down all around him, disposing of the next two Ranger batters in similar fashion. He had not looked this imposing, this indomitable, all year. It took the Baby Bazooka just eleven pitches to complete the Rangers' half of the first frame; now it was the hometown boys' chance to try and put a mark or two on the pristine scoreboard.

When Lefty Rogers trotted out to the mound for the home half on the inning, the mood of the ballpark changed drastically. Those who had just spent the previous minutes laughing and cheering morphed without warning into a hideous monster, a poly-headed creature with countless arms, a pernicious, rabid beast that hurled both invectives and an assortment of loose objects at the surly turncoat. Nobody had forgotten the role he played in last year's scandal with their beloved Mickey, and nobody forgave his subsequent defection to the Rangers. Rogers loved every second of it, placing his hand to his ear while shrugging his shoulders, something that enraged the unruly crowd even further. They continued to pelt him with hot dog buns and apple cores, and yelled as loudly as they could all the horrible things they would do to him if they caught him outside, stopping only when Pee Wee McGinty's name was announced.

There was certainly no love lost between Rogers and McGinty. The diminutive shortstop stepped into the box like a demon, his eyes ablaze with loathing and retribution. He wind-milled his bat around several times, then set his hands and prepared for the first offering. Rogers showed no emotion, except for a fain't smile that was barely visible behind the webbing on his glove. The truth was, he had owned McGinty all season; made him look foolish just about every time he had faced him. The only blemish on the fire-balling left hander's record was a bunt single that proved to be of no consequence in one of the last contests of the year.

"Game on," Lefty whispered, rocking back.

The impudent pitcher brought his hands over his head, pivoted on the rubber with his left foot, and with one swift woosh, fired the ball at the catcher's glove. It was certainly a good fastball—not nearly as awe-inspiring as the ones Mickey had just thrown—but it was hard and heavy and placed artfully over the outside corner of the plate. All McGinty could do was wave at it. Lefty got the ball back, and with the deliberation and skill of a surgeon, let fly again, this time shaving the inside half of the dish for a called strike two. An intoxicating confidence began to blossom before Lefty's eyes. He was feeling it. His ball had that extra little hop it always had on days when he was almost un-hittable.

The entire Brewer team recognized the fire in Lefty's eyes, and the impressive nature of their nemesis' first two tosses. Each man lifted himself off the bench, and climbed to the top step of the dug-out, where they all proceeded to rally behind their teammate.

"Come on now, Pee Wee," Finster shouted, clapping his hands wildly. "This guy ain't nothin'. He's nothin', Pee Wee."

"Hey now, number one," Danvers added. "Little bingo now. Stroke 'em kid."

Even Mickey, who usually occupied himself during their at bats with pitch counts or puzzle books, got into the act, squeezing himself in between Danvers and Lester.

"Hit the ball, Pee Wee," he yelled. "Hit the ball."

Pee Wee heard the cries of support, and dug in harder with every one that followed. Lefty was equally focused. His next delivery was strictly a "show me" pitch—a sharp breaking ball in the dirt designed to get the batter to chase or, if nothing else, alter his timing. McGinty wasn't fooled. He just stood there, fully aware of Lefty's transparent stratagem. Then, mindful of Lefty's fragile ego, he asked the umpire to check the ball. The man in blue slid the mask away from the front of his face until it rested on top of his head. Then he rolled the ball around in his hand, examining each side with a critical eye.

"Nah, this ball's okay," he finally said, rubbing out a smear of dirt caught in the laces. He looked it over again for good measure before slamming his mask down and tossing the object of his inspection back to Lefty.

The crafty pitcher wasted no time. He got the ball back from the umpire and immediately positioned himself on the rubber. He peered in at the catcher, filled with a restless irritation that distorted his already misshapen face. He shook his head once. Then again. He shook it a third time, now with more animation, prompting McGinty to step out of the box while the disjointed battery tried to get together on a game plan.

The crowd, already disenchanted with the antics of their former idol, booed heartily. Finally, on the fourth try, the Rangers' backstop put down something to Lefty's liking. Fastball away. It was exactly what Lefty wanted. He had beaten McGinty all year on hard stuff away, and having just shown him something off speed, the likelihood of blowing a heater right past him was never better.

Lefty placed the ball exactly where he wanted it—less than an inch off the black on the outer half of the plate. He watched and admired his handiwork, as the spinning sphere whizzed through the air en route to its intended destination. He was all set to turn his back and begin watching the celebratory around-the-horn tossing when, over the steady hum of the crowd came a sharp crack, like a large, dry twig being snapped in half. Lefty, perplexed by the unexpected fly in the ointment, watched with jaw agape as the ball rocketed up and over the first baseman's glove. It rose steadily as it traveled, like a fighter jet just launched, increasing in speed as it flew until finally touching down directly on the foul line, kicking up a plume of white powder before rolling into the right field corner. McGinty was halfway between first and second base when he heard the call. "Foul ball!" screamed the first base umpire. Pee Wee's immediate instinct was to go after the man—punish him for botching such an important call—but Murph was in midflight already from the dugout and arrived on the scene before McGinty could get anywhere near the guy.

"What are you, kidding me? You blind or something?" Murph wailed. "You have to be kidding me! I can still see the dust in the air."

"The ball was foul, Mr. Murphy," the umpire said, brushing an errant wisp of silver from his eyes and tucking it back under his cap.

"Foul? Foul? How do you figure that? The goddamned ball hit the line. That's a fair ball."

His eyes were distant and tepid.

"Look, I call 'em as I see 'em. The ball was foul. End of story."

"You can't call crap with your eyes closed," Murph fired back, moving in so close to the official's face that he could smell his tobacco-laden breath.

"Watch yourself now, Mr. Murphy," the umpire warned. "I'll run you just as sure as I'm standing here."

Murph continued his protest, joined now by the crowd, which had become completely unhinged, pelting the field once again with anything it could get its hands on, including cigar butts, chewing gum and soda bottles. Both Murph and the umpire danced through the shower of debris as they continued their heated exchange.

"Call 'em as you see 'em?" Murph repeated. "Really? That's your damn answer? Maybe you should get your eyes checked. Or maybe you need to consult the rule book. You do know the rule, right? Because I have never seen you before on a baseball field. Guy your age, just starting out? Makes me wonder if—"

"It was foul."

The legion of Brewer faithful continued to voice their disapproval, littering the area around first base with merciless rage. Pee Wee, who had been restrained almost instantly by Matheson and Arky Fries, was still barking from a distance.

"Bullshit," Murph fired back, turning the bill of his cap around toward the back so that he could get even closer to his target's face. "That ball was as fair as the day is long and you know it."

"I said the ball was foul," the umpire repeated, stepping backward. "Foul ball. Now get your ass back to the dugout or I'll run you right now."

With his hands affixed to his hips, and a head that now hung limply between his shoulders, Murph capitulated, exhausted from the frantic swim against the current.

"The ball was fair, and you know it," he said one more time before turning toward the dugout. "Bullshit."

Murph was steaming, and had to force the rational portion of his brain to function. There was still an entire game to play, and he would have to be lucid enough to manage the rest of it. He had all but reached the dugout steps, and regained his poise, when Mc-Nally took the opportunity to rub a little salt in the wound.

"Sure is a shame, Murph," McNally called from his perch in the opposing dugout. "That had triple written all over it."

Murph said nothing.

Pee Wee, still reeling from the horrible injustice, continued his at bat after the grounds crew cleaned up the remnants of the debacle that had just ensued. The fleeting success he had just enjoyed buoyed his resolve and he dug in now even deeper. Lefty, who had watched the entire spectacle from a safe distance somewhere behind the mound, hopped back eagerly on the rubber and set his sights on disposing McGinty once and for all. He got his sign, reared back and fired even harder this time. The ball jumped out of his hand and sped toward the plate in wild fashion, missing the mark by a healthy margin. Lefty cursed himself for evening the count and for giving the overmatched batter and his teammates a tremor of hope.

"Atta boy, Pee Wee!" they screamed from the top step. "You got him. Do it again, kid."

Lefty took the return toss from the catcher and walked behind the mound once again. There, with his back turned to McGinty, and glove tucked neatly under his arm, he rubbed the ball vigorously with both hands while chastising himself. The bizarre ritual went on for a minute or so, until the mercurial hurler put his glove back on his hand and banged the ball inside the pocket, grunting loudly before assuming his regular position atop the hill.

The next pitch was masterful, a two-seamer with extra mustard that began in the center of the plate before tailing away suddenly just as it burst through the hitting zone. Pee Wee could do nothing but wave at the elusive offering once again, ending what was a most protracted, laborious at bat. The outcome reopened the wound from minutes before. "Bull!" Murph screamed again in the direction of first base. "Absolute bull! You're killing us out there. Let the players play. He should be standing on third base right now."

Lefty retired Arky Fries and Woody Danvers in routine fashion to close out the Brewers' half of the first. With the score knotted at zero, Mickey skipped out to the mound to face the middle of the Rangers' lineup. He was never better, electrifying the partisan crowd with pinpoint accurate balls pitched at dizzying and inexplicable speeds.

This went on, batter after batter, inning after inning. And despite a couple of appeals to first base on check swings that went in favor of McNally's boys, Mickey had a choke hold on the Ranger offense. Through the first six innings, he retired all eighteen batters he had faced, twelve by strikeout. The kid was simply un-hittable.

For all his bluster and supercilious antics, Lefty was almost as good, shutting down the Brew Crew in similar fashion. The home team had managed only two hits and a walk, but all three men died an uneventful death on the base baths, leaving Murph and Matheson scratching their heads as to how they were going to push a run across.

The top of the seventh promised to hold more of the same. Mickey jumped out quickly to an 0–2 count on Clyde Rivers, burning two fireballs right past the Ranger right fielder. With the batter now in a hole, Danvers dropped back at third, even with the bag. For a moment, Mickey glanced around and scanned the crowd, as if he were momentarily blinded by the lights and fevered activity. His eyes danced from placard to placard, and the raucous cheering filled his ears.

Mickey! Mickey! Mickey!

He smiled a little, and was feeling, in the most private chambers of his heart, that Oscar was looking down on him; it felt good, but he wished that that Daphne and Duncan could be there watching too.

With thoughts of his beloved creatures fresh in his mind, he uncorked his next pitch. Lester had called for a bender, low and outside, but Mickey's arm sagged a bit during his follow-through. The ball helicoptered a bit, hovered right in the center of Rivers' happy zone. His eyes widened. The stunned batter took advantage of the fortuitous miscue, smashing a bullet right down the third base line.

Danvers, anticipating a late swing on the part of the right handed hitter, had moved off the line, leaving a gaping hole between he and the bag. Out of position now, and with only a mere fraction of a second to react, the slick fielding keeper of the hot corner laid out, fully extended, his yawning glove turned in backhand fashion. The scorched ball skipped like a skimmed stone before lodging itself in Danvers' web. The force of the smash was so great that it carried his body back a step or two toward the outfield grass. In the infinitesimal time it took Danvers to realize what he had just done, he spun to his feet, cocked his arm and fired a pea over to Finster just before the runner stepped on the bag.

Danvers stood across the diamond admiring his handiwork, and was just about to pump his fist in celebration of the highway robbery, when the first base umpire began gesticulating wildly, throwing his arms to the side as if he were tossing out a bucket of bath water.

"Safe!" he cried, pointing his finger at Finster's back foot. "Off the bag."

The man had barely completed his call when Murph, resembling one who had just been shot out of a cannon, tore onto the field once again. He was waving his arms frantically this time and his eyes bulged from the swell of blood that pulsed behind them.

"That's twice now! What kind of a bullshit call is that?" he thundered, firing his cap in the dirt before the umpire's feet. "You've been screwing us all night. Jesus Christ! There is no freakin' way his foot was off the bag."

"His foot was off the base, Mr. Murphy," the umpire said. "I was standing right here."

"I don't give a crap where you were standing! You missed the call again!"

A breathless attention suddenly seized the man in blue. He stood now, arms folded, his eyes narrowing.

"Go back to your dugout, Mr. Murphy," he said deliberately. "That's enough."

"I'll say it's enough!" Murph fired back. "Friggin' idiot! You're killing us here! Killing us!"

Murph continued to harangue the umpire, spurred on by the rousing ovation from the frustrated crowd. He spit, kicked the dirt, and removed first base from its mooring and flung it into the outfield. It seemed that years of frustration and misfortune had all at once welled up inside his heart and had taken the shape of this incompetent numb skull standing before him.

"Holy crap! You are awful! Awful! I'd have better luck calling the game from the other side of the friggin' field."

The umpire, having entertained enough of the attack, abandoned the high road and answered back. His breath was heavy now, and laden with anger and exasperation. He unfolded his arms, and pointed to the Brewers' side of the field. As he extended his hand in the proper direction, the glow from the right field lights caught something on his little finger and flashed painfully into Murph's eyes.

"I told you," he said, shoving his hand passed Murph's face while pointing to the Brewers' side of the field, "to go back to your dugout. Do it now, or you're done for the night."

Murph stopped his tirade suddenly and directed his gaze toward the man's hand. Fancy, black onyx ring with a diamond shaped baseball in the center. He shook his head like a boxer after absorbing a deft roundhouse. It took him a second or two to remember exactly where he had seen it before. Then it him like a brick. Victor Bryant, Rosco's friend. Why hadn't he realized it sooner?

"Oh, that's just great," he said out loud, shaking his head in the direction of Rosco's seat. Now it all made sense. "Beautiful. Just beautiful. A ringer."

Mickey was rattled a bit by Murph's explosive demonstration. He had never seen the man act that way before.

"Are you okay, Murph?" he called out as Murph made his way off the field, still muttering under his breath. "Mickey will help you."

Murph stopped for a moment, just long enough so that Mickey could see that order had been restored.

"I'm fine, Mick," Murph answered. "Everything's fine. Just pitch the ball, Mick. It's all good."

Once he was off the field of play, Murph sat down, leaned up against the dugout wall and sighed. This was the final insult. It was bad enough that Dennison was putting the screws to him, and that McNally was threatening to vanquish him from the game he loved so much forever. But now, to learn that Rosco had played him as well, had arranged for a little insurance policy so that both he and McNally would get what they wanted? That was unbearable.

"Looks like we got ourselves a ringer at first, Farley," Murph said, as he and Matheson watched while Mickey got set to deliver his first pitch from the stretch.

"Well, if that don't beat all," Matheson griped. "How do you like that? What's an old guy like that doing playing the part of McNally's bitch?"

"Oh, he's not only taking it from McNally, Farley. Rosco's got his hand in the mix too."

"That dirty, rotten—"

"I tell you what though," Murph went on. "If I go down, I am bringing both of them with me. You can bet on that."

The two of them bantered a while longer in hushed whispers, with Matheson doing most of the gabbing. Murph had moved past it for the moment, concerned more now about Mickey and the runner at first. He had delivered one pitch, a ball outside. Murph toyed with the idea of a pitch out, but did not want to put Mickey in a hole. It was a moot point soon enough when Mickey missed again on his next pitch, up and way.

It was the first trouble the kid had seen all day. Murph scratched his head, and whispered something in Matheson's ear. It was time to earn his money. With the way Mickey was throwing, and given the late stages of the game, Murph was certain that McNally would try to play small ball on him; however, he was not quite sure exactly how to combat it. Danvers and Finster pinched at the corners, and he called to Lester to remind the middle infielders that the rotation play was in effect. But Mickey was slow to the plate, and even slower off the mound when fielding his position. It worried him, although he guessed that McNally would let his batter see at least one more pitch before he put on a bunt and put the runner in motion. Hell, that's what he would do. Murph's hunch was incorrect. As soon as Mickey lifted his hands and brought his knee to his chest, Rivers took off. The ball was an easy one for Lester to handle—pipe fastball letter high—but the jump that Rivers got was just too much to overcome. He was already on the bag at second when Lester's throw arrived.

With a 2–1 count, and the go ahead run on second base, Murph readied his field for a bunt. Again, he pinched his corners, and Lester signaled to McGinty and Fries about the coverage. The plan was simple—field the bunt and cut the runner off at third.

"Hop off that mound on a bunt, Mick," Murph screamed. "As soon as he squares." Mickey smiled. He loved the word *hop*. It made him think of Duncan and Daphney again. They loved to hop, especially in the morning, when Mickey would let them out of their cages to scamper around in the cool morning grass.

"Okay, Murph," Mickey said. "Hop."

Mickey came set, with his hands resting awkwardly at his waist, and checked Rivers at second. It bothered him that the Rangers' runner was dancing back and forth, and once or twice Mickey almost stepped off, but Murph's instruction was foremost in his mind. *Hop off the mound and field the bunt.*

So with his eyes still fixed on the runner, Mickey lifted his leg, brought his hands up, turned to face the batter who had squared around prematurely, and fired. It was a dart, destined for the center of the plate, where the batter's bat hung extended and limp, flat, ready to deaden the ball somewhere on the infield grass. With Murph's admonition ringing in his ears, Mickey flew off the mound like he was pushed from a ledge. The boy had done exactly what he was told to do. Executed the plan to perfection. But he moved so effortlessly, so adroitly, that by the time he realized the batter had pushed the ball between the mound and second base, instead of in the traditional place in front of the plate, it was already past him.

With the well-placed bunt, the Rangers were in great shape. The first pitch to the next batter resulted in a steal of second base, placing runners on second and third with nobody out. Murph just shook his head and sighed.

"Pull the infield in, Farley," he said. "Try and cut down the runner at home."

FRANK NAPPI

Dutifully, each of the Brewer infielders crept forward so that they were now standing on the infield grass. They all pounded their gloves, and assured Mickey that they had his back, but it was of no real consequence, because the next pitch was lofted high in the air to centerfield. Jimmy Llamas darted back to the warning track and tucked the ball away neatly, but had no chance of throwing out the runner tagging from third. Rivers practically walked home. A silenced throng of Brewer faithful watched in horror and disbelief as the Rangers grabbed a 1–0 lead.

Mickey, spurred on by the sudden misfortune, regained his prior dominant form and fanned the next two hitters. Murph tried to use Mickey's prowess as motivation for some sort of an offensive stand, but Lefty appeared to have their number, retiring the Brewers in order in the seventh and the eighth. Mickey did his part the rest of the way, sitting down the next six Rangers to face him. He left the field to a rousing ovation, one that carried into the home half of the ninth as the Brewers sent up the top of the order in a final attempt to stave off elimination.

McGinty lead things off with a terrific at bat, working the count full after falling behind 0–2. He proceeded to foul off the next three pitches before finally grounding out weakly to second base. Everyone in the ballpark sagged.

Arky Fries was next. He did not fair much better, lofting a hump back liner that teased initially, only to fall harmlessly in the outstretched glove of the shortstop. Under a sky that appeared to darken now, an entire city seemed to sink into the deepening night, an early October pall that signaled ominously the long, approaching winter weeks ahead. The bewildered masses looked on breathlessly, wanting desperately to believe that there was still time, as Lester Sledge came to plate for what was more than likely the final at bat of the Brewers' season.

Lester had done nothing all night, save for a long fly ball in the fifth inning that drove the Ranger centerfielder up against the fence before dying a quiet death. Despite his lack of productivity on this night, it had been quite a memorable season for the young African American catcher. He led the American Association in homeruns and doubles, and posted the highest slugging percentage in the team's history. His defensive prowess was also well documented, punctuated by the meager success rate of all of the would-be base stealers who fell victim to his lethal arm.

Lester had also become one of the fan favorites both in and around Borchert Field, something that those close to him found utterly remarkable, given the tumultuous start to his Brewer career. But that was months ago, before he and Mickey had become the "dynamic duo," the "terrific tandem," and the heart and soul of a Brewer team that, as the season wore on, promised better things than were about to transpire.

A steady but guarded buzz began to surface as Lester dug in to take his cuts. Lefty postured on the mound, puffing out his chest and tossing the ball up with one hand, all while delicious thoughts of a complete game shutout against his former team, one that would nail down the pennant and send droves of Milwaukeans to the exits, sick and teary-eyed, swirled magically in his head.

Lester was still, focused and humble, the very antithesis of his dance partner. His eyes were calm and his jaw set. He had traveled a long way to this fantastic lawn, had weathered controversy and hardship and unfathomable ugliness. Standing there, scanning the many faces lit softly by the stadium glow, he felt complete. Satisfied. Lester Sledge was at peace. Each muscle was patient and primed, ready to combat whatever it was that Lefty had in store.

Lefty began his sequence to the potent Brewer catcher with a riding fastball, up and in. Lester, who had been looking for something middle-in, pulled his hands in and fired the bat head through the hitting zone, pulling the ball thirty feet foul into the leftfield stands. The crowd, sensing their hero's readiness and resolve, stirred a little louder, hoping against hope that the wondrous season that had treated them to so many phenomenal feats had just one more miracle left to reveal. The slow bender that Lefty offered next surprised no one in the park, including Lester. He was on that one too, lacing it viciously down the line, where it landed in virtually the same spot as the previous pitch. Lefty had not fooled Lester a bit, but he was now in command, needing just one more strike to finish off the Brewers once and for all.

An eerie hush fell across the ballpark like a burial shroud. All around, people sat in their seats zombie-like, some with hands covering their eyes, others with their heads hung in front of them so low that there was no chance of witnessing the unspeakable. The sounds alone would tell the story. Others, those who possessed a sort of masochistic need to see the tragedy through to the end, stared straight ahead, their bodies tense and stiff, bracing for the final, fatal blow.

Lester was still composed, although his heart beat with more purpose now, almost as if it were suddenly too big for his chest. He had no fear of failure, for he had done his part all year. But now, looking out at Lefty's smugness, and the premature celebration that had begun in the Rangers' dugout, he decided that he would not yield, in any way, to this hopelessness.

Lester always thought like a catcher, even when he had a bat in his hands. He knew, all too well, that the pitcher-batter show down most often had nothing to do with physical skill and musculature; that it was really about cerebral dexterity, the ability to be a student of the game, a tactician, one who despite physical gifts, approached his work with the methodical maneuverings of a chess champion.

Lefty had been in the game long enough to recognize this as well. He stood on the mound, ruminating over what was brewing in Lester's mind. 0–2 count. He was probably expecting him to follow the same sequence he had employed the last time he had him in this position. Climb the ladder with a fastball, just to get him thinking. Then, take advantage of his keyed-up bat and drop a slow, sweeping hammer on the poor bastard. Yeah, Lester was definitely thinking that way. Lefty knew what he had to do. The lanky southpaw spun the ball behind his back as he peered in for his sign. He shook off the first one, then did the same with the second, mindful that his ostensible indecision would add to the mystery of what was really coming. He loved the power, that feeling of control, and toyed briefly with the idea of making Lester wait even longer. But he was ready to pop the champagne corks now. It was time. So when the Ranger catcher placed down two fingers, and pointed to his inner thigh, Lefty nodded in agreement.

The ball came out of his hand effortlessly. It was a clean pitch, one that rolled out of Lefty's hand with a tight spin. It was the perfect pitch for the occasion—the perfect pitch to dispose of a batter who was looking fastball. Oh, how the beauty of the choreography thrilled Lefty as he watched his handiwork unfurl. Yes, it looked like a fastball up and out of the zone, but soon it would dive down, into the strike zone, freezing Lester Sledge and leaving nothing left to do except hurl his glove into the air and wait for the pile-on at the mound.

Yes, it would have been the perfect plan had Lester not been one move ahead of Lefty. He knew that the cocky southpaw would be expecting him to look fastball, followed by the breaking stuff. It had worked so well, why change? Unless, of course, you were trying to out-guess your opponent. Then all bets were off. Lefty liked to be cute. And Lester knew that he wanted to end the game with a strikeout. So he made the adjustment, kept his hands back, and watched dutifully, waiting for the true orbit of the tiny white sphere to reveal itself.

The moment the ball began its descent into the hitting zone, Lester loaded his hands and thrust his front foot forward. He caught the pitch with the sweet spot of the bat, lofting a high, majestic streak of white somewhere far into the night. In the seconds that followed, Lefty's face melted away like it was made of wax. He could only watch, and dream about what could have been, as the ball landed well beyond the centerfield fence, sending Lester around the bases for a game tying trot and igniting a brush fire of tearful exultations and raucous chants all around the ballpark.

Sledge Hammer! Sledge Hammer! Sledge Hammer!

The crowd was roaring its approval. It was complete pandemonium. The emotional tide had swept away everyone, but none as violently as Murph.

"Hey, how 'bout that McNally!" he screamed, the veins in his neck threatening to burst right through his skin. "Yeah baby! Yeah!"

His was pumping his fist wildly, first in the direction of the opposing dugout, then toward first base.

"Let's see you call *that* friggin' one foul, you friggin' snake."

They were all overwhelmed by the sudden turn of fortune. The entire Brewer dugout, lead by Jimmy Llamas, who was waving his cap like a victory flag, erupted explosively, jumping and hollering and laughing like a band of school boys, stomping their feet and clapping their hands as Lester finished his jaunt, finally touching home plate before jogging back to the bench, where he was assaulted by a barrage of bear hugs and slaps on the back.

Danvers, who had been on deck at the time of the fortuitous blow, was the first to peel off the mob and stood now just outside the batter's box, waiting for the insanity to subside. The tiny ballpark continued to rock, unable to regain its composure for several minutes. He watched with amused absurdity, his heart now aflutter with visions of replicating Lester's heroic feat; stood there, savoring the pain on Lefty's face and the jubilation rioting through the crowd until the frenzy slowly dissipated to a level that would now allow the game to continue.

Danvers took Lefty's first pitch for strike one. The second pitch was also called a strike. Recognizing the familiarity of this development, and believing it to be some sort of omen, the throng of Brew Crew stalwarts rose to their feet, ready to lose themselves in what would no doubt be the most exciting game ever played at Borchert Field. Lefty was enraged by the static and bore down now even harder. Deep inside his brain was something like a grain of sand that would not go away—would not let him be.

His mouth was dry but everywhere else were signs of nervous moisture. He took a long, deliberate breath, set his feet carefully on the rubber, accepted his sign, wound up, and fired.

This time, he was the victor. The pitch was well placed, a cut fastball that slipped past the tardy bat of Danvers, dashing everyone's hopes of a walk-off pennant party. Sure, there was a little disappointment, but in the wake of Lester's eleventh-hour miracle, nobody could feel too bad about having to go to an extra frame to determine a winner. Mickey trotted out happily for the tenth. Even though he was a little fatigued, the swell of excitement was just too much to resist. The Brewer brain trust was happy to have him on the hill, but their decision to stick with the young ace was not made without some trepidation. He had never gone this long in one game before and it was cause for a little concern.

"Are you sure you're not tired, kid?" Matheson asked him before he went out. "It's okay to be gassed. Only natural ya know. You've thrown quite a gem today."

"Mickey is not gassed, Coach," he said to Matheson. "A little hungry, and thirsty, and my arms are sweaty, and I would like to go home and pet my rabbits, and maybe—"

"Okay, okay, kid," Matheson said, pushing the boy in the direction of the field. "I get it. I get it. Geez, just get out there."

Mickey picked up right where he had left off; he fanned first two batters with relative ease, running his total for the game to a staggering fifteen. Now the hungry crowd rose to its feet, lead by the Baby Bazooka Brigade, with Mickey placards in hand, waving them so that all that was visible from section to section was an undulating sea of white. They wanted more and were trying desperately to will their favorite son to complete the mission.

Here comes sixteen! Here comes sixteen! Here comes sixteen!

Mickey heard the chant and was happy, mostly because he thought that only *he* had been counting. He knew all his stats for the day: 15 strikeouts, 1 walk, 2 hits, 98 strikes, and 27 balls. It was quite a line score. He was pleased, although the number fifteen bothered him too. He much preferred to end the game, or at least his outing, with one more punch out.

If he was going to accomplish the feat, however, he was going to have to do it against the Rangers' cleanup hitter. No easy task by any means. With the yellow windows from neighboring houses looming out in the still, black distance like hopeful eyes, a disorderly house of rabid fans hung on Mickey's every last movement. It was an anxious waiting, the kind you feel right before Christmas or the birth of your first child.

The kid did not disappoint, revving the crowd's collective engine even further when he jumped out in front on a fastball that the batter fouled straight back. Mickey's second toss missed just outside, but the one after that caught the inner half of the dish, placing the Rangers' slugger in a 1–2 hole.

Sensing the kill, the legion of Mickey worshippers roared even louder.

Here comes sixteen! Here comes sixteen! Here comes sixteen!

They screamed and stomped and twisted themselves into all sorts of pre-celebratory positions. They were about to witness something truly amazing. Sixteen strikeouts. And then, after that, one final at-bat to capture the long anticipated pennant.

When Mickey rolled his arms and lifted his leg, it set off a flurry of popping flashbulbs, courtesy of the local press who were determined to capture the fantastic achievement and preserve it forever. The display was indeed magical, and imbued the moment with an ethereal air, but seemed to disrupt Mickey's normal routine, causing him to stumble a bit and let go of the ball prematurely. Fortunately, the flight of the pitch was still true, and everyone followed its path with mouths open and hearts afire, certain that this was the moment they had all waited for.

So when they heard the thunderous sound, something like dynamite in a canyon, nobody flinched. It just did not seem possible. The pitch was perfect. Uncharacteristically up in the zone, but perfect nonetheless.

Even when they saw Jimmy Llamas turn, drop his head and race back to the wall, they still refused to believe that Mickey had been tagged that way. The ball just kept going, rising like a some sort of ground to air missile, destined for touch down somewhere deep into the night.

Llamas was swift in his pursuit, continuing the chase with his head turned and tilted skyward, his eyes wedded to the spinning sphere. With each step, he gained more and more ground on the ball, and in doing so, roused the stunned spectators from their momentary stupor and captured their imaginations once again. It was the ultimate race, man against ball. And with so much riding on the show down, the chase became that much more compelling. The only concern for all who watched with arrested breath was whether or not Llamas would run out of real estate before he could snatch the potential heart-breaker. The fleet footed centerfielder was now one step ahead of the ball, and appeared to be lined up and in perfect position to make the grab. But then the great green wall that had been looming in the distance emerged, and threatened to put a violent end to the dramatic pursuit.

Llamas was so focused that when he began his leap, he did not even notice how close he was to the eight-foot wooden barrier. He just bounced off the ground, as if the warning track were made of foam rubber, and used his free hand to grab the top of the wall, balancing long enough to position himself so that he could extend his other hand, the glove hand, just past the wall, a tiny stretch of no man's land, the forbidden zone, the place where leather webbing and ball arrived simultaneously.

The last thing the crowd saw, before Llamas' arm disappeared momentarily behind the highest of the wooden slats, was the ball peeking out from the centerfielder's glove. It was the most amazing feat any of them had ever seen. It was highway robbery at its finest. Then gravity reasserted itself, and a winded and slightly bruised Llamas fell, collapsed in a heap, hat askew, glove closed. Everyone in attendance broke into thunderous applause as the second base umpire, still trailing the play, raised his thumb high in the air and made the call.

"Out!"

The batter, however, refused to relent. He continued to run the bases, even as the Brewer players began jogging off the field, insisting that the powers that be check Llamas glove for the ball. They all laughed at him, but Llamas, sitting with his back up against the wall and his legs outstretched, wilted now, like the last rose of summer. "Show me the ball," the umpire called. "Hold it up for me."

An odd sensation flowed through Llamas. He hesitated for a moment, an arresting feeling seizing his will to move. He just sat there, lifeless, until the umpire asked again for the ball. Then Llamas held up his glove, opened it, and exposed the barren pocket, much to the dismay of thousands of Brewer hopefuls.

"No catch!" the umpire yelled. Then he held his index finger high in the air and drew several imaginary circles in the air, signaling a homerun.

The Rangers celebrated wildly, while Mickey went white with the staggering realization that he had surrendered the lead. His stomach hurt and he was feeling increasingly uneasy. It had been so long since he had faced any sort of adversity that he was scarcely able to handle the swell of anxiety that was now suffocating him.

"It's okay, Mick," Murph called from the bench. "Not a problem. Just get the last out. We're the home team. We got the hammer here. Then we score and go home."

Mickey liked what he heard. Home sounded alright to him. He breathed rapidly through partially opened lips, and his legs labored a bit, but managed to compose himself with the help of Lester's prodding and the raucous cheering that began to rise again in recognition of the boy's stellar effort. They were all still calling for that last K. One more strikeout, and then they could go to work, trying to produce yet another miracle. Mickey made sure he did not disappoint this time, disposing of the next batter with three straight fastballs.

Once inside the dugout, all of the players rallied around Murph. The scene resembled something like a going away party. All around Murph were faces, long and bloodless, desperate for something to cling to.

"Now or never, guys," Murph said, glancing up at the score-board. "There ain't no tomorrow."

The Brewers had the bottom third of the lineup due up against Lefty, who had convinced McNally only minutes before that he was still good to go. The despicable Rogers smelled the blood in the water, and wasted no time going in for the kill. He fanned Fin-ster to begin the inning, retired Faber on a routine one hopper to third, and had gotten ahead of Jimmy Llamas 1–2 before finally stepping off the rubber to compose himself one last time. He had been cast as a pariah in Brewer folklore, ridiculed and blamed for the team's misfortune the previous year. Sure he had his hand in it, but it wasn't all his fault. And nobody wanted to hear his side of things. They just rode him out on a rail. It hurt, worse than anyone ever could know. But this felt good. Yeah, this felt right. Being the instrument of the Brewers' demise was more than right. It was sweet justice.

Carried away now by the emotional cocktail of pride and ven-geance, Lefty Rogers climbed back on top of the hill, stared in at Llamas, who had shortened up and was crouched over the plate, and fired his shot. It was a fastball, not unlike the dozens of others he had thrown that day, except for the significance which floated behind it. Llamas saw the pitch the whole way, could even see the spin of the laces, and loaded his hands at just the right time. His stride was perfect too, right in time with the ball's approach. It was all as it should be, except when the rotation of the laces caused the ball to cut sharply outside. What had appeared to be a strike was now heading well off the plate. Llamas, in midswing, halted his at-tack, straining to hold back the bat barrel before it passed through the zone. The crowd gasped, but the home plate umpire awarded Llamas' efforts with the call "ball two, no swing," but Rogers, who was already wedded to a game-ending punch out to capture the crown, immediately pointed down the first base line, imploring his catcher to ask for an appeal. The gesture produced an instant numbing of Murph's spirit. His whole body buckled under the fatigue of his utterly vain efforts, so much so that he could not bear to watch any longer.

"When I go down, Farley," he whispered in the old man's ear, "I'm taking them with me."

Then he pulled his cap down over his brow, hung his head, and slipped out of the dugout and into the clubhouse, just as Victor Bryant rung up Llamas, pounding the final nail into the Brewer coffin.

Borchert Field was benumbed. There was an odd, piercing effect of quietness amidst the cavalcade of noises coming from the visitors' side of the diamond. There would be no celebration, no champagne shower or pennant waving. They had fallen short yet again. Chip McNally's Rangers had repeated last year's torture of their most storied rival, only somehow, in the flatness that followed what was becoming a dubious tradition, it seemed a little worse this time.

POSTGAME

The rain the next morning had chilled the air so that when Murph got into his car to meet with Dennison as agreed, his hands were already cold and deadened. The icy drizzle peppered the landscape and rolled steadily down the farmhouse windows along Diamond Drive, distorting the golden glow of the lamps inside, creating what looked to Murph to be a row of mournful candles, set there no doubt to acknowledge the occasion of his professional passing.

When Murph arrived at Dennsion's office, the petulant owner was seated at his desk, his face mostly hidden behind a towering stack of papers. When he heard the door open, he did nothing to acknowledge Murph's entrance, just kept working behind his pile, every so often releasing ringlets of cigar smoke into the air, tiny white ribbons that hovered briefly and stretched high above the mess before fading quietly into the dimly lit atmosphere.

"Uh, Warren," Murph said with notable irritation. "We had a meeting?"

The silence in which Dennison received Murph's greeting spoke volumes about the man. He continued to scribble away, not uttering a sound or lifting his head until he had completed the task on which he was working.

"I'm well aware of our meeting, Arthur," he finally said. "You lost again. That was the deal, remember? But holy Christ, I am getting a little tired of it all. Maybe if you had won once in a while we could have cut out some of these meetings."

Murph was tired of holding his tongue.

"Are you kidding me? That's a bunch of bullshit. You know what happened last year. Was that my fault? And there's something you should know about this year. I only learned during the game that I had been—"

"The only thing I know, or care to know, is that you lost—to the Rangers. Again. Save the song and dance Arthur. Results. Results are what matter."

Something inside of Murph burst. It was warm and painful. He thought for a second it was his heart. He had had episodes before. But this felt different. Worse. It was worse.

His soul was bleeding.

"So that's it?" Murph said. "Just like that? Nothing we accomplished the last two years means anything to you? You honestly think somebody else could have done a better job with these guys?"

"Somebody else will be managing the Brewers next year. That's it."

"Just like that? You have no problem with your decision? None at all?"

"What was our agreement, Arthur?" Dennison asked, tapping the end of his cigar into a glass ash tray.

"I know what the agreement was, but—"

"And did you lose?"

"Yes, yes we lost today but I'm trying to tell you that—"

"Then there's nothing more to talk about. I told you that if you did not win, someone else would be my manager. I expect you to have your office cleaned out by tomorrow night."

The callous, perfunctory manner in which Dennison's comments were delivered only added to Murph's angst and frustration. In his misery, everything seemed to come to an abrupt halt, still and silent, save for the laborious sound coming from the clock on the wall. The incessant ticking was filled with all sorts of malignant implications, like lost opportunity, squandered chances and now, as he stood there pondering the evanescence of baseball life, the hour of his demise.

He was tired of all of them. Dennison. McNally. Sheriff Rosco. All of them. His mind was whirling with myriad thoughts, but he knew exactly what he was going to do as he turned for the door. They would rue the day they crossed him.

"Oh yeah," Dennison announced just as Murph was about to exit the room. "Before you leave, I should tell you that you are expected in Boston first thing Monday morning." The owner's expression softened for just a second.

"Meeting with the Braves' brass. You, Mickey, and Lester. All three of you. Hell if I can figure it. Must be some sort of twisted, pathetic charity stunt. Who knows. But don't be late. You've made me look bad enough already."

Hearing this, Murph thought he was the victim of some ill-timed, temporary hallucination. A two-time loser, catapulted to the pinnacle of baseball hierarchy? He turned back to face his executioner, possessed of clashing thoughts.

"What did you just say?" he asked.

"You heard me, Murph."

"They're calling us up?" he questioned. "Are you telling me that we got the call? All of us?"

Murph inhaled purposefully and narrowed his stare.

"So why all the damned mystery and drama then, Warren? All the talk of me 'leaving' next year? Do you really enjoy seeing me suffer that much?"

"Relax, Arthur—have a sense of humor. It's all good, right? We both got what we wanted, no?"

"Are you kidding me? Hell yes. Yes. This is the most—"

"Easy there. Good God. There you go again, breaking your arm patting yourself on the back. Sure, they want you. But you can be sure as hell that once you screw up, you'll be out on your ass again, lock, stock, and barrel. If I've told you once, I've told you a thousand times—"

Murph heard nothing after Dennison's acknowledgment. He just stood there, as Dennison droned on, scratching his head in amazement. After all the years of broken down buses and second-rate hotels, of greasy truck stop food and the ignominy attached to the moniker of minor league lifer, he was finally going to get his chance. He would take Mickey and Lester far away from the small town ignorance and ugliness. He would leave McNally and Rosco to suffer at the hands of their own devices. Yes, it *was* all good. He was on his way. They were all on their way.